THE STAND IN

A SINGLE IN SEATTLE NOVEL

KRISTEN PROBY

&
AMPERSAND
PUBLISHING, INC.

The Stand-In
A Single in Seattle Novel
By
Kristen Proby

Single in Seattle Character Glossary

With the Single in Seattle series quickly growing, and the size of the entire family, I figured it was time to include a who's who in this huge world, listed by family. Please know that this may contain spoilers for anyone who hasn't read all of the books, but it's a great reference for those who want to make sure they read about everyone.

The Williams Family

Parents: Luke and Natalie – {Come Away With Me}
    Olivia 'Liv' Williams – Works for her father's production company, Williams Productions, as the lead costume designer. Married to Hollywood celebrity **Vaughn Barrymore.** – {The Secret}

Keaton Williams – Restores rare vehicles. With country music star **Sidney Sterling** (Siblings are Gray and Maya Sterling). – {The Setup}

Haley Williams – Book to come.

Chelsea Williams – Book to come.

Parents: Mark and Meredith Williams – {Breathe With Me}

Lucy Williams – Book to come.

Hudson Williams – Book to come.

Aunt & Uncle: Samantha and Leo Nash – {Rock With Me}

No Children.

The Montgomery Family

Parents: Isaac and Stacy Montgomery – {Under the Mistletoe With Me}

Sophie Montgomery - Nutritionist and social media influencer. Married to **Ike Harrison**, quarterback for Seattle professional football team. – {The Score}

Liam Montgomery – Book to come.

Parents: Jules (Montgomery) and Nate McKenna – {Fight With Me}

Stella McKenna – Interior designer. Married to attorney **Gray Sterling** (Siblings are Sidney and Maya Sterling). – {The Scandal}

Parents: Caleb and Brynna Montgomery – {Safe With Me}

Maddie Montgomery – Accountant. Married to **Dylan**, a travel writer. – {The Scramble}

Josie Montgomery – Nurse. Married to **Brax Adler**, a musician. – {The Surprise}

Michael "Drew" Montgomery –Professional football coach. Married to **London Ambrose,** owner of the football team. One child, Caleb.

Parents: Will and Meg Montgomery – {Play With Me}

Erin Montgomery – Heroine in the first novel of the **WILDS OF MONTANA series, Wild for You.** Married to Remington Wild, rancher and single dad.

Zoey Montgomery – Book to come.

Parents: Matt and Nic Montgomery – {Tied With Me}

Abby Montgomery – Book to come.

Finn Montgomery – Book to come.

Parents: Dominic and Alecia Salvatore (Montgomery brother) – {Forever With Me}

Emma Salvatore – Book to come.

Five Years Ago

"How many fingers am I holding up?"

"Two."

The doctor narrows his eyes on me. "But how many can you actually *see*?"

I want to lie and tell him that I only see two fingers. That I'm not dizzy as fuck, nauseous, and seeing double of every damn thing.

But I don't lie because my mom would kill me.

"I see four."

He purses his lips as he types into his computer. It's been a week since I took a hit on the field during the fourth quarter when we were up by three points.

Thanks to my pass before the hit, we won by nine.

1

But I got hit hard enough to give me one hell of a concussion. It isn't my first, but I hope like hell that it's my last, though football is a tough sport, and quarterbacks get hit *hard*.

My uncle Will taught me that from an early age when I realized that I didn't want to follow in my dad's footsteps by joining the Navy. Instead, I wanted to play professional football.

"What's the prognosis, doc?" Dad asks. He's sitting in a chair in the corner of the small exam room. I had to have him drive me to the appointment since I can't see well enough to drive myself.

"Brain injuries are always a mystery," the doctor replies as he closes the laptop and turns to address the two of us. "Unfortunately, it's going to take time for your brain to heal, Drew."

"I have a game tomorrow night."

"No." The doc shakes his head slowly as he looks me square in the eye, his own eyes hard and serious. "You don't."

"Don't tell me that I'm out the rest of the season."

Dad shifts in the chair, and I scowl at the two older men.

"Come on, it's just a concussion."

"This one isn't minor," the doc replies. "It's your third this year, Drew, and it's bad. What did you have for breakfast the morning of the game?"

I sigh in frustration. I can't remember. That entire

day is completely gone from my memory, and it frustrates the hell out of me.

"At least I can play for my senior year next fall."

The room is quiet again until the doctor clears his throat. "Drew, it's time to walk away from football."

"Fuck that."

"Drew—" Dad begins, but I shake my head and then immediately regret the movement when the room spins and my stomach revolts.

"Football is my *life*. I'm damn good at it, and I'll be going pro. There are already scouts watching me. You can't tell me that I'm done. That's not possible."

"Another concussion could lead to neurological issues, permanent memory loss, and personality changes. You'll be at higher risk of early-onset Alzheimer's and Parkinson's disease." Doc sighs grimly. "I know that football is important to you, Drew, and that you're a damn good player. But your *life* is worth more. I'm sorry to deliver this news, but your days on the field are over. I'll want you back here in a month for another CT so I can see how your brain is recovering."

He shakes our hands, and then he's gone, and before I know it, I'm sitting in the passenger seat of my dad's truck, headed toward my childhood home in the suburbs of Seattle.

"I'll get another opinion," I mutter as I close my eyes and will the dizziness away. Christ, being dizzy is the *worst*.

"That *was* the second opinion," Dad reminds me gently. "Drew, switching career tracks when you're twenty-one isn't the end of the world."

"What am I going to do?" I demand. "You and I both know that I was never expected to perform well academically. I'm a jock, the star of the team, and I'm expected to win games. No one gives a shit about my grades. I'll have a degree in *business*, but I couldn't even tell you how to fill out a spreadsheet. It's a joke."

"You can coach."

I scoff at that and turn my face to the window so he doesn't see the tears in my eyes.

"I can't coach quarterbacks. Not when I want to be doing what they are. When I know that I'm better than they are."

"Well, your ego is healthy." Dad reaches out and pats my leg. "You get that from me. Look, sometimes the right choice isn't the one we think we want to make. Leaving the SEALs fucking sucked for me. I didn't want to do it. I didn't know anything else, and I *liked* my job. Sure, it was hard, but I was good at it."

"Then why did you?"

I look over in time to see him swallow hard.

"You never told me why you left the SEALs."

"Injuries." He shrugs. "And I was getting older. I'd seen a lot of shit, and it messed me up in the head some. Coming home was the right thing, and then I met your mom and your sisters, and I knew that it was the way my life was supposed to go."

"Coaching doesn't pay what being a pro athlete makes."

"Not much pays like that, son." Dad laughs. "But you never played ball for the money."

"No, but it's a damn nice perk."

He laughs again and pulls into the driveway. "You have a point. Coaches don't do too badly, though. You can talk to your uncle Will about that. And you don't have to decide today. You need to rest and heal up before you start thinking about which track you want to hop over to."

"Dad." My voice stops him before he opens the door to get out of the cab.

"Yeah?"

"I'm scared."

He blows out a breath and nods, then leans over to kiss my hair the way he's always done since I was a kid.

"I know, buddy. Don't worry. We've got this."

CHAPTER 1

DREW

"*I* don't know how to say this without sounding disrespectful." I push my thumbs into my eyeballs and wish that I were anywhere but here, in my own damn office. When I move my hands, London Ambrose is still standing on the other side of my desk, waiting expectantly.

"What?" She raises a perfect eyebrow. Jesus, the woman is gorgeous. And she's the new co-owner of the professional football team that I coach for.

Which makes her and her brother, Rome, the youngest owners of a professional team, in any sport, *ever*.

She's a billionaire in her early thirties and is absolutely stunning, but she drives me fucking crazy.

"I don't care about the uniforms," I reply simply. "I don't *care* that they're changing. And I don't understand why you'd want my opinion on them."

Her face, all smooth porcelain with lips the color of ripe raspberries and eyes as blue as the sky on a clear summer day, doesn't change in the least. She doesn't seem to be offended or affected in any way at all.

"You're going to have to look at them," she points out. "Every single weekend. More than that, actually."

"Did you run it by Will?" My uncle, Will Montgomery, is the general manager of the team, as well as the president of operations. I was originally offered the defensive line coaching position, but when the spot for a quarterback coach came available, he hired me for that position a few months ago, and despite the raised eyebrows of the press and fans, I happily accepted. This is my dream job. "He's the GM. He should be the one you talk to."

"He suggested I come talk to you." The side of her lips tips up into a small smile, showing just the hint of a dimple on her left cheek. "It seems the Montgomery men are putting me off."

"I think you should choose whatever you like and send it through for approval from the league. As long as they don't burn our retinas out, we won't care. Players included."

"Fine." She sighs and checks her watch. "Crap, I have to go. See you tomorrow."

She waves and hurries out of my office, moving as quickly as her sky-high heels and skinny black pencil skirt will carry her.

Which, I have to admit, is remarkably fast.

I check the time myself and see that it's only about two in the afternoon. That's another thing that irritates the hell out of me when it comes to the new bosses.

They're never here.

I guess if you're a billionaire, you can keep the hours you want while the people you hire dig in and do the dirty work.

I don't know why that grates on me, exactly.

"Why are you scowling like that?"

I glance up and see Will walk through the door and then sit across from me.

"I'm not scowling."

"Oh, yeah." He grins and crosses an ankle on his knee. "You are. Did London piss you off again?"

"Why did you tell her to come ask *me* about the damn uniforms? Again."

He laughs and shrugs. "Because I don't give a shit."

"Well, I don't either. She hangs around my office, around *me* far too much for my liking. Aren't owners supposed to just show up for games and talk to reporters and shit? Why is she always here?"

"She wants to take a more hands-on approach," Will says simply. "Her brother handles things on the weekends."

"That's the other thing." I stand and pace my small office. "He shows up to all the games, but she doesn't. That doesn't make any sense to me. She's here all week but can't be bothered to show up when we're actually doing what we're paid to do?"

"You're awfully worked up about this."

I blow out a breath and shove my hands into my pockets. "You're right. It's stupid. Let them do what they want."

I shake my head and sit once more.

"What's up?"

"Well, we're halfway into the season, so I thought I'd check in to see how you're doing."

"Are you making the rounds to all the staff?"

He just waits for me to reply to him.

"I love my job." I frown a little, realizing for the first time that it's absolutely, unequivocally the truth. "I understand that at twenty-seven, I'm not much older than the players. Hell, some are a little older than me, but they're respectful."

"That's because you're fucking good at what you do, and they respect you for it. Age doesn't matter."

"It can matter. We get along well, and I think we've hit a good stride. But I have moments of imposter syndrome."

"You're doing a hell of a job. We're happy with the performance of the quarterbacks. There's always room for more training, but you're having a great season. Shake off the doubt. It won't serve you in this position."

"I was surprised when the plan changed, and I was offered the quarterback coaching position rather than defense."

"But you never wanted defense," he points out.

"That's what you did because it was available at the time."

"I just wanted to work in football," I admit with a shrug. "Hell, I'd just mow the field if that was all I could get. So, yeah, this is my dream job, and I'm damn grateful for it. Now, why do I feel like I just got an A on my report card?"

Will grins. "Because you did."

"Does this mean I get a raise?"

"Next year." He winks and stands. "Go home, Drew. I know you've been here since five this morning."

"I had shit to do."

"Go home," he repeats and turns for the door. "It's going to get busier this week. Get out of the office for a while."

And with that, he walks out of my office, whistling as he makes his way to the elevator to head back up to his own office, which happens to be about four times the size of mine, with a killer view.

Of course, he's earned that.

I think of the paperwork I still have to work my way through. The training schedules to assign, and the performance evaluations to study.

And then I decide that Will's right. It's Tuesday, and as the week progresses, we'll only get busier as we approach game day.

So, I grab my keys, lock my office, and make my way down to the garage where my new-to-me Jeep awaits.

I had my cousin, Keaton, work his magic on fixing up a vintage two-door Jeep for me. Sure, I can afford a new one, but this one is just…cool.

And with Keaton's help, it's extra cool.

But now that we're into November, I've had to put the doors and roof back on, closing it up in an attempt to stay warm in the winter, which means that it's still drafty.

I love Seattle, but winters are long and wet here.

I'll have to garage the Jeep for the winter and break out the Range Rover I bought when I got my first check from the team.

I know it's cliché to get a big check and then immediately buy a car, but I didn't give a shit.

After leaving the parking garage, I head toward home but then reconsider. I love my new condo. It's right on Lake Washington, with a great view, and it's less than half a mile from the training facility and headquarters for the team. It doesn't get any more convenient for work.

But I don't want to be alone this afternoon. I'm used to living at what my family affectionately refers to as the *Cousin Compound*, where it's always a hive of chaos. Full of friends and music and chatter.

My room was back in the former guesthouse, so I had privacy when I wanted it. But I always knew that family was nearby.

It's not that I regret moving out. Not at all. But

sometimes, you don't want to be alone with your own thoughts.

So, I hit the freeway and make my way over to Alki Beach, on the western shore of Seattle. A few years back, the parents bought the house next door to the original one so they could open up the yards and make it a true compound for all the cousins. I don't know what they'll do when everyone is off and living their own lives, but that will be a while yet.

Because we have so many celebrities in the family, the parents thought it would be safest to have the cousins live together, with a lot of over-the-top security, thanks to Uncle Will and his OCD about such things. And, of course, the cousins didn't complain.

It's a sweet setup, with a pool and plenty of space. It's basically a Montgomery fraternity.

What's not to like about that?

But when I park and go inside, I frown because I don't hear any voices. It's still and feels completely empty.

"You've got to be kidding me. There's always someone here."

I walk out the back door, intending to cross the backyard to the other house to have a look around, but I swing by the guesthouse, just in case.

And when I open the door, I feel a scowl form on my face.

Erin and Haley are rolling up yoga mats, and both grin when they see me in the doorway.

"Hey, Drew," Erin says as she tucks her mat away on a low shelf against the wall. "What are you doing here in the middle of the day?"

"No, that's not the question." I lean my shoulder on the doorjamb and cross my arms over my chest. "The question is, what the fuck have you done to my room?"

"Not your room anymore," Haley says with a shrug. "We converted it into a Zen yoga, library space."

"A she shed," Erin adds with excitement. "Isn't it great? It's so pretty."

"Why are there rocks on the windowsills?"

"Those are *crystals*," Haley replies coolly. "And they're there to bring good energy into the space. To protect it."

I narrow my eyes on my younger cousin. "Protect it from what? Are they going to snag the clothing of an intruder?"

"You don't get it." Haley pats my cheek and grins up at me. "But we love you anyway. Besides, you don't *have* to get it. This is our *she shed*. And the last time I checked, you're not a she."

"Nope, not a she."

"I have to go. I'll catch up with you guys later."

Haley waves and then takes off for the house, which leaves me here with Erin. At just a couple of years younger than me, Erin and I have always been close. I haven't seen her in a while, so this is a good opportunity to catch up.

"How are you?" I ask as I step inside.

"Come sit on this couch thing," she replies, gesturing for me to sit on what looks like a beanbag. "It'll change your life."

"I don't know that I need my life to be changed." But I oblige her, and I have to admit, it's damn comfortable. Erin sits across from me, her knees drawn up to her chest, and smiles serenely. "Okay. Talk to me."

"What do you want to talk about?"

"What's been going on with you? I haven't seen you much lately. We used to talk all the time."

"You moved." It's not said with any censure at all, just a statement of fact. "But I have missed you. Not much is happening. Nothing much *ever* happens."

"Hey." I frown as she casts her eyes down. "You don't sound like yourself."

"I don't think I belong in Seattle." Her eyes widen, as if she can't believe she just said that out loud.

"Okay, now we're getting somewhere. Why not?"

She blows out a breath, and if I'm not mistaken, her eyes get glassy.

"Don't cry. If I could manage to pull myself out of this death trap, I'd come over there and hug you. Don't cry, okay?"

"I'm not." She clears her throat and sniffs. "I'm not crying. I love our family, Drew. And I'm grateful that I have them. That I have all of you in my life. But it's not an easy family to be a part of. Particularly, it's not easy to be Will Montgomery's daughter."

"Yeah." I nod slowly. "I know it's been rough for you

in that department. Did the sports broadcaster come sniffing around again?"

"No. But I did meet a guy a few weeks ago who seemed nice. On the second date, he asked when he could meet my dad."

I wince. "Ouch."

"I'm just so over it. I get it. I have a cool father, but don't most guys dread meeting a girl's parents?"

"Usually," I confirm. "I can't say it's something most guys get excited about."

"That's all they ever want from me. To meet my dad. And I *love* my dad. I'm proud of him. But sometimes I just want to be...normal."

"Our family definitely isn't normal."

"No." She plucks at a string on her jeans. "Sometimes I think I should find a small town somewhere, where it's quiet and slower paced, and I can just be, you know?"

"There are a lot of small towns in Washington."

"*Not* in Washington." She shakes her head. "Somewhere new and different. I don't know where that is, but I think it's out there, and I just have to find it. In the meantime, I'm spinning my wheels. I have a business degree that I don't give a shit about."

"Why did you major in business if you hate it?"

"Because I didn't know what I wanted."

"Well, what *do* you want?"

"I don't know!" She covers her face with her hands. "I'm almost twenty-five, Drew, and I have no idea what

I want or who I am. I work full time as a barista. Sure, the tips are good, but I'm not going to make pumpkin spice lattes for the rest of my life."

"Probably not. But if you did, I'd still be proud of you."

She bites her lip as she gazes over at me, those pretty green eyes filling with tears again. "It feels like everyone in our family has their shit together, you know? They know what they want to be, or they're doing what they're passionate about. They're figuring it out. Our parents have given us awesome opportunities that a lot of kids don't get—to be who we want to be."

"Sweetheart, I don't think you sound ungrateful. If that's what you're worried about, you need to stop that. Yes, we're privileged. It's the luck of the draw with birth. It doesn't make us bad people. And it doesn't make you a bad person to be a little lost right now."

"Yeah, that's how it feels. Like I'm just *lost*. And I know it won't last forever, but I don't like it right now."

"You'll figure it out. I have all the faith in the world that you'll discover what's best for you, E. Just remember, your path is *yours*. Not any of the parents' or the other cousins'. You're your own person, and I think it's easy to forget that in this family because we all get so swept up in the amazing things that everyone is doing. I mean, look at us. Liv is an Academy Award-winning costume designer, and she married a movie star. We have athletes and music sensations, and hell, Keaton's building a car for Garth Brooks as we speak."

"It's nuts," Erin replies simply. "But I'm so fucking proud of all of you. You're the youngest quarterback coach in the entire league, Drew. That's freaking amazing."

"And you're going to find what makes you happy, too. But you're amazing *now*. You don't need to be a celebrity or work a job that gives you lots of publicity, or even a lot of money. Find what makes *you* happy."

"Thanks." She smiles softly. "Thank you for that. I think I needed the reminder."

She takes a deep breath and looks around the new she shed.

"Do you really hate this? We worked hard on it."

"I don't hate it. I don't want to use it, but I don't hate it."

"Fair enough."

CHAPTER 2

LONDON

"*W*hy is it," I demand as I stomp up the steps to the second floor, speaking loudly, "that during the summer, you're up before the birds and demanding breakfast, but during the school year, you fight me like crazy every single morning?"

I stomp into my son's bedroom and press the button on the wall that opens his curtains, letting the dim November light into the room.

"Come on, Caleb Rome Ambrose, you need to get up and get ready for school. We're already going to be late."

"Tired."

My gorgeous ten-year-old rolls over and pulls the covers over his head.

"Too bad." I rip the covers off him, grab a foot, and start to tickle him.

"No! Stop! I don't want to go to school!"

"You have to go to school." I release the ankle and then pull him to his feet, giving him a squeeze. "Go on. Get dressed. You'll have to eat breakfast in the car."

"Why can't it be Saturday?" he groans as he stomps into the bathroom and slams the door.

"Don't dillydally! I mean it, buddy. We have to go."

"I'm coming," he says from the other side of the door. Hearing the toilet flush and the water come on, telling me he's washing his hands and brushing his teeth, I make my way back downstairs to finish packing his lunch.

It's already been a crappy morning. I slept through my alarm because I was up into the wee hours of the morning, making my way through my email.

I didn't even get halfway finished before I couldn't keep my eyes open any longer.

My toaster oven gave up the ghost, but not before burning my English muffin first, and when I pulled the milk out of the fridge for cereal, I found that it had expired.

If this is indicative of how the day is going to go, I should just call in sick for both Caleb and me and enjoy the day with him.

But responsibility weighs heavily on my shoulders, and I know that we both have places to be today.

So, work and school it is for Team Ambrose.

"Where are your shoes and socks?" I ask when Caleb makes his way into the kitchen. "And you didn't comb your hair."

"No one cares if my hair is combed," he says with a negligent shrug.

"*I* care. Buddy, we are *so late.* Please get your socks and shoes on."

"Fine." He stomps to the mudroom, and I can hear him shuffling around in there.

"I would give my kingdom for a kid who's a morning person."

"I am a morning person," he replies as he returns to the kitchen. "Just not when I have to go to school."

"Don't you like school?"

"It's fine." He shrugs again and accepts the foil-wrapped breakfast burrito I pass him. "But why does it have to be in the morning?"

"Good question. One I don't have an answer for. Come on. We need to get our shit together and get out the door."

"You said shit."

I stop and close my eyes, counting to five. "Yes, I did. And please don't say it again."

"Why can you say it, but I can't?"

"Because I'm a lot older than you, kiddo. Come on. Let's go."

He always moves slowly when I need him to *hurry.*

When I see that he's buckled in, I put the car in gear and back out of the garage, then head for the school.

We have to wait for the gate to rise at the entrance to the neighborhood, and after waving at Harold, the security guard, we're off.

"Mom, what did you study in school? You know, in the olden days?"

"It wasn't *that* long ago," I reply and give him the mock glare in the rearview, making him giggle. "I studied the same things as you. Math, spelling, reading. The usual stuff."

"Weird."

God, I love this kid. No matter how my day is going, he can always make me smile.

"Here you go," I say as I pull up to the drop-off spot in front of the school. "If you hurry, you'll get in there just before the bell."

"I forgot my lunch."

I sigh and close my eyes again.

"Are you going to say shit?"

"Maybe." I wave him out of the car. "Get hot lunch today. There's money on your account."

"'Kay. See ya."

"Have a good day. Be good. Love you." It's the same thing that I say to him every single day.

"Love you, too, Mom."

After breathing a huge sigh of relief that I got him to school on time, I drive over to the football team's headquarters. As part owner of the team, I'm not required to keep an office there or stay abreast of the day-to-day operations of the team. But I enjoy it. I've learned a lot in the few months that Rome and I have owned the team, and I enjoy being in the middle of the hustle and bustle.

I used to keep my office at home, but that was lonely. Isolating.

Depressing.

I can do most of my work from my office at headquarters, both for the team and for the other companies I head. Getting dressed in business attire, slapping on makeup, and doing something with my hair makes me feel productive.

And, so far, no one has had an issue with me being around a lot of the time. Not that they'd tell me if they were against it. I am the boss, after all.

I pull my Mercedes into my parking space, and as I walk to the elevator, I lock the car behind me. I'm only running a few minutes behind the time I usually get to the office, so given the way this day started, I'm not doing too poorly.

To my surprise, the elevator stops on the second floor, and a sweaty, sexy Drew Montgomery walks on to join me.

"Ms. Ambrose," he says with a terse nod.

"Coach." I smile over at him. Drew is the one person on staff that I've had trouble winning over. He's not rude, but he's not warm and fuzzy either.

I don't plan to stop working on him.

"I had a new idea for uniforms," I inform him and have to press my lips together so I don't laugh when that scowl forms between his eyebrows. "What do you think of sequins?"

"Like I said, yes—*sequins?*"

"Sure. I thought it would be pretty on the field, all the twinkling and such."

His mouth twitches.

"Don't look now, Coach, but I think you're about to smile at me."

He inhales and lets the smile come before glancing over at me, and the impact of that smile, with those intense blue eyes, is almost enough to knock me off my axis. I know I've only met two of the Montgomerys, but based on Will and Drew, the family is *gorgeous*.

"I trust you had a good workout?"

He glances down at his sweaty shirt and then nods. "A grueling one."

"I should take advantage of the facilities here sometime. I never use the stationary bike I bought for my house. Isn't that always the way? Spend a bunch of money on workout equipment and never use it?"

"It's your facility," he replies. "You should take advantage of it."

I nod in agreement. "Please be sure to let me know if any of the equipment needs to be replaced or updated."

"Okay."

The elevator stops at his floor, and he walks out. "Have a good day."

Just as the doors close, he turns and offers me another of those grins.

When I'm alone, I pat my chest.

"Coach Hottie McHotterson is what they should

call him," I mutter, and then step out of the elevator when it stops on the top floor.

My heels click on the tile floor as I make my way down the hallway to my office. All the administration has offices up here, along with publicity, accounting, and HR. We also have a huge conference room where we hold most of our meetings, but the press room is on the main floor. I'm in the corner, with a great view of Lake Washington. My office is big enough to house my own workout equipment of its own, but where would the fun be in that?

When I pull my phone out of my bag, I see that I have a missed call from my brother, so I give him a quick call as I boot up my computer and long for a cup of coffee.

"Are you in the office today?" Rome asks when he answers.

"I'm in the office most days. What's up? Are you stopping by?"

As the CEO of several companies of his own, Rome keeps an office in downtown Seattle, but sometimes he stops by headquarters. Mostly, he goes to the games, brings the woman of the moment and some friends, and has fun in the owner's box.

Which is fine by me. One of us should be at the games, and I can't make them.

I have a son who needs me, and I'm doing my damnedest to keep him out of the public eye.

"Probably not today, but I'll do my best to be at

Caleb's soccer game on Saturday. That's tomorrow, right?"

"Yes, tomorrow is Saturday. He'd like that. Why did you need to know if I'm at the office?"

"Dad was asking me this morning over our breakfast meeting."

I scowl. "Why would he want to know?"

"Couldn't tell you. I didn't ask. Anyway, I have to get to a meeting. Have a good day."

"You, too."

Rome ends the call before I can, and I sit back in my chair, frowning.

I don't have a tight relationship with my father for a myriad of reasons. We don't hate each other, and we're not estranged. We just don't see eye to eye on much of anything, so we avoid each other.

It's worked for more than a decade.

So, I have no idea why he'd ask Rome if I was in the office today. Besides, why wouldn't he simply pick up the phone and ask me himself?

And then I smirk at myself and sign into the computer.

Because it's my *dad*.

Blowing out a breath, I stand and poke my head out of my office, looking for my assistant, Louise, but she's not at her desk. That doesn't bother me much because I can fetch my own coffee, so I walk down the hallway to the employee lounge and stop short.

Louise is lying back on a table, her skirt shoved up

around her hips, her purple panties hanging from one foot, and her hands gripping onto a pale white ass as she's ridden hard.

Not at all embarrassed, I lean on the doorjamb, my arms folded over my chest, and wait for them to finish.

"Oh, fuck yeah. I love it when the boss doesn't show up," Louise announces, digging her nails into that white flesh. "I wish she *never* came in."

Wondering idly if I should shoot Louise's husband an email, I examine my nails and realize that I need a manicure.

"Oh, yeah, baby," Patrick, one of our publicists, groans. "God, your pussy is so good."

"It's all yours."

Not wanting to stand here all damn day, I finally clear my throat, which has them scrambling. Patrick pulls out and fumbles with his pants. Louise falls off the table, seeming to grapple with her panties while pulling her skirt down, and when they turn toward me, their eyes are huge, and Louise's cheeks are flushed.

Whether it's from the sex or embarrassment, that remains to be seen.

"Oh, shit," Louise stammers. "We were just—"

"I'm not blind," I assure her coldly. "Both of you can gather your things and get the hell out of my building. You're fired."

"But, no, just—"

"You can't—"

"Oh, yes, I can. And I just did. You have five minutes

to get the hell out before I have you escorted out. And Louise, you might want to let your husband know what kind of woman he's married to."

"Don't tell him." With wild eyes, she runs to me and grabs onto the lapels of my suit jacket.

I raise a brow and stare down at her hands until she lets go.

"Please don't tell him. It's just an office romance."

"I thought we were in love," Patrick interrupts, bordering on whining.

"I don't give a shit what you are. Get out. Now."

"But—"

"I will not say it again." I turn cold eyes on both of them. "You thought you could take advantage and disrespect me like this? You thought wrong. Goodbye. Your last check will be wired to you by tomorrow."

Still without a drop of coffee in my system, I stride down to my office and call security to ensure that Louise and Patrick leave and their team property is collected. Then I call Sherry in HR to pass along the news and ask her to find me a new assistant.

"Geez, I'm sorry," Sherry says. "I'll get started on it right now. Do you want to borrow someone else's assistant in the interim?"

"No, I'm fine for now. Thanks, Sherry."

I hang up and press my fingertips to my forehead, trying to alleviate one hell of a headache. Then I remember that I'm still without coffee, but I refuse to go into that lounge until it's been thoroughly sanitized, so I call Ed in janitorial and explain the situation.

He assures me that it'll be detoxed in no time.

To tide me over, I place a delivery order for Starbucks, and I've just started making my way through *more* emails when there's a knock on my door.

"I'm busy this morning, so if it's not an emergency, can we do this later?"

"But I came a long way to see you."

My blood runs cold, and when I glance up at the doorway and see Felix Winningham III standing on the threshold, I feel faint.

Not in a good way.

"Like I said, I don't have much time today. What do you want, Felix?"

He clucks his tongue and walks inside my office slowly. "That's not a very nice way to welcome me, sweetheart. I know it's been a few months since we last saw each other, but I'm here now."

"What do you want?" I ask again.

"Well, I spoke with your father this morning. I always did love him, you know."

Bile rises up in the back of my throat. *This* is why my dad wanted to know if I was here today.

So he could sic Felix on me.

Dad would love nothing more than to see me marry Felix. The *right* kind of man.

And by that, he means the right kind of money.

But I don't answer. I simply watch him with cool

eyes, knowing exactly how to school my features so that it seems like I'm not bothered in the least.

I perfected this move at six years old.

"Honey, I'm sorry for everything that went down before. You know that I would *never* intentionally hurt you in *any* way."

"Right, so are you saying that you accidentally put your cock in that woman in *my bedroom*? Did you slip and fall?"

"Don't be snide."

"I don't know why you're here. I made it clear, more than once, that I want nothing at all to do with you ever again."

"Well, your father thinks I'm good for you."

"My father has never known what's good for me," I counter sharply.

"You're being unreasonable." His voice is soft again, but there's an edge there, almost as if he's desperate. "Don't be overly emotional about this, babe."

"Honey, sweetheart, babe. None of those things applies to me where you're concerned."

"You and I both know that you haven't fallen out of love with me."

"I don't think I was ever *in* love with you. And I definitely know that I'm not now. What I want is for you to leave my office."

"I have your father on my side, London."

"Good for you. Go try to charm him because it's not working on me."

There's a knock on the door, surprising both of us, and I'm startled, and not a little embarrassed, to see Drew standing there, holding my Starbucks.

"Delivery for you," Drew says, his eyes intense on mine, although he has a cocky grin on his lips. "Is everything okay in here, babe?"

Babe?

I blink, and then suddenly realize what Drew's doing.

"You didn't have to bring me coffee."

Drew walks around Felix to me, passes me the coffee, and wraps his arm around my waist.

"You had a rough morning," he says and kisses my temple, then turns to Felix. "Oh, hello. I'm Drew. Who are you?"

Felix is practically vibrating with fury, and it fills me with delighted glee.

"This is Felix," I reply before the angry man can manage to sputter out a word. "He's a former acquaintance. I'm still not sure why he dropped in today."

Drew and I wait expectantly, but Felix narrows his eyes menacingly at Drew.

"I wouldn't try it," Drew says tightly. "You won't win."

His stance, his tight jaw, and every taut muscle in Drew's body radiates alpha energy, and I'm *so* here for it.

"I came to ask London if I can escort her to the fundraiser dinner tonight." Felix's voice is strained. If

I'm not mistaken, I'd say he's afraid of Drew, which fills me with even more glee.

"She already has a date," Drew replies. "Sounds like you came all this way for nothing."

Felix looks at me, and I simply nod, and then he turns on his heel and marches out of my office, slamming the door shut behind him.

Drew doesn't immediately pull away from me, and I don't mind.

"What an asshat," he mutters and scowls down at me. "You used to fuck that?"

No, I didn't, but I simply shrug a shoulder. "I realized that he's an asshat pretty quickly."

"Good." He steps away, and I take a long sip of the coffee.

"I'm sorry you had to witness that, but I'm not sorry that you got him to leave."

"What time should I pick you up tonight?"

That makes me grin as I take another sip of my coffee. "Drew, you don't have to escort me tonight. It's really okay."

"Do you think he's not going? He'll be front and center, likely as your father's date, so he can keep an eye on you. I know guys like this, and they piss me off. I'll take you."

"You don't even like me."

"Says who?"

I laugh now and shake my head, and then the laughter comes harder, and I can't control it. I have to sit and cross my legs so I don't pee myself, and all the while, Drew just stands there, his arms folded, watching me with humor in his own blue eyes.

"You can't stand it when I come to your office," I say when I can breathe again. "And now you're going to willingly spend the evening with me?"

"I don't dislike you. I *do* dislike him. What time should I pick you up?"

"We can meet there."

"London." That's the first time he's ever said my name, and it's the sexiest sound I've ever heard in my life. "What time?"

"Seven?"

"I'll see you then."

CHAPTER 3

DREW

I'm not entirely sure how I ended up in this situation.

I wasn't lying to London when I told her that I didn't dislike her. She's not my favorite person on the planet, but even if I hated her guts, I would have stepped in this morning when I heard that smarmy voice in her office.

I happened to be in the lobby of the building when her coffee was delivered, and I offered to run it up to her. No big deal.

But as I walked down the hall, I heard him, and it was plain as day that he was an asshole. Before I knew it, I had my arm wrapped around her, had kissed her head, and had given the other man the impression that she and I were an item.

The kicker is, despite the fact that she can grate on

my nerves faster than anyone else in the known universe, she felt good against me.

And she smells like cinnamon, which intrigues me. Is that normal? Does she bake a lot? Where does that come from?

I guess I inherited the urge to swoop in and help a woman from my dad and uncles, and the thought of escorting her to the charity dinner tonight doesn't bother me. As a member of the staff, I have to go anyway. She's going, and I'm going; we might as well just ride together.

Like I said, no big deal.

I have to check in with the security guard at the gate of the neighborhood as I pull onto her street.

"Drew Montgomery for London Ambrose."

"Yes, sir. Her home is two miles in, at the end of the road."

"Thanks."

He nods and presses a button to open the enormous iron gate, and I pull through.

I'm not a stranger to wealth. While my parents are not wealthy, I have aunts, uncles, and other family members who are. I'm used to big homes, fancy cars, and luxury goods of all kinds. We understood that we were a privileged family, but it was never really a big deal to any of us cousins.

But the kind of wealth that London's family has? That's foreign to me. I don't know a lot about them, or how they amassed such a huge empire, aside from knowing that their father was one of the tech guys that made it really big in the nineties. They have access to billions of dollars, which is a concept that I can't really wrap my head around.

Not that I need to.

At the end of the road is a smaller driveway with a brick mailbox, and I turn to follow it through some trees that have lost their leaves. It winds around for another quarter mile or so before the house comes into view.

The sun has just gone down, and the house is lit up from the inside out. It's a two-story estate, and it sprawls with beautiful, old trees surrounding it. There's even a fountain in the middle of a circular driveway.

Fancy.

I climb the steps to the front door and press the doorbell. I can hear some shuffling inside, and then the door opens.

But it's not London who answers.

"Who are you?" a young voice asks as he peeks out from the side of the door.

"Caleb!" That's London's voice yelling out from inside the house. "You can't just open the damn door."

"She said *damn*," the boy says with a snicker, and then the door opens wider, and London's frowning down at the kid. She's in a white terrycloth robe, with one eye made up and the other one naked. I can still smell the soap from her shower.

"Hi," she says and huffs out a breath. "Sorry, I'm running a little late, which seems to be the norm today. Come on in."

She steps back, making room for me to step inside, and I feel my eyebrows climb, despite myself.

My entire family would fit in the foyer. And that's saying something, given that my family is massive.

"Your home is lovely."

"It's big," the boy named Caleb says with a shrug. "Come on, I'll show you my game room."

"You don't have to—" London begins, but I shake my head and offer her a wink.

"Go get ready. We've got this." London's a mom. I had no idea. How didn't I know this?

She sighs, seems to weigh her options, then shrugs. "Okay, thanks. I won't be long, and Miss Quinn is in the kitchen fixing a snack, so she'll join you in just a few."

"Don't worry. Go."

Caleb gestures for me to follow him and leads me into a room that is, indeed, a game room.

There's a big couch facing a huge television, and I see he has his game console on, and Mario Kart is ready to go.

There's a popcorn machine and a candy station that seems to be locked, and that makes me grin.

"How often do you get to raid the candy box?"

"Only when Mom and I watch movies in here. I

guess the last people used this as a movie room, but I mostly play games in here. What's your name?"

"Drew. And you're Caleb?"

"Yeah. Caleb Rome Ambrose. I'm named after my uncle. He's the *best.*"

"I've met him," I inform him and sit on the edge of the couch. "He's a really nice guy. My dad is named Caleb, too."

"Is his middle name Rome?"

"No, it's Andrew. Like me."

"Do you work for the team?" I can already tell that I'm in for a bunch of questions, and that doesn't bother me at all.

"Yep. I'm a coach."

"But you're not a player? You look like a player."

"Used to be." I smile at him. "How about you? Do you play any sports?"

"Soccer right now. Hey, you should come to my game tomorrow. It's going to be a lot of fun. I'll probably score a lot of goals."

This kid doesn't have any confidence issues.

"I might just do that."

"Have you ever played soccer?"

"Sure, when I was about your age. I like to watch it on TV, too."

"Me, too! Mom watches with me sometimes. It's cool."

"Does Miss Quinn stay with you a lot?"

"Only when Mom has to go do stuff for work." He

shrugs and picks up a controller. "I heard her tell Uncle Rome that she doesn't want to have a nanny because we're a team, and we do just fine by ourselves. I'm probably old enough to stay home by myself. I don't really need a babysitter."

"I think, according to the law, that you do."

That makes him smile, and then he shrugs his slim shoulder once more. He's going to be a tall kid, and he's got his mom's dark hair and blue eyes.

Before he can ask me more questions, we hear female voices coming down the hallway.

"He should be in bed by ten because he has a soccer game tomorrow morning." London walks into the game room, followed by a woman, whom I'd guess was college age.

And my tongue sticks to the roof of my mouth.

London's in a black dress with a high neckline, but her arms are bare, and her legs... I get glimpses of her long legs through the slits in her form-fitting dress. She's lean and toned, and I suspect she works out more than she let on in the elevator earlier today.

She's usually in suits at work, not showing any skin.

"You're beautiful, Mom," Caleb announces and wiggles his eyebrows.

"Thanks, buddy. You and Miss Quinn have fun, okay?"

"I'll let her win at least one game," he says with a smug smile, which makes Quinn laugh.

"That's a lie. He never lets me win. Don't worry about us; just go have fun."

"Ten o'clock," London says sternly. "Don't give her a hard time when she tells you it's bedtime."

"I wouldn't do that," Caleb replies, trying to look earnest.

"Yeah, right. Okay, I'll see you in the morning." London kisses his head, ruffles his hair, and turns to me. "I'm ready when you are."

"Let's do this." I gesture for her to lead the way and then turn back to Caleb. "It was good to meet you, Caleb."

"You, too!"

I follow London out to my car—I broke the Range Rover out for the winter—and open the door for her, then walk around to the driver's side.

"I didn't know you had a son," I begin as I start the car. "And before you reply to that, I have to tell you, you *do* look beautiful."

Her lips tip up into a smile. "Thanks. You look good in a suit yourself."

"I try not to wear them often," I confess as I pull away from the house.

"I don't advertise Caleb," London says. "He's no secret, and at one point, it was a hot topic in the press —me being an unwed mother—but that press has died off, and I like keeping Caleb out of the spotlight altogether. I know that I can't shelter him forever, but for now, he's not the topic of interest, and I'm happy to keep it that way. He goes to a good private school and lives a pretty normal life."

I raise a brow and turn to her as I slow at the security gate. "Come on."

"Okay, it's as normal as it can be. He plays soccer, has play dates with his friends, and goes to the movies. And I am with him as much as I can be."

"Which is why you come to the office at nine and leave by two."

I feel like an ass. I assumed she kept those hours because she was the boss, and she *could.* I pegged her as spoiled and indulged and, therefore, a slacker.

"I want to be the one to take him to school and pick him up. I don't have a nanny. Not full time, anyway. Quinn helps out a lot, and she travels with us if I have to go out of town for work. She's great, and the job works for her and her college schedule."

"He's a cute kid."

Now that makes her light up. "Thanks. I might be biased, but I think so, too. And smart. Holy shit, he's smart. I can't get anything past that kid. Anyway, I'll stop gushing about him."

"You're a mom." I still can't quite believe that. "It's your job to gush. My mom *still* likes to talk about her kids."

"How many siblings do you have?"

"I have two sisters. They're twins and older than me. Technically, they're half sisters. My mom had them with her first husband, but my dad adopted the girls right after they got married. If anyone heard me refer to them as *half*, I'd get my ass chewed."

"As it should be," London says with a nod. "So, you're the baby of the family."

"Of the immediate family. But I have about a dozen or so cousins, and we're all really close. We were kind of raised as siblings. You're the baby, too."

"Yes, Rome is less than a year older than me."

"What's up with the city names?"

That makes her laugh as she fiddles with the handbag in her lap. "It was my mom's idea. We weren't conceived there or anything weird like that. She just loves those cities and wanted to name us after them. Dad didn't care."

"Where's your mom now?"

I feel her turn to watch me. "You don't watch the news much, do you?"

"Not really," I admit.

"My mother is in the south of France with her new husband, who happens to be five years older than me. Jacque. I've never met him."

"Wow. You don't speak to your mom?"

"Once a year. On my birthday, she calls to sing to me. On Caleb's birthday, a delivery comes with way more toys and crap than he needs. On Christmas, I get diamonds of some kind. This necklace was last year's gift."

Her fingers clasp around the large diamond pendant just under her collarbone.

"Aside from that, no. She's pretty wrapped up in her own life, having fun in Europe."

"You don't sound too torn up about it."

London clears her throat, showing the first sign of any emotion during the entire conversation. "My parents didn't raise me. Mrs. Olson did. She was my nanny from the day I came home from the hospital. She raised both Rome and me until we were in college. I speak to her often and see her several times a year. Sometimes, she and her husband vacation with us."

I nod, getting a better picture of how London grew up, and it only gives me more respect and appreciation for how she's chosen to raise her own son.

"I feel like there's a hell of a lot more to talk about," I say as I pull up to the valet, "but we're here, so I'm going to bookmark where we are and pick it up later."

Someone opens both of our doors, and there are flashbulbs going off and questions called out.

And when it's discovered by the press that we arrived together, there are even more questions.

"Ms. Ambrose, are you and your coach an item?"

"How long have you and Coach Montgomery been dating?"

"Is this a conflict of interest?"

We avoid all the questions, and with my hand on the small of her back, we make our way down the red carpet.

I start to move away to let her be photographed

alone, but she turns to me, smiles, and holds her hand out for mine.

Her eyes say, *don't go.*

So, I take her hand, and we smile for the cameras. Once inside, London takes a long, slow breath and then turns to me, glancing around to make sure no one is listening in.

"I'm sorry," she hisses. "I just get so nervous, and I instinctively pulled you back, and if that made you uncomfortable, I apologize."

"I'm fine." I shake my head down at her. "If I didn't want to be here, I wouldn't be."

She nods, but I see the nerves and uncertainty still in her face.

"London, you've got this. You look amazing, you're smarter than anyone else in that room, and you're the *boss. You* are the boss. Don't forget that."

Her eyes jump to mine in surprise, and then she squares her shoulders, those diamonds winking at her neckline, and nods once.

"You're right. Thanks for the reminder."

"Let's go find our seats."

The ballroom is *fancy.* It seems tonight is the night for that term, because I can't think of another one. The crystal chandeliers hang low over round tables dressed in crisp, white tablecloths covered in silver and crystal.

A string quartet plays live music as we wander through the room.

London smiles and greets everyone who

approaches her, remembering their names and little tidbits about their lives, which surprises me.

"Oh, hello, Marshall. It's so lovely to see you and your wife, especially after that nasty spill you took on that ski trip last year."

"Nancy, you look marvelous. How is that new puppy settling in?"

"Greg, you're as handsome as ever. How are you and your husband getting on? I keep meaning to invite you over for dinner."

She's flawless as she moves through the room, making small talk. You'd never know that she was a ball of nervous energy just thirty minutes ago.

When we make our way to our table, I'm relieved to see my uncle Will and my aunt Meg already seated, and walk over to say hello.

"You're so damn handsome," Meg says as she pats my cheek and smooths down the lapel of my jacket.

"And you're gorgeous. What are you doing with a dud like him?" I gesture to Will with my thumb as he grins widely next to me.

"He charmed me with his rapier wit."

I snort at that and turn to shake my uncle's hand. "No one else is here yet?"

"Henry and his wife should be here soon."

I nod. Henry is a defensive line coach and has become a friend of mine over the past few months.

London makes her way to my side, and I smile down at her. "Meg, have you met London Ambrose?"

"Briefly," Meg replies and reaches out to shake London's hand. "It's great to see you again, London."

"You, as well. That gown is beautiful. Blue is your color."

"Thank you."

"There's my girl."

I feel London stiffen beside me, but she pastes on a smile and turns at her father's voice.

"Hello, Dad."

"You're a vision," he says as he leans in to buss her cheek. "But you look like you might be putting on a few pounds."

Appalled, I glance over at Will, who shakes his head. *Don't respond.*

"Actually, I'm down five," London retorts. "But who's counting, right?"

"Felix joined me this evening," her father goes on, not even missing a beat. Chandler Ambrose is an ass. "He said he saw you this morning."

"He interrupted my day, yes."

"Come, sit with him, and you two can get things sorted out."

"Not on your life." London smiles up at her father, who's raised an eyebrow at her. "I will not now, nor ever, sit with him and sort anything out. But if you would like him to be your friend, that's your choice."

Will clears his throat, and Meg looks down at her drink, but I don't move my eyes from Chandler.

"I believe our seats are right over here," I say,

gesturing to two chairs on the opposite side of the table from Chandler and Felix, and London smiles up at me as if I just cured cancer.

"I'd love to get to know you more, Meg," London says as she turns her back on her father and sits next to the other woman.

"It won't last," Chandler says to me in a low voice before walking away to try to charm someone else.

Meg and London are already chatting about music as Will gestures me over as he stands.

"What's going on here?"

"It looks like we're on a date."

Will's eyes narrow. "I thought you didn't like her."

"Feelings can change. I like her just fine."

He exhales and shoves his hands into his pockets. "Be careful, Drew. Chandler isn't exactly the man you want to try to go toe-to-toe with."

"I'm not trying to do that."

He nods and then takes his seat next to his wife. I glance up and see Felix watching us with an angry, narrowed gaze.

I lean over and whisper in London's ear. "I'm going to be very attentive tonight because that asshole over there has wolf written all over him."

She laughs, playing the part, and cups my cheek in her hand. "I don't mind. But we should probably talk about all of this later."

"Later. For now, just play along."

CHAPTER 4

LONDON

I'm freaking exhausted. It's been three hours of smiling and pretending. Talking and remembering small, insignificant tidbits about acquaintances so they feel special.

The hardest part, though, is keeping a smile on my face, even when my father is acting like a complete ass. He's embarrassing.

Always has been.

He's so arrogant and thinks he's the most beloved, most important person in the room. And usually, he is. He's charming, and people like him.

But more than that, he's rich. Beyond rich. And because of that incredible, unreal wealth, people gravitate his way.

It's the only reason that Felix has affixed himself to my father's side. He thinks that he can milk my father for a whole bunch of money. It's the only reason he tried to talk me into a relationship with him. He doesn't want *me*; he wants my family's money, influence, and contacts.

He's a user.

And either my dad doesn't see that, or he doesn't really care. But the fact that he's so sure that I should be with Felix, and won't let go of that ridiculous notion, frustrates the hell out of me.

"You hanging in there?" Drew asks, whispering in my ear.

"I'm okay," I reply honestly and smile over at him. "You've gone above and beyond this evening."

"I don't know if you realize this, but being near you isn't exactly a hardship, London."

That makes me flush with satisfaction. When was the last time someone told me that they enjoyed being around me for *me*? Not because of what I can do for them, or because of what I own or who I know, but because they enjoy my company?

I don't remember.

And isn't that just pitiful?

"Still, thanks a lot, Drew."

He winks at me, and that makes my stomach jump. How is it possible for a man to be so handsome? His parents must be gods because Drew is *hot*.

I've thought so since the day he started working for the team. Of course, I've been nothing but professional, but a girl can look.

And I've *looked.*

"Let's dance, shall we?"

My heart sinks when I look up and see that Felix has walked around the table to me.

I glance over and see my father watching me with narrowed eyes and decide that I'll appease him with one very public dance.

"Fine." I stand from my seat and turn to Drew. "I'll be right back."

"I'll be right here, babe."

Felix leads me to the dance floor and pulls me into his arms. He's stiff and uncoordinated.

And I absolutely *hate* the way he smells.

After I found him fucking some chick in my bed, I replaced the entire bed, the linens, *everything* because that smell seemed to linger behind.

It makes me gag.

"I know you're not really dating that coach," he says calmly.

"Says who?"

"Says everyone I asked tonight. Maybe you're fucking him, but you're not in a relationship with him."

"That's absolutely none of your business."

"It's absolutely *all* of my business. Because your father has approved of me dating you and, after an appropriate amount of time, marrying you."

"This isn't the sixteen hundreds, Felix." My voice is as dry as the Sahara. "My father can't just betroth me to someone. He doesn't have any say in who I date."

"Oh, I think we both know that your father has

quite a bit of influence on your life. Do you want him to sell the team? To take away your trust fund, your home? It would be a pity if you and Caleb were homeless."

"You're insane," I hiss and pull out of his arms. "There's no way in *hell* my father would do any of that to me. Not for anything."

"I bet I could talk him into it." He winks. "It's all about what's best for business, after all."

"Fuck this." I storm away from him and over to my table, but rather than join Drew, I approach my father. "You do realize that Felix is a smarmy bastard, right? He basically just told me that if I don't date him, he'll talk you into ruining me."

There are gasps around us, and my father's eyes flick to the side before he stands and leans in to speak quietly in my ear.

"You're making a scene, London."

"You're damn right I'm making a scene. I will *not* be spoken to like that, and I expect my father, whom I love very much, to have my back."

"Of course, I have your back," he assures me, and his eyes soften. For the first time in a long time, I feel like it's true. *This* is the dad from my childhood. He turns to Felix, whom I can feel vibrating with fury behind me. "You can go, Felix. Any friendship or relationship we had is now done."

"She's lying," Felix insists, but my father shakes his head and kisses my forehead.

"No. She's not. And I was a fool to think that you might be good for her. Now, I advise you to leave peacefully, or I'll have you escorted out."

Felix snarls—actually *snarls*—before he turns and stomps away, shoulder-checking people on his way out.

"We'll discuss this later," Dad says softly, and then sits down to enjoy the rest of his evening, as if he's just flicked off a pesky fly. "Don't worry, darling. We'll find someone...*suitable.*"

He glances at Drew and smirks, then turns and talks to someone else at the table.

This night is over for me.

"Would you mind if we make it an early night?" I ask Drew when I return to my seat.

"You're the boss," he says, and we take the next thirty minutes to say our goodbyes and make our way out to the valet.

We're quiet as we wait for his car, and the whole time, I can't get my dad's last shot out of my head. *We'll find someone suitable.*

As if Drew would be an *unsuitable* match? Why? Because he's not as wealthy as my father? I hate to break it to him, but there are very few people in the world as well off as he is. If that's what he wants me to find, we're both going to be horribly disappointed.

We're still quiet in the car as Drew pulls onto the interstate.

"Do you want to tell me what happened during that dance?" he finally asks.

"Felix got too confident in his influence with my father and threatened me with poverty and homelessness. Not that my father has any say in such things because he didn't buy my home, and I've amassed wealth on my own, but the fact that he mentioned Caleb, that my son's name crossed his lips, was too much for me to stay quiet about. I just lost my shit."

I see Drew's hands tighten on the steering wheel in temper. "I should have punched the fucker."

"*I* should have punched the fucker," I reply. "Hopefully, he's gone for good now. I'm just tired."

"You put on quite a show."

My head whips around, and I stare at Drew in surprise. "What do you mean by that?"

"Exactly what I said. It's impressive to watch you work a room. You know everyone's names and details about them and then bring it up in conversation."

"I was trained from a young age to be very good at socializing."

"The training worked."

"I hate it."

Now he glances my way in surprise. "Why?"

"It's exhausting. I'm not an extrovert. I like quiet, and I like to be by myself. I don't want all the noise, all the questions, all the prying eyes. I'm used to it, but that doesn't mean that it's fun for me."

"Fascinating," he murmurs, and I settle back against

the leather seat to watch the city lights fly by as he drives me home.

When he pulls up to a stop in front of my door, I move to get out of the car, but he holds up a hand.

"Wait."

He doesn't wait to see if I followed his order before he gets out of the vehicle and walks around to open my door.

That should have irritated me, but all it did was make my core tighten in the most delicious way.

Drew holds his hand out for mine and helps me out of the vehicle, then walks me to the front door.

"Thanks for escorting me tonight."

His lips twitch as he places his hand on the door and leans into me. "You're welcome. I actually had a really good time."

Holy baby Jesus, he's going to kiss me.

"You don't have to," I blurt out, and he cocks an eyebrow.

"Have to what?"

"Kiss me."

Those lips, those sexy as sin lips, tip up on one side in a cocky grin, and without a word, he dips his head down and touches those lips to mine. He just presses them there, chastely, and then in the span of a nanosecond, the kiss warms up.

I open up to him, and his hands are suddenly cupping my face as he kisses me urgently, hungrily, and presses my back to the door.

My head spins. I want him to boost me up so I can wrap my legs around his waist and lose myself in him.

And then my wits return to me, and I press my hand to his chest.

That's all it takes to have him lift his head away and stare down at me, breathing as hard as I am.

"Do I need to apologize?" he asks.

"I hope you don't," I reply with a small laugh. I can't resist reaching up to cup his cheek. "That was really...*good.*"

He nods, that cocky grin still on his ridiculously divine face, and waits while I unlock the door and disarm the alarm system.

"Have a good night, Drew. Drive safe."

"Good night."

I smile and close the door. It's a few minutes until I hear his vehicle start and head down the driveway.

Leaning against the door, I take a long, deep breath.

Holy shit, Drew Montgomery can *kiss.*

ROME: *Sorry, can't make the game today. Work complications. I'll come see Caleb later.*

I sigh as I read the message from my brother, send a quick reply, and toss my phone into my handbag. Caleb is running on the field, kicking the ball and pointing at one of the other kids. He obviously wants to pass to the other boy.

"You've got this, Caleb!" I yell out and clap my hands. It's chilly this morning, but it's November in Seattle, so that's a given.

I'm just grateful that it's not raining.

"Can I sit here?" I tip my head back and look up into the bluest eyes in the country.

"How did you know we'd be here?" I scoot over, making room for Drew.

"Caleb invited me yesterday," he says. "It wasn't hard to figure out where you'd be. Is it okay that I came?"

"My son will be thrilled."

"How did you sleep?" he asks, passing me a cup from Starbucks.

"I actually slept like the dead." I sip the coffee and look up at Drew in surprise. "How did you know how I take my coffee?"

"I read the sticker on yesterday's delivery," he replies easily, watching the boys run around on the field. "How are you today?"

"I'm fine. A little tired and a bit mentally drained from all those people, but otherwise, no complaints. How about you?"

"Same as you." He frowns when he sees Caleb fall, but then relaxes when my boy gets back up again and continues down the field. "Where's his dad?"

"I'm surprised that wasn't your first question last night." I take a sip of my coffee and sigh. "Caleb's dad wasn't a bad guy. I was rebellious in high school and in college. I loved dating guys that my dad didn't approve of. Theo definitely fit that bill. He was wild and loud and silly. But he could be really sweet and kind, too. I got pregnant at twenty-one, and boy, did that piss my dad off."

"Was that the goal?" Drew asks evenly.

"Probably, at that time. I liked making my dad mad. It was the only time he paid attention to me. I made it clear that I'd be keeping the baby, but Theo wasn't ready to be a dad."

"He split?" Drew asks.

"Kind of. He and I broke up, but he still took an interest in the baby. He helped with things, but I didn't need or want his money. He loved holding Caleb while he slept. And I didn't mind having him around."

"So, where is he now?"

Watching my son laugh with his friend, I blow out a breath. "Well, he got mixed up with some bad people, developed a drug addiction, and overdosed when Caleb was three."

"Jesus, London, I'm sorry."

"Me, too." I smile over at him. "I really am sorry that Caleb won't ever know him because, despite the demons he fought, he was a good person. But we have Rome in our lives, and he's a great male figure for Caleb."

"What about your dad?"

I snort and shake my head. "He may have a house here in Seattle, but we don't see him much. My dad would say that's not true, and I think that he loves Caleb as much as he's able to love anyone."

"You and your dad have a...different relationship."

"Yeah. We do. This is a really deep conversation to have over soccer."

That makes Drew smile. "Sorry, I just had questions."

"I don't mind answering them."

"I want to see more of you, London. I want to see a lot more of you."

"Okay, I'm not saying no, but I am going to warn you that my life is complicated, and I have a kid. I'm a *mom*, Drew. That comes first, always."

"I get that and respect it. What are the other complications?"

"I don't want to disrespect you in any way, but my dad won't like it."

Now he laughs and drags his hand down his face. "I think that's a first for me, but would it offend *you* if I say I just don't give a flying fuck if your dad likes it or not?"

"No, it doesn't offend me."

"Does it bother you if your dad doesn't approve?"

"No, I just know that he might try to make waves. He thinks I should be with, and marry, a man with a certain status. Oh, God, not that I'm suggesting we'll get married or anything, I'm just saying. I mean, of course, we're not getting married. You hate me."

"I don't hate you. I don't plan on getting married

today, but who knows what might happen? And lastly, what will your dad do if you don't end up with someone he approves of?"

"He could cut me off." I tap my chin, thinking it over. "I don't think he would, but he could. And that doesn't scare me much because I have businesses of my own, not to mention plenty of investments and wealth that don't depend on him in the least, but I'd worry about Caleb. Although, it could be good for us to continue to pretend to date so that he doesn't try to hook me up with another of his smarmy, rich friends."

"Is that what you want? For it to be fake? I just told you that I want to see more of you, and I didn't say anything about pretending."

That makes my stomach flutter. "Why? Why do you want to see me?"

"Because you make me fucking crazy, but then you turn around and make me laugh. I've seen you in three different looks in the past twenty-four hours, and I can't decide which is the hottest. You look amazing in those professional suits you wear to work, but then last night, you were the sexiest woman in the room in that dress that just screamed to be ripped off and tossed onto the floor next to the bed."

I swallow hard, but he's not even close to finished.

"Now, this morning, here you are in jeans, sneakers, and a hoodie. Your hair is undone, with no makeup on, and I'll be damned if this isn't the look I love the most. And you didn't even *try*."

"I didn't even think about trying." I'm glowing. That's the only way to describe the sensation of hearing Drew tell me how attracted he is to me. "But those are just looks, Drew."

"You're smart and kind. You love your kid, and you run the team well. You're respected. As far as I'm concerned, that's a good place to start. I want to know more about you."

"Can we talk about the team jerseys?"

"That's where I draw the line."

I can't help but laugh at that. "I've really annoyed you with those, haven't I?"

"I almost spiked your coffee with poison."

That makes me snort. "This could make waves at work, you know. Rumors, looks, blatant talk."

"I won't be a secret." He tips my chin back so I'm looking at him. "I didn't sign anything in my contract that says I can't date someone at work. Plus, you're the fucking *owner*. You can do what you want."

"Well, there's that."

"If you're not attracted to me—"

That makes me laugh again, and I shake my head. "I wanted to climb you like a damn tree last night. If my ten-year-old hadn't been in the house, I might have."

"So, we're on the same page, then."

"Yeah, Drew, we're on the same page."

He nods, and we're quiet for a moment as Caleb dribbles the ball down the field and kicks it into the goal.

"That's my boy!" I yell as I jump up and clap. "Good job, Caleb!"

Caleb's grin is huge as he smiles my way. And when he sees Drew sitting next to me, that smile spreads with joy.

"Hey, Drew!" he yells, waving.

Drew waves back, and we take our seats once more.

"He's one hell of a kid," he says, still watching my boy.

"Yeah." I nod, feeling better than I have in ages. "He is. You and the team fly out this afternoon for LA, right? For tomorrow's game?"

"I have about four hours until I have to be at Boeing Field," he confirms. "Is Caleb the reason that you don't go to any of the games?"

"Yes. I spend the weekends with my son." I nod and look over to find him watching me. "But we always watch the games on TV."

"Caleb would probably enjoy going and sitting in the owner's box."

"He asks every weekend if we can go," I confirm. "And I know that I won't be able to tell him no forever. But for now, I like keeping him out of that spotlight."

"I get it," he says, and I can tell by his tone that he means it. "My uncle Luke was adamant about keeping his kids out of the public eye."

"And who's Luke?"

"Williams." He watches me for a second and then

grins. "*Luke Williams.* The movie star, producer, production company owner."

"Oh, *that* Luke Williams. Wow. He's your uncle?"

"Yeah. We're a family full of celebrities. Anyway, he had the same stance as you, and they all turned out great."

"Good." The whistle blows, signaling the end of the match. "Do you want to join us for lunch before you leave for LA?"

"Hell yes, I do."

~

"Ms. Ambrose, this is your new assistant, Lucy Williams." Sherry has just stepped inside my office and gestures for Lucy to join her.

I smile at the younger woman, already approving of her sharp pink suit and the way she's styled and put together. Lucy smiles back at me and walks forward, steady on her heels, and offers me her hand.

"Hello, Ms. Ambrose. It's a pleasure to meet you. I'm looking forward to working with you."

"The pleasure is mine." I glance up at Sherry and give her a nod, signaling that she's free to go. "I'm going to be showing you around, Lucy. I know that someone from HR would normally do that, but you'll be working directly for me, so I think it's best if we start together right away."

"Sounds good to me," Lucy assures me. "I'm eager to get started."

"Let's jump right in, then, and start with your desk area." I lead her out of my office to the desk on the other side of the door. "This is your home base. I also have a new iPhone here for you, with my number, all the coaches' numbers, and a few other key people in the contacts. You're welcome to use this phone for personal use if you want to, as I ask that you keep it on you at all times."

"You don't want me to simply use my own personal phone?"

"No. I'd rather you had a company phone. You can stow your handbag and coat here before we move on."

We start our tour on this floor, and I show her the lounge, introduce her to everyone in each and every office, and then we make our way to Will Montgomery's office.

"Will?" I knock on his door, and he looks up with a smile. "I'd like to introduce you to my new assistant."

"Great." Will nods politely, and then his eyes widen. "Lucy? What the hell are you doing here?"

He rises from behind the desk and hurries over to wrap up Lucy in his arms, giving her a tight hug.

"Uh, hi, Uncle Will." She winces and looks at me like, *please don't fire me.*

"*Uncle?*" I raise an eyebrow at Will as he backs away.

"Yeah, Lucy's my niece. Why didn't you tell me you wanted to work for the team?" He frowns down at his niece, who now has her eyes closed. "I could have put in a good word for you."

"Because I wanted to get this job on my own merit, that's why. Not because of who I know. Even if you *are* impressive."

"Well, I'm glad you're here," Will says as he backs away. "Lucy's pretty badass," he assures me.

"So far, I agree. We'll see you later."

Lucy and I walk out of Will's office, and she stops and takes a deep breath. "I apologize, Ms. Ambrose. I didn't disclose who my family was because I really wanted to get this job on my own. I've wanted to work for you for a long time, and when I saw the opening, I jumped at it. I respect you so much as a strong businesswoman."

I nod slowly. "Thank you. Personally, as long as you do a good job for me, I don't care who your family is."

The truth is, I can relate to Lucy. Sometimes, being related to influential people isn't as helpful as everyone thinks it is.

"Okay, let's keep going. There are still quite a few people to meet before we get to work."

"It's a big building," she says.

"And trust me, it's *full*."

CHAPTER 5

DREW

"*I* know it's late notice," Mom says into my ear. I have the phone crooked against my shoulder as I type out a response to an email on my computer. I love the woman dearly, but she always manages to call me when I'm at work and in the middle of something. "But I miss my children. I want to have dinner tonight at six. Both of your sisters and their guys are coming, and it won't be the same if you tell me you can't make it."

There's absolutely nothing in the world like mom guilt.

"I can make it," I reply. "I'll be there at six."

"You don't, by any chance, have a date to bring with you, do you?"

"No." My lips twitch when she sighs heavily. "Sorry to burst your romantic bubble."

"Well, I heard that you escorted London to that fancy dinner the other night."

"Yes, I'm sure Aunt Meg called you from the car on her way home."

"We're not amateurs," she replies with a snort. "She texted me during dinner and managed to take a photo with her phone while she was at it."

"Of course, she did. Sorry, London won't be with me."

"Another time, then. I'll want to hear all about it. You looked so handsome in your suit. Okay, I know you're working, so I'll let you go. See you tonight."

"See you later, Mom."

I hang up and turn my attention back to my email when suddenly, London is in my doorway.

"Hey." I stand, but London just grins and motions for someone to join her. And that someone is my cousin, Lucy. "Luce?"

"Hi," Lucy says with a little smile.

"This is my new assistant, Lucy Williams," London says with a big smile. "Today is her first day, and I'm showing her around."

"I might not remember everyone's names, or even where the bathroom is, for a few days, but I'll get there," Lucy says with a half laugh.

"I don't even know everyone's names," I assure her. "I didn't know you put in for that job."

London and Lucy share a look and then laugh.

"What? What did I say?"

"Uncle Will said the same thing. I wanted it this way," Lucy assures me. "If you still lived at the compound, we could carpool to work."

"The compound?" London echoes, raising an eyebrow in question.

"I'll tell you all about it another time," I assure her. "Welcome aboard, Luce."

"Thanks." I can tell by the bright smile on Lucy's face that she wants to jump up and down and squeal with excitement. The fact that she's keeping it together is admirable. "I'm really excited to work for you, London. I think there's a lot I can learn from you."

"I appreciate you saying that. We still have some things to see and people to meet, but we're almost done," London assures her. "Drew, would you like to join us while I show Lucy the training center?"

"Sure." I put my computer to sleep and join the two women as we make our way to the elevator. "You're going to love the training center, Luce. London and Rome have been generous enough to let all the employees use the facilities when the team isn't in training."

"I don't work out often," Lucy admits and bites her lip. "But maybe I'll find time to hop on a treadmill now and then."

"We have trainers," London says as we step off the elevator and make our way to the double glass doors that lead to the gym. "In case you need extra motivation."

Although *gym* is too simple a term for it.

"There are also locker room facilities for both men *and* women, so feel free to snag one of the empty lockers and keep your things in there so you don't have to haul it back and forth from home." London smiles and waves at Jill, the manager of the training facilities, who happens to be manning the front desk. "Jill will get you set up with the appropriate credentials on your employee badge so you can just swipe on through."

"Happy to," Jill says, smiling at Lucy. "Welcome."

"Thanks." Lucy's smile is at least a thousand watts. "This place is amazing."

"We're a professional sports team," I remind her with a wink. "It had better be."

"I'll take your badge and load it with all the goodies while you get the tour," Jill says, accepting Lucy's shiny new card when it's passed to her. "And if you ever have any questions, just find someone wearing these stylish blue polo shirts. We're the training staff."

"Thanks," Lucy says again as we walk away.

"There's a pool, sauna, and hot tub," I begin as I lead the two women into what I consider my domain. I spend several hours every single day in here. "All the cardio machines you could ever want, along with weight machines or free weights. There are spin classes, yoga classes, and even physical therapy, should you ever need it."

"Basically," London adds, "if you so much as have a

crick in your neck, feel free to come in and have it worked on."

"Wow," Lucy breathes.

"You can make appointments with a massage therapist, acupuncturist, or chiropractor. Do you need someone to talk to? We also have a psychologist that you're welcome to see."

"Do all these things come out of my check? Or will I be billed?"

"Oh, I'm sorry, I should have been clear," London says with a smile. "There's no charge for any of this. It's part of your benefits package."

Lucy's mouth opens and then closes again. "Holy shit, the person before me really messed up." Then her eyes go wide. "I'm so sorry. I didn't mean to say that out loud."

London just laughs and nods. "You're right. She messed up. I don't think I'll have the same issue with you."

"No, ma'am."

Once we've made the rounds through the facility, and Lucy's had the opportunity to meet several of the players who have stopped in for training, we run into Ike Harrison, our superstar quarterback.

And cousin-in-law.

"Lucy?"

"Hey, Ike. Congrats on the win yesterday. You *killed* it."

Now London simply laughs. "Do I employ your entire family?"

"Only about five percent of it," I inform her with a grin as Lucy and Ike catch up. "I know you didn't do this as a favor to my family, but thanks. She'll do a good job for you."

"I had absolutely *nothing* to do with it. Sherry in HR hired her. She got this job on her own merit."

"I know that means a lot to her," I reply, watching as Lucy and Ike share a laugh. "I'm having dinner with my family tonight, but will you be in your office this afternoon? I'd like to pop in and say hello when we're not surrounded by a bunch of other people."

"I'm having lunch brought in around one. Why don't you join me?"

"I can make that work." I nod and shove my hands into my pockets so that I don't reach out for her. She's dressed in another power suit, red this time, and it stirs things in me. Her hair, dark and short, skims the neckline and begs for my fingers to run through it.

I want to kiss her and feel her against me.

"Let's move on, shall we?" London says to Lucy, completely pulling me out of my reverie.

"I'm ready when you are," Lucy assures her.

"I'll see you later," London says to me and smiles softly before leading Lucy away.

All I can do is stand here, feet planted and hands in my pockets, and watch them go. London's ass sways enticingly in that tight skirt.

"You okay?" Ike asks as he steps beside me.

"I'm fine. You?"

"Oh, I'm great. You have a weird look on your face, my man." Ike claps his hand on my shoulder.

I raise an eyebrow and turn to him. "Is that so? What kind of weird look?"

"A gooey, lovesick look. I should know. I get that same look whenever I see my gorgeous wife."

"I don't want to know the perverted thoughts that go through your head when you see my cousin."

I glance over, and he's just grinning at me.

"Don't make me punch you out, man."

Now Ike laughs and turns away to sit at the weight machine again. "I'm not saying a word."

"You had *sushi* brought in?" I ask as I take in the massive spread of food on the table in the corner of London's office.

"Sure. I was hungry for it. If you hate sushi, I can order something else."

"No, this is fine. I'm just surprised. Although, I shouldn't be."

"It's just sushi," she reminds me and flips a button on a remote so the glass between her office and the other areas of the building goes smoky, leaving us all alone. "And I don't like to eat with an audience."

"And here I thought you just wanted me all to yourself."

London laughs and takes her suit jacket off, lays it nicely on the back of her desk chair, and walks over to me.

"How's your day going?" she asks.

"It's going really well. How about you? You look happy."

"Are you kidding? My team won yesterday, and I have a new, *competent* assistant, who doesn't seem like the type to fuck around with anyone in PR—"

"She better not."

"My kid is great, and I'm having lunch with a handsome guy. Oh, and I have a new handbag waiting for me at home."

"That one's important."

"We don't fuck around when it comes to handbags," she says, her face deadly serious. "Certainly not when it comes to Dior."

She grabs several rolls with her chopsticks and sets them on a plate.

"Help yourself," she says, gesturing to the table.

"This will feed a small country," I inform her before stuffing a California roll into my mouth.

"Whatever we don't eat, I'll take home to Caleb. He loves sushi."

"Will it still be good?"

"Well, the chef is coming back in about thirty

minutes to gather this all up in coolers and take it to my house."

I nod, trying not to choke on the roll in my mouth. "Right. The chef."

London tilts her head to the side, watching me. "You're not going to get all weird on me for things like that, are you?"

"Weird? No. It makes sense. You're a single mom who works a lot of hours, with responsibilities I don't even know about. You can afford to hire all the help you can get, and I think you should."

"Exactly," she says with a smile. "The chef is a must-have for me. Without her, we'd be in trouble. I never learned to cook well. I can do PB&J and macaroni and cheese from a box. And I handle breakfast just fine, as long as I can just add milk or pop something into the toaster oven. But when it comes to meals? No, I need help with that, and it's not good to eat fast food every day, although my son would love that."

"So, the chef doesn't live with you and follow you around with platters of fresh food?"

"Jesus, does that happen somewhere?" She licks something off of her thumb. "Because if that's a thing, I want it."

She laughs now and reaches for a napkin.

"No, she makes us dinners and stows them in my fridge or freezer. She also handles Caleb's lunches, although I pack them, and if she has extra of something, she'll bring me lunch here. Today, she called and said she'd made too much sushi and asked if I wanted some. Of course, the answer is always yes to sushi."

"Naturally. You don't have to explain your lifestyle to me, you know."

"That's not why I did it," she replies, kicking off her shoes and stretching out her toes. "I'm not ashamed of anything. I'm definitely not ashamed of being rich. I may be indulged, but I give a lot back to this community, as well."

"I know you do."

"I was just sharing with you what Cher the Chef does—ya know, making conversation."

"Her name is Cher the Chef?"

"Well, she's a chef, and her name happens to be Cher, but Caleb calls her Cher the Chef, and it's stuck."

"I like it. What other staff do you have?"

"Well, it's a big-ass house, so I have a housekeeper who comes in weekly to help with the big stuff, but I do our own laundry and such. I also have a gardener. And Lucy, my assistant. That's about it."

"That's not outrageous," I inform her. "You don't have stables of horses with a guy to keep them brushed, shoed, and ready to go for you?"

"No horses."

"You don't have a chauffeur?"

"Nah, I like to drive."

I grin at her. "See? You're not extravagant at all."

That makes her laugh and shake her hair back, running her fingers through it.

"If you're trying to seduce me, it's working." I can hear the strain in my voice, and her eyes widen as she looks over at me in surprise.

"I'm just relaxed, to be honest. I never let myself relax in this office. It feels kind of nice."

"It's sexy as fuck."

"We probably shouldn't have sex in my office in the middle of the day."

I lick my lips. Yeah, I want her, more than I've ever wanted anything in my life.

"The first time I have you won't be here, in the middle of the day. It'll be somewhere soft and comfortable, where I can take my time, with the security of knowing that we won't be interrupted for a very long time. I want you, London, but I'm a patient man."

She blinks rapidly and lets out a gusty laugh.

"Well, damn, now I wish we were doing it here in the middle of the day."

"You're late," Maddie accuses me as I walk through the front door of the house we grew up in. She's sitting with Dylan, her husband, on stools at the kitchen island. Mom's stirring something in a pot at the stove and beams at me as I walk over and kiss her cheek.

"I'm not too late for food," I reply and lean over to sniff the pot. "Is that taco soup?"

"Yep."

"It's my favorite, and it's not even my birthday."

Mom chuckles and stirs the soup again. "I wanted to try something new, but your father told me that he'd like for his kids to want to come back again, so I stuck with the tried and true."

"Where is Dad?"

"He's out back with Josie and Brax," Maddie says and pops a chip loaded down with salsa into her mouth.

"What are they doing?"

"No idea," Maddie replies before carefully selecting another chip. "Go get them. I'm starving. I'm *always* starving these days."

I head for the back door and find Dad with Josie and Brax on the back deck, drinks in hand, talking.

"It's a little cold to be hanging out on the deck," I inform them as I join them. "Shouldn't you be doing this inside?"

"It's not raining," Dad points out and looks up at the sky.

"You have a point." I sit across from them and accept a drink from my dad. "Maddie says we should go in because she's hungry."

"I'm hungry, too," Josie says with a sigh. She looks nervous, but before I can ask her why, she hops up. "Okay, let's go in."

She takes her husband's hand and pulls him to his feet, and they go in through the sliding glass door.

But Dad and I stay where we are.

"Tell me about London," is all he says, but his eyes are watchful.

"You already know who she is."

"I don't think that means much," he replies. "Tell me about who she is to *you.*"

"Right now, she's someone I'd like to get to know better. I haven't slept with her, and I really don't know her that well, but I like her. I respect her. So, we'll see where it goes."

He nods and starts to stand. "Good enough."

"She's a mom."

That has his eyes narrowing on me as he lets his butt fall back into the seat.

"She's a single mom, and the dad's out of the picture permanently. He's deceased." I swallow. And stare out at the backyard. "The kid's name is Caleb, which feels...I don't know...serendipitous, I guess. He's about ten, cute as hell, and smart. And she's an excellent mom."

"Is this a problem for you?"

"No." The answer is immediate, right from the gut. "It's not a problem. It's just different. I've never tried to date a mom before, and there is a whole different set of rules."

"Yeah, there is." He nods and leans forward, elbows on his knees. "You can't just fuck around with a single mom, son."

"I don't plan to just fuck around with her at all, kid or not."

"But you have to decide, before you take things any further, if you're okay with it being a package deal."

"I know that, Dad. She's already told me that Caleb comes first, always, and damn if that didn't make me like her more."

"Because she reminds you of your mom."

I snort at that. "I understand the sentiment, but I've never looked at Mom the way I do London."

He just lifts an eyebrow, and I shrug my shoulders.

"Sure, there are similarities. I figured that if anyone had any advice for dating a single mom, it would be you."

"Hell, I fell in love with your mom so fast and hard, and with those girls just as fast, that I don't know if I have any advice on that. I didn't have a choice. I knew I wanted them. I didn't think I deserved them, but I wanted them."

"I like her, Dad. And I like the kid."

"Does it irritate you when he's around?"

"Not at all. I had lunch with them on Saturday before we left for LA, and I had a great time."

"Kids are hard, and they change the game. But they're worth it."

I nod, already feeling better.

"Your mother and I would like to meet them," he adds.

"Oh, don't I know it." I laugh and stand with him. "As soon as Mom hears about Caleb, she'll be planning a dinner party."

"She's wanted to be a grandma for a while now."

"Hey, Josie and Maddie are freaking *married*. They can take the reins on that first."

We're laughing as we step inside and then stop cold.

All three women are crying, holding on to each other. Brax and Dylan just look uncomfortable.

"What the fuck is going on?" Dad demands, his Navy SEAL voice on.

"Oh, honey," Mom says, wiping at her eyes. "Our girls are gonna have babies."

My mouth drops. "Like, *both* of you are pregnant?"

"We just found out," Maddie replies, nodding. "We were both going to tell the family tonight and didn't know it."

"You two tell each other everything. It's annoying."

Josie laughs and hugs me. "We wanted it to be a surprise."

"Talk about a surprise," Mom says as she walks into Dad's arms. "I'm going to be a grandma."

CHAPTER 6

LONDON

his week can kiss my ass.

Work-wise, I have to admit, it's been great. The team has won the last three games. The clothing boutique that I'm a silent partner in New York went viral on a social media site, and they've never been busier. The podcast I back is more popular than ever, and I have agreed to be a guest for them next week.

Not to mention, my financial portfolio, the one that has absolutely *no* ties to my father, couldn't be doing better.

But my father is driving me up the freaking wall, and since the charity dinner several weeks ago, he has decided to take a vested interest in my love life.

My phone dings, and I hope with all my might that it's Drew. I haven't seen him in close to two freaking weeks. We haven't even run into each other at work.

Then, the team went to the East Coast to play games on back-to-back weekends there and stayed for the week in between to practice at a facility we rented so they didn't have to fly back and forth.

So, Drew's been with the team on the East Coast for the past ten days. But he's coming home today, and the team was victorious after both games.

We've been texting here and there, and he even called a few times, but it's not the same. I want to *see* him. How did I suddenly become so ridiculously attached to him?

Picking up my phone, I deflate when I see that the message isn't from Drew, but from my father.

Dad: This is Henry Burton's number. He's a bit older than you, but he's rich as hell and interested.

I scowl. "When giraffes fly out of my ass. Henry Burton is sixty, has children older than me, and the last time I heard, was in a wheelchair after losing his leg to diabetes."

Rolling my eyes, I shake my head and immediately call my brother. But he doesn't answer. In the middle of leaving a message on his voicemail, the man himself walks through my office door with a big smile on his face.

"I guess I don't need to leave this message because you just walked into my office."

I click off and frown at my brother.

"I thought you'd be happy to see me."

"I'm so fucking frustrated."

81

That makes him lift a brow, and he looks over his shoulder, as if he's making sure that I'm not speaking to someone behind him.

"With me?"

"No, with the sperm donor we call a father."

"Oh. Him." He shrugs and takes the seat across from me, resting his ankle on his knee. "There are few days of the week that I'm *not* irritated with him. What did he do now?"

"Let me ask you a question. Does he constantly bombard you with the names and numbers of eligible women for you to date and eventually marry?"

Rome blinks, then drops his face into his hand and laughs until his sides must ache.

"It's not funny. I'm being serious, Rome. Does he?"

"Of course not. That would be ridiculous." He wipes at a tear in the corner of his eye. "Why would he do that?"

"You tell me." I pull up the text I just received and show it to my brother, who now frowns. "And this isn't the first one of these. He sends them several times a week now. The other day, a dude named Drew Houston called me out of the freaking blue."

"Drew Houston?" His eyebrows shoot up. "Really?"

"Who *is* he?"

"Sis, he's the guy who started Dropbox. He's a billionaire."

"Well, I politely declined and called Dad and told him to absolutely *not* give anyone my number. So now all he does is send me the contacts. It's annoying. Doesn't he have anything better to do? He's running an empire, for Christ's sake. And why the sudden interest? As far as I've ever known, he didn't give a shit who I dated."

"Well, that's because you mostly haven't dated at all since Caleb was born," Rome points out. "Except for that idiot—oh, what's his name? Rolex?"

"Felix." I snicker. "And that was a huge mistake. One I won't make again."

"I have a hypothesis," he says. "I think Dad's decided to be interested in your love life because you attended that gala with Drew Montgomery."

"So?"

"Don't get me wrong," he says, holding up his hands. "I like Drew a lot. His family's great. I have no issues at all with him, and at the end of the day, it's none of my business."

"Okay."

"But...you know Dad. Drew isn't the *right* kind of guy for his daughter."

"Uh, what the fuck, Rome?"

"Hey, I agree with you. But Dad's a snob from way back."

"So, if you attended an event with someone like, say, my assistant, for instance. Actually, that's a good analogy because she's Drew's cousin. Nice girl, from a good family, attractive. Dad would say she isn't good enough for you?"

"Well, no. He wouldn't. He would probably slap me on the back, wink, and check out her tits."

"Exactly. It's completely ridiculous."

"It'll blow over," he assures me. "I agree with you. It's stupid and beyond sexist. But he'll lose interest soon and move on to the next thing to fixate over. Don't worry about it. Ignore him. So, are you dating Drew?"

"I wouldn't call it dating," I mutter. "I haven't seen much of him lately, but I'm interested."

"Does he know about Caleb?"

"Yeah, and he's been really nice to him. Caleb asks about him and seems to like him."

"Then I say see how it plays out. If he hurts you or the kid, I'll kill him and have it covered up, but otherwise, I'm happy for you."

That makes me laugh. Rome always knows how to lighten the mood.

But when I glance his way, he's not smiling.

"Okay, caveman. Why did you come to my office today?"

"Because we heard back from the league on the uniform changes for next year."

I raise a brow. "And?"

"They approved them."

"*Yessss.*"

"Do you have the movie cued up, buddy?" Carrying an enormous tub of buttered popcorn from the machine in the corner, I approach the couch where Caleb's lounging.

"Why haven't we seen Drew in a long time?" he asks, rather than answering my own question.

"Because he's a coach, and the team has been traveling the last week or so." This is one of the reasons that if I do start dating someone, even if it's casually, I don't introduce them to my son. He asks questions and gets attached. "Do you like Drew?"

"Sure, he's nice. He's funny. And he knows a lot about sports."

I grin. These days, sports reign supreme in my son's life. "Yeah, he does know a lot about sports."

"Maybe we should see if he wants to come over for movie night."

"It's getting later in the evening, and you have to go to school tomorrow, kiddo."

"It's not that late," Caleb disagrees, checking the wall clock. "It's only six. I don't have to go to bed until nine. There's time."

Before I can reply to that clever comeback, my phone rings, and Drew's name is on the screen.

"It's him! Invite him over," Caleb hisses.

"You know, life was easier before you knew how to read."

That makes my child grin as I answer the phone.

"Hello."

"Hey, am I catching you at a bad time?"

"Not at all." It's *so* good to hear his voice. "Caleb and I were just settling in to watch a movie."

"How do you feel about having company?"

"Yes!" Caleb shouts, loud enough for Drew to hear. "Yes, we want company."

Drew chuckles in my ear. "I guess he can hear me."

"Yes, he can hear you." I can't help but grin. It's a relief that my kid likes the man that I seem to like very much, too. "We have plenty of popcorn here, if you'd like to join us."

"I'll be there soon."

I don't have to call down to the security gate because I've already put Drew on the permanent list of people who can just come on through to the house.

"Well, what a coincidence," Caleb says with a big grin. "It's like we manifested him, or something."

"First of all, your vocabulary is impressive. But you might be hanging out with Quinn too much."

"She's really smart, and I like the idea of wishing for something so hard that you can make it happen. We're magical beings, Mom."

"Right." The doorbell rings, surprising me. "That was fast."

Caleb races me to the door and beats me, but before he can pull it open, I stop him.

"You have to ask who it is," I tell him sternly.

"Mom, we already know who it is." Caleb rolls his eyes. "It's *Drew.*"

"Ask anyway."

He sighs, as if this is the biggest chore of his life. "Who is it?" he yells out.

"It's Drew Montgomery," we hear in response.

"Told you." Caleb pulls the door open. "I knew it was you, but Mom still made me ask."

"Probably a good rule to ask who's ringing the doorbell," Drew says as he steps inside. His eyes immediately find mine, so blue and vibrant and full of *hunger.* They move up and down my whole body, as if he's soaking me in. "You look great."

"Dude, she's in her *sweats.*" But Caleb hops on the balls of his feet. "Come on! We have to start the movie."

"I have some things here for you guys," Drew says as he follows us down the hall. "First, flowers for a beautiful woman."

"Barf," Caleb mutters, but I can see the happy smile on his adorable face as I bury my nose in a bloom and fuss a little.

"And a little something for the man of the house," Drew says as he passes a wrapped package to my boy.

"It's not even my birthday," Caleb says as he rips the paper. "Whoa, Minecraft Legos! Oh, man, there are so many pieces. I won't be able to do this by myself."

"I'll help you," Drew offers with a shrug, as if it's no big deal and he offers to help kids put Legos together every day of the week. "Want to get started on it now? While we watch the movie? If it's okay with your mom, that is."

Caleb turns hopeful eyes to me. "Please?"

"Fine with me."

"Yeah! I'll go get the platform."

Caleb races out of the room, and Drew looks at me in surprise. "Platform?"

"He has a special board that he puts his Legos on so he can carry them throughout the house and work on a project without being stuck in his room. My kid is social."

"Smart." He moves in closer, sliding his hand over my hip. "I missed the hell out of you. Being away that long is *too long*."

"I missed you, too," I admit and reach up to cup his cheek. It seems to be my signature move with this man. I love the way his slightly scruffy skin feels against my palm. "Your boss is a tyrant for making you stay away for so long."

His lips twitch with humor. "I'll tell her you said that."

"Did you have a good trip?"

"A successful one," he says, his eyes intensely glued to my lips. "How was your week?"

"Long."

Satisfaction shoots into those blue eyes, but before he can kiss me, Caleb comes running back, holding his Lego board high in the air, over his head.

"I have it!"

He zooms past us, headed straight for the big square

ottoman in front of the couch so he and Drew can sit on the floor while they build.

"Want to join us?" Drew asks, but I shake my head and press play on the movie already pulled up on the massive wall TV.

Sure, I could join them, and likely have fun, but I kind of want to sit back and watch them work together. Do they aggravate each other? Do they really get along well when it's just the two of them and I'm not directing a conversation?

The reality is, if Drew and I continue to see each other on a personal level, my son is in the equation. Because I spend as much time with Caleb as possible, I won't give up time with him to accommodate Drew or any man.

Before long, I'm pretty much watching the movie by myself as the guys build their work of art. They giggle and tease each other. Once, when Caleb realizes that he made something wrong, he gets frustrated with himself.

But Drew calmly explains that it was an easy mistake to make and helps Caleb correct it.

All in all, I don't think it could have gone any better.

When the credits roll, Caleb looks up at me with pleading eyes. "*Please,* can I stay up longer to keep working on this?"

"Sorry, buddy, but you have school tomorrow. No can do. Go put your pajamas on and brush your teeth. I'll be up in a few."

Caleb sighs. "Okay."

"Hey, whenever you want to work on this, just have your mom call me. If I'm not working, I'll come help."

That cheers Caleb up. "Okay, cool. Thanks, Drew."

Now he runs out of the room, and I can hear his feet, which aren't all that tiny anymore, stomp on the stairs up to the second floor.

"You were really great with him this evening." I smile at Drew as he boosts himself up on the couch and takes one of my bare feet in his hands to massage it.

"Caleb is a great kid. It's not hard to hang out with him at all. Besides, Legos are the best. I think my mom still has some of my old sets in her attic."

"Would you say that if Caleb was a brat?"

"No. If he was a brat, I wouldn't be here. But I don't think you'd put up with a disrespectful child for long."

"He's a normal kid," I reply with a sigh and close my eyes when his thumb digs into the arch of my foot. "He pushes buttons, and if he's hungry or tired, he can be a handful. But no, on the whole, I don't tolerate my son being a jerk to anyone."

"It shows."

"I have to go up and say goodnight to him. I'll be right back." I have to pull my foot away and stand up before the relaxing massage puts me to sleep.

"How about if I pour us a glass of wine?" he offers as he stands with me.

"Excellent idea. The kitchen is this way."

He follows me as far as the kitchen, and then I

branch off from him to go upstairs. I find Caleb already in bed, his sidelight on.

And he's already asleep.

I can smell toothpaste when I lean in to kiss his forehead, and it makes me smile. He actually brushed his teeth.

"I love you so much, baby boy."

"Love you, Mama."

He doesn't open his eyes with the words. He's already too sleepy for that. And for just an instant, he's not a ten-year-old with smelly socks and a mop of brown hair that's screaming for a haircut.

He's my baby. I can see the pudgy cheeks and smell that baby smell. It's in moments like these that my heart fills to almost bursting with all the love that I have for this little human that I created.

"Sleep good."

"Hmm." He rolls onto his side as I turn out the side-light and walk to the door. I close it behind me because Caleb always demands pure darkness at night.

I tried a nightlight when he was little, but he wanted none of it.

My kid isn't afraid of the dark at all.

I don't make it back to the TV room because I find Drew still in the kitchen, casually leaning back against the countertop, a glass of wine in his hand.

When I walk into the room, his eyes light up, and it sends a jolt right through to the very core of me.

"He's already out," I inform him as I step forward

and take the offered glass of white. "Do you want to go chat in the game room?"

"Honestly, I'd like a tour of this incredible house. I want to see it through your eyes."

"Showing off this house is one of my favorite pastimes," I inform him. "I bought it about five years ago, but before we moved in, I had a major renovation done to update everything. The house was built in the nineties, and it was pretty outdated."

"This kitchen is great," he says, looking around. I follow his gaze.

It's a white kitchen with a massive island that I absolutely love for baking Christmas cookies.

"Check it out."

I move to the tall cabinet next to the stovetop. It looks like a small pantry, but when I open the door, I reveal a massive butler's pantry behind it.

"Whoa," Drew says in surprise. "A secret room."

"That's exactly what Caleb said," I reply with a laugh. "I *love* this space. I don't host parties often, mostly during the holidays, but it's so nice to be able to hide the mess back here. People tend to congregate in the kitchen, and this makes it possible for me to keep my kitchen clean while still using it, if that makes sense."

"Makes sense," he replies with a nod. "What else do you have hiding around this place?"

"There are quite a few fun things, actually. Here,

let's start at the front door and work our way through from the beginning."

"Deal. Wait."

He hurries past me, opens the front door, and steps outside. Thankfully, he doesn't ring the bell and wake my son, but he knocks on the door softly.

"Who's there?"

CHAPTER 7

DREW

"Who's there?"

I can't help but chuckle. God, is this the same woman that irritated the hell out of me just a short time ago? She's completely wormed her way into my life and my thoughts, and she didn't even *try*.

She's now a fixture that I can't imagine doing without.

"Drew," I reply loud enough for her to hear, and she swings the door open, grinning up at me with humor.

And I realize, without a fucking doubt, that she's *mine*.

"Drew?" she asks, her brows pulling into a frown when I don't say anything.

"Sorry." I clear my throat. "It must be the wine. Lead the way, madam."

Her face relaxes once more, and she offers me her

hand. I link my fingers with hers, and she shows me the entryway that still knocks me back a half step. The ceiling in here is *impressive*.

Then she leads me into a study, an office, and a guest suite complete with a walk-in closet and an en suite bathroom.

This suite alone is bigger than most apartments.

"My favorite part of this room..." London says with a grin as she pushes on a panel in a bookshelf. It pops open, revealing another room. "Is this."

A *library*.

"Should I just call you Belle?" I ask as we walk into the hidden room.

"It's not *that* big," she replies as she lowers herself onto a plush reading chair. "I like to hide in here sometimes."

"Hide? From what?"

"I don't know." She shrugs, looks unsure, and stands. When she turns to walk back out again, I catch her elbow in my grip and turn her to me. "I don't even know why I said that."

"What do you hide from, London?"

Her eyes drop to my lips before lifting up to mine. "Life, I guess. Sometimes, when Caleb is tucked away in the game room, or even in bed, I come in here and just *be*. It's quiet, and I like books, so it's a good place to hide in. And no one bothers me when I'm in here."

I reach up, brush a strand of her hair off her cheek,

and take a tiny step toward her, closing the gap between us.

She licks her lower lip in anticipation. I haven't kissed her since the night of the gala. I've wanted to, but there was always a reason that I shouldn't.

There's no reason not to now.

With my finger under her chin, I lift her lips to mine. Just like last time, the kiss starts soft and slow and then builds to hungry and all-consuming. My hands drift down her sides to her ass and then up under her shirt.

She's not wearing a fucking bra.

I groan against her mouth, and she wiggles against me in invitation as I move us over to the wall and boost her up with my hands planted on her spectacular ass so she can wrap those long legs around me, and I can continue to feast on her mouth.

"God, you're sweet," I murmur against her as I kiss my way to her neck. She lets out a little moan, and then her hands suddenly stop moving.

She stops moving.

"Drew."

"Okay." I set her on her feet but keep my hands on her shoulders to steady her. "I'm sorry."

"No, please, don't apologize. It's just, my son is upstairs, and if he came looking for me—"

"I get it." I cup her face and lean my forehead against hers. "I understand."

"Thanks." She sighs and closes her eyes.

"But I have a question."

That has her opening those pretty eyes once more and watching me warily. "Okay."

"When can I take you on an *overnight* date? I like Caleb a lot, and I'm happy to do things with the three of us, but maybe I could take you somewhere overnight."

Her lips tip up into a soft smile. "I'd like that. Let me get with Quinn, and we'll figure out a time that works."

"Thanks." I kiss her again, but much more chastely this time, before pulling away. "Okay, there's still a lot of house to see."

"Let's go see it."

She licks her lips, and I see her take a long, slow breath as she leads me out of the hidden library, which makes me grin. It's satisfying to know that I have the same effect on her as she has on me.

"You've seen the kitchen. There's another big living space and dining area back here."

I follow her through the rest of the first floor, and then we climb the stairs to the second floor.

"That's Caleb's room," London whispers as we tiptoe past. "These are more guest rooms."

Finally, at the end of the hallway, she opens a set of double doors that reveal her massive main suite.

"This is my room," she says, gesturing. "I love it because I have a great view of Mount Rainier."

The furniture is muted and pretty, the carpet plush.

And, I realize, the bathroom is the size of my condo.

"Holy shit, you could have a party in here."

London laughs. "This tub is a lifesaver for my sore feet. Even Caleb still likes to take baths in here."

"Who wouldn't?" I catch a glimpse of her closet as I pass by and have to stop and back up for another look. "This might be the biggest closet I've ever seen, and that's saying a *lot*, given how fashion-obsessed the women in my family are."

She doesn't laugh as she walks past me and runs her hand over the marble top of an island that rivals the one in the kitchen.

"This, aside from Caleb and the football team, is my pride and joy. I *love* fashion, as I'm sure you realized when I hounded you for weeks about the uniforms. The league approved them, by the way."

"Congratulations."

She walks past the racks and racks of hanging clothes and shelves loaded down with handbags and shoes, and she caresses everything as if it's a treasured lover.

"I own a clothing boutique in New York," she continues. "I'm a silent partner, but I love it. I go out there four times a year to look at what's new and bring those new things home with me. I attend fashion week in both New York and Paris every fall, building that into my trip to the boutique. It's one of the few times that I don't feel guilty when I leave Caleb with Quinn for a little longer than normal. He wouldn't want to go with me. It would be boring for him, and I want to soak *everything* in. It just feeds my soul in a way I can't really describe."

"So, you love fashion, but you own a football team?"

"I also own a tech start-up and a podcast, and I back several other endeavors. I'm an entrepreneur, Drew. I guess that's the one thing I got from my father that's done me any good. I know people assume that Rome does all the work in his fancy office in downtown Seattle, and don't get me wrong, he *does* do a lot of work. I choose to keep my main office at the training facility so I can oversee everything that I need to while also working on all the other things that need my attention.

"The team itself is a lot of work. I'm constantly in meetings with the attorneys and the sales team because we rent out the stadium for concerts, shows, and other sporting events. Even private citizens sometimes rent out the stadium."

"I hadn't thought of that," I reply, feeling ashamed that I ever thought this intelligent, driven woman was simply playing at being the CEO of a professional sports team. She's not playing at anything.

She's slaying.

"I cram as much work as I can into the six hours or so that I'm in the office, then I get Caleb from school and take him to practices, rehearsals, and play dates. I always have my laptop on me so I can work while he's otherwise occupied."

"London." I step forward, to the opposite side of the island, and lean my elbows on the marble. "Are you telling me all of this because you think that you have something to prove to me?"

"I used to see the way you looked at me," she admits. "The way pretty much *everyone* looked at me when we took over the team and I moved into the owner's office. Like I was a joke, like I was no better than that piece of shit we bought the team from."

She holds up her hand when I'm about to speak.

"And I get it. I'm young, and all I wanted to talk about was uniforms. Do you know why?"

I shake my head.

"Because the current uniforms were chosen by *her*, by that woman who disrespected this organization and bet *against* it. I don't want my team to wear something that she chose for them. According to the league's rules, we can change uniforms at the beginning of the next season, and that's what I'm doing. I'm switching up the color patterns, and while they'll still be recognizable as Seattle jerseys, they won't be the same as what she chose at all. I'm also adding a throwback uniform."

"I'm sorry that I didn't take it more seriously. I really am, London."

She inhales deeply and then shakes her head. "It's okay. I got approval, and those old jerseys are out of there. The new ones can't get here fast enough. Anyway, yeah, I guess I do feel like I have something to prove. If I were a man, no matter my age, it wouldn't be so hard. If Rome and I reversed roles, I wouldn't have received so many snickers. I really respected Lucy for the way she insisted on getting her job because I've felt that same way myself."

"You two are going to do well together."

"Oh, I can already feel it. She's stepped in seamlessly and revamped my calendar, she brings me coffee and my favorite scone every morning, and she already knows everyone's name on our floor. I think she even has some of the numbers I ask her to call memorized already."

"She's smart," I reply simply, proud of Lucy. "She was the valedictorian of her class in both high school and college. She's the nerd of the family. We're proud of her."

"And what are you?" she asks.

"I'm the jock." I shrug and offer her a grin. "It worked for me."

"I bet it did. I think I veered off the topic of my closet."

"What's your favorite thing in here?"

"I have categories of favorite things," she informs me as she gazes around. "But my most prized possession? Hmm."

She taps her lips and then reaches for a simple, obviously old jacket.

"Not what I expected," I admit.

"It belonged to Coco Chanel," she says and does a little happy dance. "She wore this in the 1960s. She was a little thing, wasn't she?"

"Have you ever worn it?"

"Hell no. Do you know what I paid for this?"

"I have no idea."

"It was a *lot*. Like, a lot a lot."

"I'll take your word for it. What else do you have in here?"

She stows the jacket away and then reaches for a handbag. "This isn't vintage. It's a Hermes Birkin 30, crocodile leather, with diamond-encrusted hardware."

"Looks like a black bag to me."

She pets the side of it. "It was a quarter of a million dollars."

I about swallow my tongue as I stare at the bag in her hands. "Holy fuck, London."

"Want to hold it?"

"Fuck no. I'll break it, and I can't pay you back for it."

She chuckles and stows it away. "These are my babies, but aside from the jacket, I use them all. What's the point in buying them if they just hide away in a closet? I want to see them, touch them, use them. And I do. Okay, that's enough playtime in the closet. I'm sure I'm boring you half to death."

"Actually, no. I'm seeing a whole new side to you, and I like it."

"You like the shopaholic in me?"

That makes me laugh. "I like watching you talk about something that brings you so much happiness."

"What is that thing for you?" she asks as she turns

off the lights in the closet and follows me out to the bedroom, where we sit on the sofa by the windows in the corner of the room. "And don't say football. That's your job."

"I can't say that I've ever spent a quarter of a million dollars on anything, aside from my condo."

She tilts her head, and her eyes say, *come on.*

"I like cars. I have an older Jeep that my cousin restored for me, and I also have the Range Rover you saw. That's all I have room for right now, and I'm nothing like the cousin I mentioned, Keaton, but I think they're fun."

"I bet that Jeep *is* fun in the summer," she says with a soft smile. Her eyes look heavy as she rests her head on her hand, leaning against the back of the couch. "Tell me about your sisters."

"They're both pregnant right now."

"What?" That has her head coming up. "Both of them?"

"Yeah, I found out when I went to my parents' house for dinner. They didn't know that the other was expecting. They both planned to surprise the family. And I guess they did."

"Well, that's exciting. Are they married?"

I nod and reach for one of her bare feet. She doesn't even put up a fight this time and sighs when I dig into her arch.

"You wear too many high heels."

"That's impossible. Keep talking."

"Josie is married to Brax Adler. He's a musician. She's a nurse at Seattle General. Maddie is an accountant, and she's married to a guy named Dylan, whom she met on a flight to Iceland at Christmastime."

"That sounds like a Hallmark movie," London says with a yawn.

"Now that you mention it, it does." I laugh and squeeze her heel. "It sounds like they'll be having babies about a month apart next year. My mom is over the moon."

Her eyes have closed, but I can tell that she's still listening.

"In fact, I think my mom is going to go shopping for baby stuff this weekend."

"I have stuff," she offers softly. "Happy to pass it along."

"Thanks. I'll let them know. You should go to bed, sweetheart." I just don't want to leave her. I want to stay like this all night, talking and laughing, comparing stories about our families. I want to hear more about the boutique she owns in New York. My cousins and aunts would probably all love to make a trip over to check it out.

But she's already breathing evenly with sleep, so I stand and lift her into my arms and carry her to the bed. She snuggles down, her face half-pressed into her pillow, and hardly stirs as I cover her with the blanket.

Pulling another blanket and pillow out of a hall closet, I lie down on the couch and fall asleep myself.

"You're still here."

My eyes flutter open, and I find a ten-year-old boy smiling down at me.

"Hi," he says cheerfully. "You and Mom slept in."

"Caleb?" London sits up, confusion on her still-sleepy face, and she checks the time. "Caleb! Damn it, we're late. Go get dressed right now."

"Drew's still here," he points out, and I am grateful that I didn't join London in the bed last night like I wanted to.

"Yes, I see him. Go get ready *right now.* We have to leave in twenty, or you'll be late for school."

"I guess I'll miss breakfast again," he says to me with a shrug and then hurries off to his bedroom.

"Shit," London mutters as she stumbles out of the bed and heads straight for the bathroom.

I decide to go downstairs and be useful.

I find milk that hasn't expired in the fridge, some cereal in a cabinet, and a banana. Caleb comes hurrying into the kitchen just as I finish slicing the banana.

"Eat this," I say, pushing the bowl to him.

"Wow, Mom's never made it like that before."

"Do you like bananas?"

"Sure."

"Then you'll like this. Start shoveling it in your piehole, kid."

Caleb smirks and does as I say, taking a huge spoonful of cereal, and crunches happily.

London runs in five minutes later, looking put together but rushed.

"You're eating." She blinks at Caleb and then turns to me. "You did that?"

"It's just cereal, but it'll get him through until lunch."

"You're a lifesaver," she announces as she wraps her arms around me and hugs me tight. "Thank you. I'll throw your lunch together, buddy."

"Can I get hot lunch today? It's pizza day."

"Even better," I say with a wide grin. "Pizza day."

"That works," she says with a nod. She looks frantically around, like she's searching for something.

"What do you need?"

"Coffee. For God's sake, I need coffee."

"Already poured." I pass her the mug and watch as her glazed eyes fixate on the liquid, and she pulls it to her lips, taking a long sip.

"I might marry you after all," she decides as she sighs. Then her eyes widen in horror. "I didn't mean—"

"I know what you meant." I pat her shoulder as Caleb stops eating his cereal and watches us with serious eyes.

"Are you getting married?"

"No, buddy," London replies and kisses his head. "Are you about done?"

"Why don't you want to marry my mom?" he

demands. "She's a catch. And she's nice. And she makes really good cookies."

"All good reasons to get married," I agree, nodding. "But she was just kidding. That's all."

"Adults are weird," he decides and jumps down to go get his shoes on.

"Thank you," London says as she grabs her handbag and her computer bag. "You can let yourself out if you want."

"I'll leave with you. I can walk around to my car. And London?"

"Yeah?"

"You really are a catch."

CHAPTER 8

LONDON

"*I*t's November," Caleb points out as I yank a tub of holiday décor out of the attic. "Why are we doing this so early?"

"I like Christmas." I blow a strand of hair out of my eyes and pass my son a wreath. "Put that by the stairs. It goes on the front door."

"Last year, you had a whole company come to the house to decorate."

"And they're coming again this year because I can't reach the high stuff without a ladder, and I'm afraid of heights. But there's some stuff that we should do ourselves because it's fun, and you and I have some traditions."

"Like making the popcorn strings that go on the tree."

"Yes. But you eat most of the popcorn."

He grins at me. "It's delicious. Are we doing that

tonight?"

"No, that has to be done closer to the holiday, but don't worry, I won't forget."

"I know." He sounds completely unconcerned. "You don't forget anything, even the stuff I wish you *would* forget."

I chuckle and pull out the last box for today, then close the door behind me, and we make our way to the stairs leading to the first floor.

"I'm going to scoot the heavy ones down the stairs behind me," I inform him. "Take that wreath and head down. I don't want to trip over you."

"Don't fall and break your face," he advises, his own face perfectly serious.

"Thanks, I'll do my best."

I've made it halfway down when the doorbell rings.

"I got it!" Caleb yells and runs for the door.

"Ask who it is!"

I hear my son sigh and then say, "Who is it?"

I can't hear the answer, but it must satisfy Caleb because he opens the door.

"What the hell?" Drew hurries over to me and takes the heavy weight of the tote off my back. "What are you doing?"

"Bringing Christmas decorations down from the attic. But the question is, what are *you* doing?"

"I was in the neighborhood," he replies after setting the first tote on the floor. "Are there more?"

"Two more at the top of the stairs."

Drew immediately climbs the steps, two at a time, and before I know it, he's lugged both of the totes downstairs.

"Thanks. You didn't have to do that."

"They're heavy," he says, barely winded. "You could have broken your back."

"Or your face," Caleb chimes in helpfully.

"Not that I'm not happy to see you," I say, ignoring their lack of confidence in me to do manual labor, "but what are you doing?"

"I thought I'd come see what you're up to," he says and shoves his hands into his pockets. "Probably should have called first, huh?"

"No, I don't mind if you want to come over. You're welcome anytime. It just surprised me, that's all."

"I told Mom that it's too early for Christmas stuff," Caleb says. "Do you have yours up?"

"I don't know that I'll put anything up this year," Drew replies.

"Why wouldn't you?" Caleb wants to know, looking slightly mortified at the thought of no Christmas decorations.

"Well, I just moved into my condo this year, and I haven't really thought about decorating it for the holidays."

"You have to at least have a *tree*," my son insists. "We will have five of them."

Drew's eyes fly to mine in surprise. "*Five* trees?"

"It's a big house," I remind him. "We have one in the

game room, with all the gaming ornaments Caleb has collected over the years."

"I get two new ones every year."

I grin and push my fingers through my son's hair. "There will be a big one in the foyer, one in the living room off the kitchen, and one in each of our bedrooms."

I'm ticking them off on my fingers, trying to remember them all.

"Oh, and I'm going to put a tiny one in the kitchen. So, six."

"That's a lot of Christmas trees. I'm assuming that doesn't include all the fancy lights and garland and decorations," Drew decides. "How do you have time to do it all?"

"I hire most of it out. They have ladders and nerves of steel. But there are some things that I want Caleb and I to do together. I was in the mood to bring some down and get started, but now I realize that there isn't much I can do until the trees go up, and that isn't happening until this weekend."

I chew on my bottom lip, eyeing the totes.

"We'll put these in the guest room until I'm ready for them, and for now, the wreath can go on the front door. That's a start, at least."

Drew carries the totes into the guest room, stowing them out of sight in the closet, and then I hang the wreath on the door.

"There. Done for now."

"Maybe we can work on the Lego set," Caleb suggests, watching Drew with hopeful eyes.

"I'm down for that," Drew replies and looks at me. "Okay with you?"

"Sure. You guys go ahead. It's still in the game room. I have a couple of emails to send, and then I'll be in."

Caleb happily runs off, and when he can no longer see us, Drew tugs me against him and kisses me, hard and fast, then pushes away.

"It's good to see you, beautiful." He winks and follows after my kid.

"Well then." I press my hand to my hammering heart and make my way through the kitchen to the dining room, where my computer and phone sit.

Drew is way too sexy for his own good. So far, all we've done is kiss. Sure, his hands roamed the last time he was here, and I can say with certainty that those hands are talented.

Really, really talented.

But I ache for more. I'm not too proud to admit that I've spent a moment or two getting myself off while thinking about that hot mouth and clever hands, but after weeks of flirting and banter and spending so much time together, I'm ready to get naked. Spend the whole night naked with Drew Montgomery. I mean, that sounds like one hell of a good time.

And speaking of that, I see that Quinn replied to my text earlier.

Quinn: I can totally stay the night with Caleb! Slumber

party time. Doesn't he have Friday off of school? I could stay Thursday night if you want.

I sigh in relief. Thursday is just two days away.

Me: Yes, he does have Friday off! That would actually be perfect. Thanks, Quinn!

Quinn: I'll just head that way after class. See you around 4:00.

Satisfied that Caleb's taken care of, I open my laptop and get to work. I have reports to read over and the never-ending emails to make my way through. Thankfully, Lucy has categorized my email for me. I gave her the login info to the business account so she can filter what's urgent, what can wait, and what doesn't need to be seen at all.

Lucy is now one of my favorite people in the world. I don't know what I ever did without her. She already deserves a raise.

I can hear laughter and loud voices coming from the game room, and it makes me smile. That means the guys are having fun and getting along, which is a huge relief.

Just as I'm about to wrap up work for the day, Drew comes walking through the kitchen, his phone in his hand.

"Hey." I grin up at him. "I'm just finished here. Quinn's going to stay with Caleb on Thursday night. Does that work for you?"

"*This* Thursday? As in, the day after tomorrow?"

"That's the Thursday in question, yes."

"Hell yes, that works for me. Hey, I just got a text from my mom. She invited me over for dinner."

"Oh, okay. No worries. I'll catch up with you at work tomorrow."

Drew's lips twitch. "No, silly, I'm not leaving you guys. I'm wondering if you'd like to go with me. Both of you, of course."

He blinks, watching me expectantly. Meet his parents? So soon?

"If you'd rather not, I can tell them it's a no-go for today. No big deal."

"Do you *want* me to meet your parents?"

Drew shrugs. "It's just dinner, London. I think my mom's making salmon."

"You know what?" I stand, making a decision. "Salmon sounds great. I'll tell Caleb to go wash up."

"What does he have to wash? He seemed pretty clean to me."

I laugh and cross to him, cupping his cheek. "Okay, *I'll* go wash up. Give me fifteen minutes?"

"Take all the minutes you need." He leans in and touches his lips to mine. "It's just dinner, babe. Don't be nervous."

"I'm not nervous."

"You keep biting your lip." He tugs the lip in question out of my teeth with his thumb. "Is it the whole *meet the parents* thing that makes you nervous?"

"Probably," I admit. "Most likely. But I know how to work a room, so I'll be fine."

Drew just chuckles and kisses my forehead. "They mean a lot to me. And, I'm not afraid to admit, you and Caleb do, too. I'd like for all of you to meet. But if you're not ready, I understand."

Well, when he puts it like that, how am I supposed to say no? My heart just melted all over the floor.

"I'd love to have dinner with your family. Let me just change."

"It's casual. No need for that crazy-expensive handbag."

And just like that, the mood is light, and I laugh as I walk toward the game room. "There's always a need for that handbag."

I DIDN'T CHOOSE the Birkin. I thought about it, just to make Drew laugh, but I decided to carry my favorite Dior.

Caleb is beside himself with excitement at the prospect of meeting Drew's parents. He's been asking questions nonstop since we left the house.

And Drew simply answers every single one of them with the patience of a saint.

"Did you grow up in this house?" Caleb asks as Drew pulls into the driveway.

"I did," he says and cuts the engine.

"Do they still have the same furniture and everything?" Caleb wants to know, and I turn around to look at him quizzically.

"What? Why do you want to know about the furniture?"

"I want to know *everything*," he says.

"No, the furniture is pretty new," Drew replies with a laugh. "Come on, you can see for yourself."

Before we make it to the front door, it opens, and a beautiful woman with auburn hair grins at us.

"You're here! Come in, everyone. You must be Caleb."

"That's me," my son says with a nod. "And you're Brynna?"

"Yes, I am. It's nice to meet you. You're so handsome. Come on in. I need a taste tester in the kitchen. Hello, London. It's a pleasure to meet you."

I'm suddenly swept up in a hug that surprises me.

"It's nice to meet you, as well, Mrs. Montgomery."

"Brynna, please. We're pretty casual around here. Come on. My husband is in the kitchen. I made him stay and keep an eye on things."

Drew takes my hand as we follow his mom through the house. It's a lovely home, comfortable and lived in. There are photos of Drew and his sisters at varying ages on the walls and in frames on shelves.

"Do you like cherry cheesecake?" Brynna asks my son.

"Of course, I do," he replies, making her laugh.

"Well, that's good, because I made some for dessert. Don't tell the others, but I'll give you the biggest piece."

Caleb's face lights up in delight, and for just a moment, I feel a lump of emotion form in my throat.

This is what it's like to be in a loving home.

"Hey, Pops," Drew says to his dad, who turns around from the stove and smiles at all of us. He's a tall, broad man, and I immediately see where Drew gets his looks and body shape from. He looks like he'd be formidable if you ever pissed him off. "This is London and Caleb."

"Nice to meet you," he says, nodding at me and then turning his attention to my boy. "I hear you stole my name."

Caleb's grin widens. "It wasn't my fault. She did it." He points to me, and we all laugh.

"Guilty. It's a good name. What can I say?"

"I could use some help with the grill," Drew's dad says, eyeing my son. "Would you like to be my assistant?"

"Sure." Without hesitation, Caleb joins the man and follows him out onto the deck.

"Okay, he's adorable," Brynna says. "And I'm not just saying that."

"Thanks. He's a handful sometimes, but he's a good kid. Thank you for the invitation to dinner. You have a lovely home."

"I'm glad you could come, and thank you." She glances around the house and at the kitchen. "It's been good to us. Drew, you could show her your old bedroom."

"I don't think she needs to see that."

"Wait, is it *intact*? Like, with all of your stuff from when you were a kid? Because if so, I want to see it *right now*."

"No." Drew laughs. "No, that would make Mom a psycho. It's just a guest room now."

"I did save the stuff he didn't take with him," Brynna adds. "Because I'm sentimental like that. I never thought I would be, but he's my baby."

"I understand. I've held on to all of Caleb's baby things, even though I know that I probably won't have any more children. In fact, Drew told me that your daughters are both pregnant. If they need or want any of what I have, it's all theirs."

"That's generous. Thank you. I'll definitely pass that along to them. Yes, both of my daughters are going to make me a grandmother at the same time. I can't wait. I told my Caleb about a month ago that I had baby fever, and I've never seen him go so pale."

"You don't think you'll have more kids?" Drew asks me casually before popping a piece of green bean into his mouth.

"It's not really in the plans right now." I narrow my eyes on him, thinking. Does *he* want children? This is probably something we should talk about when his mother isn't listening in. "How many cousins are there?"

"Oh, geez," Brynna says with a sigh, leaning on the counter as she thinks it over.

"A million," Drew says, making his mother grin. He has her smile for sure.

"Luke and Nat have four," she begins, ticking them off on her fingers. "Isaac has two, Jules has one, Will has two, we have three, Matt has two, Mark has two, and Dom has one. So, that's seventeen."

"*Seventeen* first cousins?" I let out a whistle. "That's a lot of babies."

"It was so fun when they were little," Brynna replies with a wistful smile. "We had so many play dates, parties, you name it. They really grew up as siblings more than cousins."

"That's what Drew said not long ago." I tilt my head to the side. "And he mentioned something about a cousin compound?"

"Yes." Brynna reaches for the salmon and begins to rub butter on it. "So, Natalie Williams, who is an honorary sister—and that's a long story—owned a house over at Alki Beach. She's owned it forever. I think she inherited it from her parents, but I'm not totally sure about that. Anyway, after she and Luke married, they never sold it. It just kind of made its way through the family. If someone needed a place to stay, they used the Alki house. Heck, even I stayed there with the girls when I first came to Seattle."

"I didn't know that," Drew says.

"It's true. When all of our kids started reaching

college age, they'd move into the Alki house so they were on their own, but still had the safety of family. Then, a couple of years ago, the house next door went up for sale, so Will and a couple of the other siblings went in on buying it. They made a few changes, renovations and updating, and took out the fence that separated the two properties, making it one big property."

"A compound," I say with a smile, loving the idea. I would have loved that when I was in my early twenties.

"That's right," she says with a nod. "The cousins live there. I think most everyone has lived there at some point, or will."

"Keaton never did," Drew adds. "He was never the social type."

"That's right," Brynna says, nodding in agreement. "Drew just moved out of there a few months ago when he took the job with the team."

"I lived in the guesthouse behind the original house," he puts in. "It was a sweet place. But I like my new condo and being close to my job. Alki would have been an awful commute every day."

I frown. "But Lucy currently lives at the compound?"

"Yeah, Luce is there," Drew confirms.

"And she commutes."

He nods, popping another green bean into his mouth. "Yeah, she does. I offered to let her stay at my place during the week, but she said she was fine for now. If the drive gets too ridiculous, she'll probably take me up on it."

"Hmm."

"Lucy is *so* in love with her new job," Brynna gushes. "I saw her the other night for our monthly girls' night, and she just couldn't say enough wonderful things about it and you. Apparently, you're the best boss that has ever lived, and she hopes to be with you for about fifty years."

"That's sweet. As far as I'm concerned, she'll be with me for a very long time. So, you have a monthly girls' night out?" The thought of that makes me grin.

"Oh, yeah, we do, with all the aunts and cousins. You'll have to join us for the next one."

"I didn't mean to invite myself."

"You didn't. I invited you." She winks at me, and it occurs to me that I don't remember the last time I felt this immediately relaxed around someone. Brynna is sweet and smart and nurturing.

Drew is lucky to have her.

"The grill is ready!" My boy comes running in from the outside. "I've cleaned it, and it's ready for the fish. Old Caleb wants to know when you'll send it out to us."

"*Old* Caleb?" I ask, completely mortified. "Please tell me you didn't call him that to his face."

"Of course, I did. We had to figure out nicknames so we don't get confused."

"Maybe we should come up with different ones."

CHAPTER 9

"*T*his is the best cheesecake I've ever had," London decrees after the first bite. "Please tell me you'll share the recipe."

"Happy to," Mom replies with a satisfied grin. "Do you like to cook, London?"

"Bake," she says with a nod. "I love to bake. I honestly don't cook a lot, but I love a cozy, warm kitchen with something in the oven, especially at this time of the year."

"She makes the best cookies *ever*," Caleb announces. "We'll bring you some."

Mom winks over at me and then smiles at Caleb. "Well, I would love that. Thank you."

When I first invited London and Caleb to dinner, I worried that I was rushing things. The look on her face was one of startled terror, and I tried to backpedal, in case she just wasn't ready for this. It didn't occur to me in the moment that she might misconstrue a casual dinner as something big. I just knew that I wanted to include London and her son in a nice dinner with my parents.

I'm grateful that she accepted. I can tell that both of my parents get a kick out of Caleb, which doesn't surprise me. He's a great kid, easy to have around and talk to. Sure, he asks a lot of questions, but he's not obnoxious about it at all.

But seeing my mom with London has been the thing that I've enjoyed the most this evening. They laugh and chat like they've been friends for a long time. They have plenty in common, and there hasn't been even a moment of uncomfortable silence since we walked through the door.

It's easy and fun.

They fit here, in my universe.

"Your sisters will be disappointed that they didn't meet London and Caleb," Dad says as he pushes away his empty plate.

"They're nosy," I reply.

"They're twins," Caleb informs the table. "Do they look the same?"

"They do," Mom says with a nod. "Come with me. I'll show you some pictures."

"Okay." Caleb stands but pauses and glances at his mom. "May I please be excused with Brynna?"

"Sure. Thank you for asking." London leans over

and kisses her son's cheek, and then he's off, chasing after my mom.

"He's a cutie," Dad says, turning to London. "You've done an excellent job in raising that young man, London. He's polite, smart, and funny."

"Thank you." London flushes in happiness at the compliment. "That might be the best compliment I've ever received."

"Is his father out of the picture?" I already informed him of this the other night, but leave it to my dad to grill someone and hear it from the source himself.

"Yes." London puts her hand on mine before I can interrupt. "He passed away when Caleb was about three. It's just been the two of us for a long time now. Well, that's not true. We have my brother, Rome, who comes around often. Caleb loves him a lot."

Dad nods, and we can hear Mom and Caleb both laughing in the next room.

"What made you decide to buy the football team?" Dad asks. Honestly, this is something I keep meaning to ask, as well, so I'm interested to hear her response.

"Rome came to me about it," she says after taking the last bite of her cheesecake. "We'd seen the mess that the former owner made in the press, of course, and we knew that the league would make her sell. Rome and I are both wealthy in our own rights, but not rich enough to buy the team. So, we made a business plan and took it to our father, and he agreed to back it. Rome and I each own 5 percent of the team, and my father owns the other ninety, but he's a silent partner. He doesn't have any interest in the sport."

"But you do."

London nods at my father's statement. "We do. We've watched football together forever. Rome played in high school and in college, and after that, we would get together on Sundays to watch. We knew it would be a good business decision, so we went for it. So far, it's going very well."

"Good for you," Dad replies with a nod. "I know that Will's damn happy there, and he tells me that the changes you've made have been excellent ones."

"That means a lot to me because I respect your brother immensely. No one knows this team the way he does. So, hearing he's happy means the world."

"Drew used to have a mohawk," Caleb announces as he comes running back into the room, a photograph in his hand. "Look, Mom."

He passes the photo to London and laughs.

"Hey, it was just for the summer," I insist. "I thought it was cool. Also, why is my mother showing you photos that old?"

"She showed me all the really old ones," Caleb informs me. "And she told me that your real name isn't Drew at all. It's Michael Andrew."

"Drew is short for Andrew," I point out. "And Michael just never stuck."

"He's definitely a Drew," Mom agrees as she joins us. "Now, who wants to play cards?"

"Poker?" Caleb asks, clearly way too excited at the prospect.

"I was thinking Uno," Mom says with a laugh.

~

"I WON'T BE IN TOMORROW," I inform Will on Thursday afternoon, just before I head out for the day. "I have things covered, and my guys know what they're working on in practice."

"Sounds good," Will says. "Doing anything fun?"

"Uh, well, I'm—"

"None of my business," he says with a laugh and waves me off. "See you Saturday."

"See you."

I wave and leave his office, ready to go to my place to grab my overnight bag, and then head over to pick up London, who left for the day about an hour ago.

She texted to give me the heads-up that she was already home, adding the little dance emoji. I think that means she's excited.

Hell, I am, too.

I make it home in record time, pleased when I see that Lucy's already there. I told her she could stay at my place tonight so she could see if she liked the shorter commute, and I wouldn't be there *hovering*, as she calls it.

"Hey, Luce," I say as I rush past her to my bedroom. My bag is on the bed and pretty much ready to go. I just have to grab a couple of things out of the bathroom. When that's finished, I quickly change into jeans and a T-shirt and top it off with a hoodie before returning to the kitchen, where Lucy's dishing out Chinese takeout onto one of the four plates that I own.

"You don't have much in this kitchen," she informs me. "*Four* plates, Drew?"

"I'm one person. How many do I need?"

Lucy rolls her eyes just as the doorbell rings, and then Erin saunters right in.

"Having a party?" I ask.

"Hey, favorite cousin," Erin says to me with a grin. "Lucy invited me over for Chinese."

"I thought *I* was your favorite cousin?" Lucy demands.

"I say that to everyone," Erin reminds her. "Hey, Drew, we're planning a cousins' ski trip to Montana in a few weeks. You need to bring London. We planned it for your bye weekend, so I know you won't have a game."

I blink at her, surprised. "That actually sounds really fun. Are we going up to Cunningham Falls?"

"No, we're trying somewhere new. Some place called Bitterroot Valley. They have a killer ski hill, and we're going to rent out some short-term rentals and stuff. I'll send you the dates. Like I said, bring London."

"What makes you think I want to bring London?"

I'll absolutely bring London.

"Dude, you're taking her out overnight tonight.

127

You'll want to bring her. The rest of us are dying to meet her."

"How did you know—?" I stop and stare at Lucy, who just smiles and waves at me. "Right. I'll mention it to her."

"I'll do my best not to interrupt London this evening," Lucy promises. "I think we have everything handled, so she can just unplug for the next twenty-four hours."

"Thanks. Don't have a huge party here tonight and disturb the neighbors, okay?"

"You're such a party pooper," Erin replies with a wink. "Go have fun. Use protection!"

"Oh, shit, the protection." I drop my bag and run back to the bedroom, listening to the girls laughing the whole way, and grab the new box of condoms I bought and toss them into my bag when I return. "Thanks for the reminder. Okay, see ya."

I wave and head out, eager to get to London's place and have her all to myself for a while.

The drive from my condo to her house conveniently takes less than twenty minutes *with* traffic, and before long, I've parked in her driveway and am ringing her doorbell.

"Who is it?" Caleb yells from the other side of the door.

"Drew," I call back, and the door swings open. "Hey, kiddo."

"Hi. Quinn's here already, and Mom has her bag by the door. Want me to put it in the car for you?"

I grin down at him. "Yeah, let's do that."

I reach for the bag, but Caleb shakes his head and muscles it down the steps himself, then waits for me by the back of the SUV. I join him, and when I've opened the hatchback, he moves to lift it in, but I beat him to it.

"Thanks for the help," I say as we walk inside. "Are you trying to get rid of us?"

"No." He laughs at that, and I see London hurrying down the stairs, looking *amazing*. I'm surprised my tongue doesn't just roll right out of my mouth.

She's in my favorite look of hers: jeans, sneakers, no hair or makeup fussed over, and today, she's wearing *glasses*.

Black-rimmed glasses.

"I didn't know you wore those." I nod to the spectacles on her nose, and she shrugs.

"I usually wear contacts, but my eyes were bothering me today. I have them with me, though, for tomorrow."

"You can throw them out, as far as I'm concerned. The glasses are sexy as hell."

She smiles, and I realize that we have an audience. We both turn our gazes down to Caleb, who's watching us carefully.

"Why can't I go?" he asks, those eyes narrowed and too observant.

Because it's time I fucked your mother into next week, and that's not possible with you around.

"Buddy, we've been through this," London replies. "It's okay for me to take a little time away now and then. It's just for one night, and you're going to have a blast with Quinn. Right, Quinn?"

"Duh," the young woman says. "Dude, we have junk food your mom doesn't even know about, and I might even let you watch a PG-13 movie. We're breaking all the rules tonight."

"And, if you want," I add, "we can do a guys' night sometime soon."

"Hey, what about *me*?" London asks.

"My mom invited you to the next girls' night out. You don't get to complain."

"That's fair," London says and smiles down at her son. "Have fun tonight, okay? Be good for Quinn. You can stay up late since you don't have school tomorrow."

"Solid," Caleb replies. "Okay, thanks for abandoning me. I'll need therapy until I'm thirty."

"Only until you're thirty?" London says, sarcasm dripping off every word. "Then I'd better try harder."

She hugs him close, gives Quinn a few last-minute instructions, kisses Caleb's head, and then we're off.

"Where are we going?" she asks once we've pulled away from the house. "I didn't even think to ask before this; I was just excited to be alone with you. Are we going to your place?"

"No. Lucy and Erin are there, eating Chinese food.

Lucy's taking the condo for a test drive tonight to see if she wants to stay there during the week sometimes. You and I are going to Leavenworth."

"The cute little Bavarian town in the mountains that has Christmas up all year long?"

"Well, it's not the prison." I can't help but laugh at my own joke. "Have you been there before?"

"The prison?" She shakes her head. "Not lately."

I take her hand and lift it to my lips, nibbling on her knuckles. "I do love your smart mouth."

She sighs and wiggles back into the seat, getting comfortable. "I've never been, but I've heard a lot about it. And it's *Christmas*."

"I know you like the holidays." I kiss her hand once more and then release it so I can change lanes. "So, I figured since you couldn't decorate your house when you wanted to, I could take you to Christmas myself."

"That's ridiculously sweet. And, dare I say, romantic."

"If I eat one more bite of this, you'll have to roll me back to the room." She sits back from the table, still eyeing the German pretzel with longing. I've just learned that soft pretzels with beer cheese are her favorite.

Then again, who doesn't love that combo?

"This little town is even more adorable than I

imagined," she says with a sigh, looking around the small tavern where we stopped for a beer and a snack. We spent an hour exploring the shops and decided to eat something before we headed back to the hotel for dinner. "And the hotel you booked? Holy shit, it's so *pretty*. It looks like it's built into the side of the mountain, and I can't wait to swim in the salt-water pool."

I'm relieved the hotel was a win.

"I have to admit, it's a little intimidating to take you somewhere overnight."

She tilts her head to the side. "Why?"

"Because you've likely stayed in the most beautiful suites in the world."

"I have." She can't resist breaking off another piece of pretzel and dipping it into the cheese. "And I *do*. I'm a travel snob, Drew."

"That likely should have been something you told me before I made the reservations."

"No way. You did an *amazing* job. That hotel is top-notch, and the suite is beautiful. I read the menu of spa services they have, on top of the healing pools and the decadent food, and it's perfect. More than comfortable."

"Where do you stay when you're in Paris?" I ask her.

"The Ritz, of course. They have other hotels?"

"One of the things I like about you is that you're so multifaceted. You can be this woman, casual and laid-back, and then you can be the traveled boss lady, with your expensive shoes and bags. You're *both*, and I think they're both sexy as fuck."

"I'm glad you do." She bites the pretzel, watching me. "Have you ever been to Paris?"

"No."

"London?"

"Nope."

"Have you been abroad at all?"

"I went to Iceland with my family last Christmas. That was fun. I've been to Hawaii, but that doesn't count. Honestly, my job has never taken me out of the country, and I don't have a lot of time to travel for leisure."

"Well, we might just have to change that. I'd love to show you Paris. It's my favorite city in the world, and that's saying something because Seattle will always have my heart."

"Did you grow up in Seattle?"

"Yes, that was our home base. Dad wasn't home much, but we were there with the nanny. I can't imagine living anywhere else full time. I can, however, imagine buying a vacation home here. It's only two hours away from Seattle, but it's so beautiful and away from the grind, you know?"

"So, you'd prefer something in the mountains as opposed to the beach?"

"I think so." She taps her lips, thinking it over. "I like the snow, so the mountains appeal to me."

"Speaking of snow. Lucy and Erin were just telling

me that the cousins are planning a ski trip to Montana during our bye weekend. I'd like for you to join us. If you want to bring Caleb, I'm cool with that."

She blinks once and then bites her lower lip.

"Whoa, what did I say wrong?"

"Nothing." She clears her throat. "You didn't say anything wrong at all. I need to thank you for being so understanding about including my son. I know it's not easy to have a ten-year-old around so much, and that dating a single mom isn't the most fun thing in the world."

"Says who?" I reach over and take her hand. "I'm having fun. If a guy has issues with a woman's kids, those issues are on *him*. Not her. You told me from the get-go that Caleb is the most important aspect of your life, and he should be. It's one of the things I respect about you. My mom was a single mom when she met my dad. It's not new to our family. If you want to bring Caleb skiing, we'll make it happen. If you'd rather he stay in Seattle with Quinn or even my parents, that's okay, too."

"Your parents would be okay with keeping him?"

"Why are you so surprised?" I laugh and kiss her hand before letting it go. "Are you kidding? They'd get a huge kick out of keeping him. But like I said, it's up to you. It honestly doesn't bother me either way. He'd probably love skiing, and we could get him lessons."

"Let me think about it," she says slowly. "I'll have to look at the dates to see what he has on his schedule."

"That works. Are we done here?"

"Oh, yeah. What should we do next?"

"I'd like to take you back to the room, get you naked, and have my way with you for about the next twelve hours."

"That's the best idea you've ever had."

CHAPTER 10

LONDON

I'm so damn nervous that I don't know what to do. My stomach is a tangle of nerves, and I swear I just broke out in a cold sweat. What if I stink? That's not sexy. Do I have time for a shower? Oh, God, he'll want to have shower sex, and that does *not* sound fun to me at all.

How do you tell the sexiest man alive, who obviously wants in your pants and thinks you're sexy, too, that you haven't actually *had* intercourse since before you had your ten-year-old kid?

"This room is seriously so pretty." I know I'm being ridiculous, but I skitter away from him when he closes the door behind us, and I make a beeline to the balcony that overlooks the pool and the river below, taking big gulps of the fresh air. The sun set long ago, but I can hear the rush of the water, and the pool area is lit up but empty. "Maybe we should go for a swim. It looks like we'd have the whole place to ourselves."

I feel Drew press himself to my back, and his arms circle around me while his lips land on my neck, sending goose bumps down my arms. "Talk to me. What's wrong?"

"What? Nothing's wrong. Nothing at all."

"Your voice is pretty damn shrill for a woman with nothing wrong." He turns me to face him and cages me in, his hands planted on the railing on either side of me. "Are you nervous?"

"Yeah." I let out a relieved breath. "Yeah, I guess I am."

"There's no need to be." He dips down to kiss my forehead, then the top of my head. "There's just you and me here. We make our own rules as we go."

"Rule number one." I press my hand to his chest and clear my throat. Geez, why does he have to be so...*muscular*?

"What is it?"

"What is what?" I look up at him with a frown.

"The rule." His lips have turned up in a satisfied smile. "You said you have a rule."

"Oh. Right. I did." Jesus, how am I supposed to remember when he's standing so close to me? I swallow hard again, probably for about the seventh time. "I don't remember what it was."

"Why are you nervous?"

"Because I haven't done this in a *really* long time."

"I think it's like riding a bike. You don't really forget how."

"And my body…" I shrug a shoulder. "I had a baby. I'm not as young as I used to be. Holy shit, Drew, did you realize that I'm older than you? By, like, five years. What does that make me?"

"Older than me," he says. "So what? I'm not a minor. You're not my teacher."

"I'm your boss." That came out way harsher than I meant for it to.

"Whoa." He takes a step back and shoves his hands into his pockets. "Have I misread the situation here, London? Do you feel like I'm pressuring you into doing something you don't want to do?"

His face and gorgeous blue eyes are cold and suddenly withdrawn. The muscle on the side of his jaw twitches, and he rocks back onto his heels.

"No." There's no hesitation in my voice. "No, we're on the same page. You're not pressuring me into anything. I'm just…out of my comfort zone, I guess is the best way to explain it. I usually know what I'm doing in every situation. But tonight, I don't know what I'm doing."

"You're no virgin," he says, and his voice has softened again, although he hasn't moved toward me at all.

"No, definitely not." I worry my bottom lip between my teeth. I should just go home. I should tell him this was a bad idea, apologize, and go back to my regular life. I've been without sex for this long. I can just keep going. My gaze finds his, and he's still cold, not encouraging at all, and I lose any courage I might have had. "You know what, never mind. Maybe this was a mistake."

I walk past him and into the room and grab my jacket.

"I'll just call for a car."

"You're not going to call a fucking car," he says, and I whirl around to find him standing just inside, his hands balled into fists at his side. "You're going to *talk to me*, damn it. Why can't you just tell me what's bothering you?"

"Ten years," I blurt out, and then feel my eyes widen in sheer horrification. "Actually, now that I think about it, it's been longer than that, because it was before I was even showing with Caleb, so probably closer to eleven."

"It's been eleven years since what?"

The bastard wants me to spell it out for him? Fine. "Since I had sex, Drew. So, sure, it might be like riding a bike, but since the last time anyone has touched me like that, I've been pregnant, had a baby, and raised that child for *ten years*. And I thought I was fine with it. God knows that I'm so attracted to you that I can't think straight, and I'm *ready* to be with you, and—damn it, stop looking at me like that."

"Like what?"

"Like you can't stand the sight of me." I reach up to push my hair off my face, and I hate that my hand is shaking.

His shoulders deflate, and he hangs his head for a moment, then shakes it and walks right over to me, *picks me up*, and carries me to the couch where he sits and settles me in his lap.

"You hurt my feelings," he admits and brushes my hair off my cheek once more. "And that made me shut down, and I apologize for that. It won't happen again. Why didn't you just talk to me about this? We had two hours in the car on the way here."

"Because who wants to admit to the guy they have the biggest crush on in the history of crushes that she's terrified of getting naked with him because she has stretch marks on her stomach and probably isn't very good at the whole thing on top of it? That's not sexy or fun or flirty."

"Maybe not, but it's necessary because, whether you like it or not, I'm not going anywhere. We have to figure this out so we can fix it. In case you missed it, babe, this isn't a one-night stand for me. If that's all I wanted, I would have simply driven you over to my house, done the deed, and taken you back home."

"Not at all romantic," I murmur and watch when he grins. That simple grin pulls all the dread right out of me.

"We're at the beginning of something really great here. Are we at least on the same page on that?"

"Yeah." I sort of melt into him and kiss his cheek. "Yeah, we can agree on that."

"Why haven't you been intimate with anyone in so long?"

I sigh and look toward the dark windows. "Because I had a kid to think about, and then the mess with his dad, and then all the businesses and travel and *life*. Sure, I went on dates here and there, but there was nothing long-term. I didn't even sleep with Felix, and that pissed him off. He retaliated by having sex with someone else in my bed."

"I'd like to punch him," Drew says.

"I *did* punch him," I reply. "He threatened to sue me for assault, and I told him I'd have him brought up on breaking and entering charges, since I didn't give him permission to come into my home."

"He has the balls to come back around again after all of that bullshit?"

"He was brave because of my father." I shrug and then wrinkle my nose. "I guess I kind of killed the mood."

He stands, as if I weigh absolutely nothing, marches us into the bedroom, and sets me on the mattress.

"I don't know if you've noticed," he says as he crawls onto the bed, urges me back against the pillows, and then hovers over me and kisses me until I can't remember my own name, "but I'm *really* into you. I don't think that anything could kill this mood unless you said that you want nothing to do with me and told me to take a hike."

"I'm not going to tell you that." My breath hitches

when his hand pushes under my sweater and glides over my ribs. "You have *excellent* hands. Like, *really* good hands."

"It's from my days as a quarterback. You have to know what you're doing."

I start to laugh, but then those clever hands slip my sweater over my head, and he makes quick work of my bra, and before I know it, I'm lying half-naked beneath him.

"Damn," he mutters, staring at my breasts. I can't help but smirk. "What?"

"I don't have the best tits. It's a byproduct of having children. I could get a boob job, but I don't really want to. No shade to anyone who does, it's just not my thing."

"So, here's the thing. You keep mentioning being pregnant and having a baby, a baby I happen to know and like, as if it's a bad thing. In fact, I haven't seen anything that I don't like, London. You need to get out of your own head for a while."

I raise an eyebrow. "I'm an overthinker from way back. How do you propose I do that?"

A slow smile spreads over those magical lips, and his hands reach for my jeans. He nudges them down my legs, tosses them aside, and then does the same with my underwear.

I wish, more than anything, that it was dark in here. But the flip side of that is, I want to see *him*.

"Look at this amazing body." He blows out a breath,

shakes his head, and nudges my thighs apart with his shoulders. "So, no one has touched you like this?"

I feel his fingers tickle my most sensitive flesh, and it makes my back arch.

"Just my vibrator."

That has his head coming up, and his eyes shine—with jealousy?—as he stares up at me.

"We'll be throwing that out right away. You no longer have a use for it. Now, where was I?" He returns to the task at hand, feeling, stroking, and kissing me until my thighs quiver and I'm holding on to the comforter for dear life.

When he pushes a finger inside of me, I cry out.

"Go over, London." He kisses the inside of my leg, just below where it meets my center. "Go over, baby."

I couldn't stop it if I tried. The orgasm rocks through me so fast and so *hard*, I see stars. And just when I think it's run its course, another fresh wave of overwhelming sensation takes over.

I can hear the tear of a wrapper, feel the dip of the mattress as Drew moves over and around me, and when his pelvis is cradled between my legs, he whispers, "Look at me now."

It takes some effort to open my eyes, but when I do, I'm rewarded with the most tender, sweetest smile from this amazing man. He's brushing the apple of my cheeks with his thumbs, and he dips in to kiss me softly.

"I've never met anyone like you," he says as he rears

back, and when his cock is aligned with me, he slides slowly, but purposefully, inside of me, and when he's seated to the hilt, he stops, our gazes still locked. "You're the most amazing woman I've ever met in my fucking life."

I lift my legs and lock them around his waist, and he begins to move as his lips descend to my own. He takes my hand, links our fingers, and pins it over my head, thrusting my breasts up so he can feast on them, tugging and biting my nipples until they're hard peaks.

I've never had a man be so completely focused on *me* and my needs. Usually, in my experience, sex is whatever gets the guy off, but not with Drew.

It's as though my own pleasure is his only job in the world.

"Jesus, you're so fucking *good*," he groans, moving faster now. Every muscle in his toned body is tightly flexed, and I can't resist feeling the hard ridges of his stomach with my fingertips.

"Back at you," I manage to moan, and I feel him grin against my skin. "Jesus Christ, Drew."

"One more time." With every thrust, he grinds the root of his cock against my clit, and it makes my toes curl and my muscles clench around him. "Come again for me."

"I'll die."

He chuckles and then reaches down between us to press his thumb to my clit. That's all it takes to send me right over the edge into another mind-numbing orgasm.

But this time, he follows me over.

~

"You know, I might have to rethink this whole *no sex with Caleb in the house* thing."

It's an hour later, and because we missed our dinner reservations, we ordered room service. We're wearing the hotel's soft white robes, sitting on the bed with the tray between us.

"I don't think you want to answer the questions that kid will come up with," Drew replies with a laugh. "Can you imagine? *'Mom, why were you screaming last night?'*"

I cringe at that. "Yikes. Yeah, I don't want to answer those questions at all. But we've been seeing each other for, what, close to a month?"

"I'm not great at math, but I'd say that's close."

"And we're supposed to wait another month for this? Come on, that's not doable."

Drew sets down the french fry that he was about to pop into his mouth and leans over to kiss me.

"No, ma'am. I'm afraid I'm addicted to you now. We'll just find ways to make it work."

"Well, I suppose my office *does* lock."

He lifts a brow. "Why, Ms. Ambrose, are you suggesting, as my boss, that I should have sex with you in your office?"

"Only if you're not going to sue me if I say yes."

We laugh at that, and then I sober when my phone starts to ring, and I see that it's Quinn.

"She must be looking for something and needs my help." I press the green button and put her on speakerphone. "Hey, Quinn. What's up?"

"I don't know what to do." Her voice is full of fear, and she's talking so fast I can hardly understand her.

"What's wrong?"

Drew immediately stands and pulls on his clothes, reaches for his own phone, and makes a call.

"I can't find him," she says, tears in her voice. "I went to the kitchen to make us sandwiches, and when I got back, he was gone. I thought he just went to the bathroom, but it took him forever, so I started looking, and I swear to God, he's not in this house, London."

"Breathe," I instruct her, and follow my own advice, taking a deep breath, keeping the panic at bay. "You have to breathe, Quinn. I'll call Rome to come over and help you."

"I already did, and he's on his way, but I had to call you. Where would he be? He was kind of pouty tonight because he didn't get to go with you."

"Did you check his bedroom? Maybe he just went to bed."

"I've looked *everywhere.* In every closet, under every bed. I even went outside to search for him. He's not here. I *know* he's not in this house."

146

She's starting to sound hysterical again, and Drew hurries over. "Quinn, this is Drew. Listen to me, okay?"

"Okay." She sniffs, obviously wiping her nose.

"My uncle is a cop, and he's on his way over there right now, along with my dad. Their names are Matt and Caleb, okay? Rome's coming, too. You're not alone. I want you to stay inside where it's safe and keep looking for him. Maybe he's hiding."

"He wouldn't hide from me."

I can hear the despair in her voice, and my own strength cracks. My eyes fill with tears.

I have to focus, so I get off the bed and hurry to get dressed, and then I toss my things into my bag and struggle to close the zipper.

"I can hear cars," she says through the phone. "It looks like two cars are pulling up."

"Make sure you know who they are before you open that door," Drew says, so calm and collected that I could just kiss the hell out of him.

"It's Rome, and they said they're Matt and Caleb. I'm letting them in."

"Okay, London and I are on our way back. It's going to take us a couple of hours to get there, and the cell service is sketchy, but keep us posted. Got it?"

"Got it." She sounds stronger now that she's not alone. "Thank you. London?"

"I'm here," I reply and wipe a tear off my cheek. "You didn't do anything wrong, Quinn. Remember that. I'll be there soon, and if he's hiding, he has some serious explaining to do."

I hang up the phone, and all I can do is just stand here in the middle of the room.

"Oh, God, Drew."

"Hey." He pulls me against him, and we take this moment to just hold on to each other. "He's fine. He's just fine. Don't beat yourself up about this."

"I shouldn't have come."

"Bullshit." My head comes up at the fierceness of that one word. "You told Quinn yourself that it's not her fault, and it's not *your* fault either. We'll figure this out, but you won't make yourself sick with guilt. No way."

"You're right." I nod and reach for my bag. "I have everything."

"Let's go."

The drive is dark. Scarily dark. There aren't even any stars in the sky as we make our way over the pass, through slushy snow, toward the city. Drew and I haven't said much, but he's held my hand and reassured me several times that everything will be okay.

He's so *strong*. He's obviously a rock under pressure and in a scary situation.

And I know, without a shadow of a doubt, that I'm completely in love with him.

"Almost there," he murmurs as we come off of the pass and are headed into the city. The roads are just wet now, so he reaches over to take my hand, pulls it to his lips the way he always does, and kisses my fingers. "How are you holding up?"

"I need to get there. I need to find my boy." I searched through the security camera footage first thing when we got into the car, and there was no sign that Caleb left the house. At least there's that.

Drew nods grimly. We haven't heard from anyone, and in this case, no news is *bad* news.

The gate is standing open when we get there, and we're waved through.

"Someone warned them that we'd be in a hurry."

"I did," Drew says simply, expertly taking the curves and corners that lead up my driveway.

Before he's even cut the engine, I push out of the car and run inside.

"Caleb!" I yell. "You'd better get your ass down here *now*!"

CHAPTER 11

DREW

"He's in so much trouble," Rome mutters and takes London's shoulders in his hands. "We haven't found him yet; we were waiting for you before we started searching the grounds and outbuildings."

"He's not technically a missing person," Matt says. "I'm Matt, by the way."

"Pleasure," London immediately replies. "Okay. I need to breathe. He's not on the security cameras as having left."

"That was my next question," Matt says.

London sucks in a breath and turns to Quinn.

"Did you look in the attic?"

Quinn nods. "Yes, and the basement, too. I even looked *in* the washer and dryer."

"He didn't say anything about playing a game with you?" my dad asks, pacing the foyer.

"No," Quinn says, shaking her head. "We were going to watch another movie, and we wanted a snack, so I said I would make us sandwiches. I've done that a *million* times."

"Wait." London holds up a hand. "On the phone earlier, you said he was pouty?"

"Yeah, super pouty. He was mad that you guys went without him, but I reminded him that we'd have fun together and that his mom deserves some time away. In my head, I was like, with a hot guy, because Drew's pretty hot."

Her face flushes, and her eyes slide over to me.

"Sorry."

"You didn't offend me."

"He has a tendency to be a brat when he's mad," Rome says and shrugs when London narrows her eyes at him. "You know it's true. I wouldn't put it past him to hide."

"Is there a shed outside? A treehouse?" Matt asks. "Did anyone check the cars in the garage?"

"I didn't think of the garage!" Quinn makes a run for the door off of the kitchen, but London and I pass her.

"I'll take the Porsche," I announce as London heads for the Mercedes. Both are SUVs, so we check the very back, as well, but come up empty.

"Damn it," London mutters, and I can see that she's starting to lose it. "I'm so mad at him, but I'm so scared, too. What if someone took him? My God, what if someone came into my house and took my baby?"

"Unlikely," Matt says. "They would have left a note, and Quinn would have known someone was here. Besides, they'd be on the security cameras."

"Well, he can't just disappear, as if into an alternate reality," my dad says.

"Wait." London holds up a hand and then runs back into the house. We're all hot on her heels as she runs right for the guest room, to the bookshelf, and presses the lever that opens the secret door to the library.

"I didn't even know this was here," Quinn exclaims as London runs inside.

"Caleb Rome Ambrose," London says, her voice hard as she scoops up her sleepy son and hugs him fiercely. "You are in big trouble, mister."

She pulls back and takes Caleb by the shoulders.

"Why did you hide in here? You know that Quinn doesn't know about this room."

"I just wanted to hide," he says and turns big eyes to the four men standing with their hands on their hips, watching him. "Who is that?"

"That doesn't matter," London replies. "You hid, and you had to have heard Quinn calling for you."

Caleb doesn't deny it, and his eyes slide over to me and narrow. "What does it matter? It was no big deal. I just wanted to come in here and wait for you to come home. That's all."

"Because you knew that when Quinn couldn't find you, she'd call me, and I'd come home."

Caleb reluctantly nods. "I wanted you to come home."

"You don't always get what you want," his mother reminds him, but he firms his chin and glares at her.

"Yes, I do."

"No." It comes out of my mouth before I can hold it back. "You don't. No one does. You scared Quinn, your mom, and all of us, Caleb. You don't get to stand there and be disrespectful when what you should be doing is apologizing."

"You're not my dad!"

"Here we go," Rome mutters behind me, but I don't turn away.

"Caleb," London begins, but I shake my head, stopping her.

"I'm not your dad. But I care about you and your mom, and I won't stand here and let you be mean to her."

That makes Caleb frown and look down, showing shame for the first time.

"She doesn't deserve that. Quinn definitely didn't deserve what you did tonight. This *is* your fault, and you'll apologize to the two women who love you the most."

He doesn't lose the frown as he looks over at Quinn, who's been crying at the side of the room.

"Sorry," he says half-heartedly. "Maybe you should have looked harder."

Quinn's jaw drops in shock as London gasps and then reaches for Caleb's arm.

"That's it," she says and drags him out of the room. "You're going to bed, and you'd better wake up with a better attitude tomorrow, or you'll be grounded even longer than you already are for this."

"I'm *grounded*?" he shrieks as London marches him up the stairs. "That's stupid! You can't do that!"

"What is this attitude?" London demands. "Where did my sweet boy go all of a sudden?"

"He's pissed," Dad says conversationally as we all stand at the bottom of the stairs and watch London haul the kid into his bedroom. "And, I'd say, jealous as hell."

"Definitely jealous," Matt agrees. "It was nice meeting you, Rome."

"You, as well," Rome replies, shaking both of their hands. "Thank you for coming to help, even though there really wasn't much to do. The moral support was welcome."

"He's *never* done something like this to me," Quinn says, tears still swimming in her eyes.

"That's a betrayal, for sure," Matt replies and pats Quinn's shoulder. "Try not to take it personally. He was trying to hurt his mom, not you."

"He did both," Quinn says, wiping her eyes. "I'm going to head home and cry myself to sleep. I was *so* scared, and now the adrenaline is wearing off, and I feel like I could sleep for a month."

"Why don't you stay?" I offer. "Stay in the guest room. Get a good night's sleep and talk to him in the morning. You might both feel better."

"Yeah." She rubs her hands over her face and then nods. "Yeah, okay. I'll do that. But I'm taking a glass of wine in with me."

"Take the bottle," Rome says. "You've earned it."

She grins and turns to my dad and Matt. "Thank you for coming. You really calmed me down and kept me that way until London and Drew got home, and I appreciate it."

"Anytime," Dad assures her.

Quinn walks off, headed for the kitchen and, I'm sure, the wine fridge.

"You did a good job of not backing down to Caleb," my dad says and claps his hand on my shoulder. "He's testing limits with you, and he's starting to have feelings about you being with his mom."

"Hell, *I'm* having feelings," Rome says, with a laugh. "Because we're all realizing that this isn't a casual thing. Personally, I like you. And Caleb does, too. He just has to be a ten-year-old for a while."

"I get it." I blow out a breath and push my hands through my hair. "Scared us, though."

"That's what he wanted," Matt says as he and my dad turn to the door. "Good luck, buddy. You'll be fine."

"Thank you both." I walk them to the door and hug each of them before they go.

"You have a good family," Rome says when I join him once more.

"I know." I let out a long breath and, like Quinn, feel the adrenaline wearing off. "I hope she's okay up there."

Rome looks up the stairs, then motions for me to follow him. "Come on, let's get some wine of our own."

Quinn is already leaving the kitchen, a *very* large glass of wine in one hand and chips and queso on a platter in the other.

"Now, that's comfort food," I say with a grin.

"I need it. Thanks again, guys. See you tomorrow."

Rome pulls down glasses, opens a fresh bottle of red, and pours.

"Did you at least have a good time for the few hours you were gone?"

"Yeah. We did. Listen, Rome, I need you to know that I'm here for the long haul. I have a thing for your sister that isn't going away any time soon."

"Nice. It's about time someone appreciated her." He sips his wine and passes me a glass, then sets another for London on the counter. "I don't have any issues at all with you, Drew. And despite what he pulled tonight, Caleb has had nothing but great things to say about you. I think he's confused."

"I'll have a talk with him tomorrow."

"There seriously needs to be a handbook on how to deal with a ten-year-old," London announces as she walks into the kitchen and immediately picks up her wine glass and drinks deeply.

"Did you have a talk with him?" Rome asks.

"I tried. He's just so stubborn, and he won't talk to me about why he was so mad. And when I explain that he scared people, especially Quinn, he just doesn't seem to care. That's not like him. I made it clear to him that I refuse to simply not go places or live my life because he's decided to act like a jerk about it, and from now on, he'll be on lockdown with a professional nanny who isn't nearly as nice as Quinn is."

"What did he say to that?" I ask.

"He fucking *sneered*. In my face." She narrows her eyes and takes another sip. "For the first time in his life, I almost slapped him. So, I told him to go to sleep, and I left."

Her phone pings with a text, and she looks at Rome. "Did you tell Dad what was going on?"

"Yeah, I gave him the heads-up, but I also shot him a quick text to let him know everything was okay."

"Then why is he texting me?"

She opens her phone and rolls her eyes.

"What is it?" I ask.

"Another man's number. For God's sake, he has to stop this."

I hold my hand out for her phone, and with a raised eyebrow, she passes it to me.

"It's time this stops," I say as I press send on his number.

"London?" Chandler Ambrose says as he answers.

"No, sir, this is Drew Montgomery. With all due respect, you need to stop trying to pair her up with someone. She's *with* someone, and I'm not going anywhere. She's taken."

There's a long pause, and then Chandler simply says, "Goodnight, Drew."

I pass the phone back to London, who appears to be speechless.

Finally, Rome laughs. "I'd bet all my money that that's the first time something like that has ever happened to that man."

"I mean it."

Rome sobers and finishes his wine. "I believe you do. Well, now that everything has somewhat calmed down, I'll head out."

He sets his glass in the sink, then crosses to his sister and pulls her in for a hug.

"Call me if you need me. I'll beat the kid up if it's necessary."

London chuckles. "I hope it *won't* be necessary. Thanks, Rome."

"Have a good night," I say with a wave, and when we're finally alone, London rubs her forehead with her fingertips.

"I'm so mad at my kid," she mutters.

"Me, too. I had a whole box of condoms to get through."

That makes her laugh in surprise, and she holds her

hand out for mine. I tug her to me and kiss her long and slow, satisfied when she melts against me. Now that I've had her naked and writhing beneath me, I can't wait to get her there again.

"I'm staying," I inform her. "I'll take a guest room, but I'm not leaving."

"Good." She bites her lower lip. "Unfortunately, I think it's best if you sleep in a guest room for tonight, at least until I figure out what in the world is going on with that kid."

"He's having feelings, and he doesn't know what to do about it." I shrug a shoulder. "I'm not going to take it personally. By the way, I told Quinn to stay. She's in one of the guest rooms."

"She's upstairs, in her room," London confirms. "I popped my head in to see if she stayed, gave her a hug, and reassured her. She was eating, drinking, and watching *Real Housewives*. You should take the guest room down here, with the library."

"That's awfully far away from you."

Her lips turn up in a soft, flirty smile. "True. But if I were to sneak down in the middle of the night, it's unlikely that anyone would hear if I seduced you and we did our best to be quiet."

"Oh, I like that idea." Her lips are soft when I kiss them. "I like that a *lot.* Let's plan on that."

She grins and checks the time. "It's late. I'll close up the house for the night."

"I'll come with you."

"She went with *you*."

"Yeah, she did. And that made you mad."

"I don't see why I couldn't go, too. We always do stuff together, and you just pushed me out. Is that how it's going to be now? You'll push me out because no one wants a kid hanging around when they want to bang that kid's mom."

"Hold up." I raise a hand and scowl at the boy. "Where in the hell did you hear that?"

"My friend, Jacob. Same thing happened to him with his mom. He said his stepdad came in and made it so his mom doesn't want to hang out with him anymore. All they wanna do is have sex."

"Caleb, do you know what sex is?"

He screws up his face in confusion. "No, but they do it all the time, Jacob said. So, you were nice to me for a while, but now you'll push me out. And that's not fair. I was here first."

"Yeah, you were. Caleb, it was for *one night*. And even if we had wanted to go for longer, your reaction wasn't fair. I'm not trying to kick you out of anything. Hell, this is *your* family. I'm just trying to get to know your mom better. I really like your mom. And I like you, too. But sometimes, we need some alone time so we can have grown-up conversations and talk about you behind your back."

That makes his lips twitch.

"It's like when you're with your friends. You don't

always want your mom to be hanging over your shoulder, watching everything you do, right?"

"No, but sometimes it's fun to have her around."

"Exactly. Although, this is a little different because we like to have you around *most* of the time. There will just be moments here and there when we do things without you. It doesn't mean we don't like you or love you or think that you shouldn't be a part of things."

He takes a deep breath, thinking that over.

"But what if, later, you decide that you don't want me around anymore?"

"Not gonna happen, bud. You and your mom are a family."

"Maybe you want to be part of our family." It's a whisper, and he looks up at me with hopeful eyes.

"Is that what *you* want? Because your actions last night said something very different."

"If you were part of our family, it would be okay." He's still tracing that line on the counter, and I see London approach the kitchen, but I shake my head just a little, indicating that she should just listen. She leans against the threshold and crosses her arms over her chest. "I mean, it's just been Mom and me and Uncle Rome forever. But if you're not going to push me out, then I guess it's okay."

"Caleb, if you don't like me, or if I've made you uncomfortable, you just have to say something so I can fix it."

"That's not it," he rushes to assure me. "I just don't want to be forgotten."

"You are *never* forgotten," London says, and Caleb's head whips around to his mom. "You're my baby, and I love you so big, even the smartest scientists can't measure it. And there's no need to be dramatic like you were last night to remind me that I have a child at home, Caleb."

He winces and folds right into his mom's arms when she hugs him close.

"I'm not raising a spoiled, entitled son," she continues and kisses the top of his head. "You're too smart and too sweet for that. You *know* better, baby."

"I'm sorry," he says, and his eyes fill with tears.

"I made breakfast," I announce and then smile at Quinn when she walks into the kitchen already dressed and seemingly ready to go. Her eyes are shadowed, as if she didn't sleep much. "Good morning, Quinn."

"Hey." She walks around the island until she's facing London and Caleb and firms her chin. "So, I had a long time to think things over last night, and I think that I have to go ahead and hand in my resignation."

"What? No!" Caleb shakes his head emphatically while London's face immediately takes on the look she has at work.

"I understand," London replies and stands. "Last night was way more than you signed on for. Caleb's behavior is inexcusable."

"I was so scared," Quinn admits, and her eyes fill

with tears. "I've *never* been so terrified in my life. What if something truly awful had happened to him on my watch? I would never forgive myself. And to know that he"—she turns to Caleb—"that you would do that to me on purpose because you were throwing some kind of a temper tantrum... It's too much for me. I don't know that I can trust you anymore, Caleb."

"I'm sorry," Caleb says and immediately runs around the island to fling his arms around her. "I'm sorry, honest I am. Please don't quit. I won't ever do it again, I promise. Just don't go."

"As you can see," London says, "we would prefer it if you'd reconsider. Quinn, we love you. You're a part of our family, and I'm so deeply sorry that Caleb pulled that stunt on you. It's not okay. Please give us another chance."

Quinn seems to think it over, and then she takes Caleb's face in her hands and tilts it up so he has to look at her.

"You can *never* do that again. When it's just you and me here, we're a team, and teammates don't do that crap to each other, right?"

"I know. I'm really, *really* sorry."

"If you ever act like that again, I'll quit, Caleb, and I'm not kidding. I love you too much, and you hurt me really bad."

Caleb, with tears flowing down his cheeks, hugs Quinn again.

"I won't. I won't do it again."

"Okay, then I'm going to trust you. Don't break my trust."

All of this because I wanted to take London somewhere nice. Spoil her. Make love to her. It's *my* fault. I should have sat Caleb down for a man-to-man talk before I took his mom out of town.

I won't make that mistake again.

"Does *anyone* want breakfast?" I ask, and all three of them nod their heads.

"Bacon," Caleb says. "It's my favorite."

"Bacon coming up, then."

CHAPTER 12

"*D*id you kill him?"

Laughing at Rome's question, I lock my office door behind us and turn to Lucy, who's typing diligently at her desk.

"Rome and I are going to go check in on some things here on campus. Just text if you need me."

"Enjoy," Lucy says with a smile and reaches to answer a ringing phone. "Ms. Ambrose's office. No, I'm sorry, she's in a meeting. Can I put you through to her voicemail? Perfect, please hold."

Rome glances back at Lucy and then down at me as we make our way down the hallway. "Your new assistant is…efficient."

"She's also beautiful, and I don't want you to lay a hand on her."

"Me?" He presses his hand to his chest and gives me his best hurt look. "I would never."

"I *like* her, Rome. You're not going to ruin this for me. I'll kill *you*."

"Point taken. But speaking of homicide, Caleb survived the night?"

"He did. And when Quinn announced that she was quitting this morning, he apologized profusely and panicked."

"Quinn quit?"

"Yeah, but I talked her into staying. Anyway, by the time Drew and I decided to come into work today, Quinn and Caleb were settled in at the house, playing video games."

"I'm sorry you ended up coming in today," Rome says. "You don't take vacation days often."

"It's okay." I shrug a shoulder as we reach the elevator. "I think I'm going to Montana with Drew and some of his cousins for a ski trip in a couple of weeks. During our bye weekend."

"That's *next* weekend."

I blink, surprised. "Really? Wow, time flies. Drew said that he was fine if I wanted to bring Caleb, but I think after his stunt last night, he hasn't earned a ski trip."

"Agreed. Tie him up in his room, and I'll push in trays of food."

I laugh and nudge my brother with my elbow. "That's frowned upon. I'll have to ask Quinn to stay with him."

"So soon after last night?" Rome frowns. "She might

not be up for it."

"Hey." I turn at the sound of Drew's voice and grin when I see him walking toward us. We came down to the practice field behind the headquarters building to look in on practice. "I was just coming up to see you. Hey, Rome."

"Drew."

The two men shake hands, and Drew turns back to me.

"I just spoke with Stella, the cousin who's actually putting the ski weekend together, and we'll be in Bitterroot Valley for four days. We have the plane lined up, and I'll make sure we have our own rental. My parents have offered to keep Caleb, if that's cool with you. I figured Quinn wouldn't be up for it, and he's grounded, but if you want him to go, that's cool, too."

I can't help but laugh. "Wow, we think a lot alike. Actually, I think he'll be better off with your parents, too. You're right, he's grounded."

"Do you want to use the jet?" Rome asks. "That might just be easier with a larger group."

"We have my uncle Luke's jet," Drew replies absently. "But thanks for the offer."

"Luke?" Rome asks.

"Williams," I reply. "The movie producer."

"That's pretty cool."

"He's the best. Anyway," Drew continues, obviously in a hurry. "I have to get back to practice. Just wanted to keep you up to date. I'll see you later."

He winks at me, nods at my brother, and then he's off, jogging back out to the practice field.

"You have a boyfriend," Rome says.

"Looks like." I grin and do a little shimmy in my pencil skirt and heels. "And he's a *hot* boyfriend."

Rome rolls his eyes, and we step over to the sidelines to watch the scrimmage.

The guys are on the field, some in white jerseys, others in blue.

Ike Harrison calls the snap, pulls back, and throws a perfect spiral down the field for a touchdown.

"Ike's fucking great," Rome says. "He's smart as hell, too. He runs plays all week on paper, calling them out aloud. He never stops working."

"It's a different language each week," I remind him. "For each game. He has to stay on top of it. His poor wife likely never sees him during the season."

"He started taking every Tuesday off," Rome replies. "At first, the coaching staff was against it, but he insisted. He needs twenty-four hours a week to rest, and it hasn't affected his performance at all."

"If anything, it's made him stronger," I agree with a nod. Another play is set up, and when Ike gets the ball, he's taken out by a lineman and hits his head *hard* on the ground. Just then, Drew yells something out onto the field and then jogs out to talk to a defensive lineman. "Oh, he's *mad.*"

"You don't fucking hit like that," Drew yells, getting

in the bigger man's face. "Not in practice, and not on the field."

"It was instinct," the player replies, shaking his head. "That hit was hammered into me for years."

"And now I'm hammering it out of you. No one leaves this field with a concussion if we can help it, got that?"

"Sorry, Coach," the player says and jogs off to join his team.

"Fucking idiot," Drew mutters while walking back to the sideline.

"He didn't like that," I murmur.

"No wonder," Rome says. "That exact hit is the reason Drew isn't a quarterback himself."

I turn to my brother, surprised. "What?"

"Have him tell you about it sometime."

"Trust me, I will."

"I HAVE to move my cousin into the compound this evening," Drew says as he walks into my office. "Wanna come? You don't have to actually lift anything if you don't want to, but I thought you'd get a kick out of seeing the place. We can pick up Caleb on the way."

I raise an eyebrow as I smile at the man I suddenly can't stop thinking about. "Why don't we just hire movers?"

"There's no adventure in that," he returns. "And it's

"Bite your tongue," Haley advises. "Your parents would kill you."

"I'm, like, in my mid-twenties. There's not much they can do. Promise me, if I do stay, you'll send me my stuff."

"I don't want Uncle Will to kill me," Haley says. "So, I can't promise to conspire with you on this."

"You're Will's daughter?" I ask, seeing the resemblance. "Yeah, good call, Haley."

We're all laughing as the guys rejoin us.

"All of Chelsea's things are in the dining room slash bedroom," Liam, who I remember because he flirted shamelessly, says. "The rest is up to Chelsea."

"It's a disaster in there," Caleb says. "It's way worse than my room."

"Your room was clean this morning."

He grins up at me. "You were gone all day."

"I like this kid," Liam says and ruffles Caleb's hair. "Y'all can stick around."

"Maybe I could go to Montana," Caleb says hopefully.

"Not a chance, kiddo. You're in the slammer."

"If I'd known about the trip, I probably wouldn't have done what I did last night," he says thoughtfully. "Maybe."

"Yep. Totally my kind of kid," Liam says with a grin.

a rite of passage to have to move your own shit into your first place. My cousin, Chelsea, is moving out of her parents' place and into the compound since I freed up some space."

He frowns now.

"What's wrong?"

"Well, now that I think about it, they already filled the space I was in with a 'Zen shed'. So, where is Chelsea bunking?"

"I would have no idea," I remind him. "But sure, we'll come with you."

"Cool. Are you ready now?"

I glance at my computer screen and the dozen or so emails that I should return, and then turn it off.

"Sure, let's go. I'll text Quinn and give her a heads-up."

I grab my computer bag, handbag, and jacket, and when I reach Drew, he doesn't open the door for me. Instead, he frames my face and kisses me, long and slow.

Of course, my hands are full so I can't lean in and wrap my arms around him, but the kiss is delicious and just what I needed.

"I've been thinking about doing that all damn day," he murmurs against my lips before pulling away and opening the door.

"You helping move Chelsea into the compound tonight?" Drew asks Lucy.

"Yeah, as soon as I'm done here for the day."

"You're done," I inform her. "Go, and we'll see you later."

"You're coming, too?" Lucy smiles and shuts down her computer. "Fun. I'll take you up on skipping out. I've been asked to buy some things on my way home."

We ride down the elevator together and part ways with Lucy in the parking garage.

Drew and I rode to work together this morning, so I climb into his car, fasten my seat belt, and turn my head to watch him navigate his way back to my place.

I want to ask him so many questions about his own football career, but I want to do it when I know we won't be interrupted by anything, and we can have a long conversation.

For now, I enjoy the quiet of the car and take some deep breaths to let go of the stressful afternoon.

"You okay?" Drew asks, reaching for my hand.

"Yeah. Busy afternoon. I'm still dealing with the aftermath of that horrible woman, Florence. She left such a mess, Drew. It's embarrassing."

"What are you cleaning up now?"

"She made a lot of promises to people. Season tickets, free tickets, facility rentals. All things that she couldn't actually guarantee but made it sound like she *could.* Now, those people are trying to cash in on those promises, and not only do we not have a record of anything, but we don't have any season tickets to give, certainly not in the middle of the season."

"She was a *mess.*"

"That's no joke." I sigh and squeeze Drew's hand. "I'll pick it back up tomorrow."

"Tomorrow is Saturday."

"So?"

"You don't usually go into the office on Saturday."

"I work from home," I remind him. "Usually while Caleb's sleeping in or playing video games in the morning. Or, if he has soccer, while he's playing. I'm an excellent multitasker."

Drew grins at me and pulls into my driveway. When I walk inside, Caleb comes running over to give me a hug and says hi to Drew as if last night never even happened.

"I just need to change," I announce as Quinn walks down the steps with her overnight bag. "Thanks for hanging out today, Quinn. Was everything okay?"

"It was just a normal day around here," Quinn confirms. "But now I have to get home because I have a date tonight."

"That sounds fun." I grin at the younger woman. "Have a great time. Be safe."

"Will do." Quinn waves, and then she's off, clearly excited about whomever she's seeing this evening.

"I'll be right down," I tell the guys and head upstairs. I need to get out of these heels. I love my shoes, but sometimes a girl just needs a pair of sneakers. Once I've changed into jeans and a team T-shirt, with some sneakers, and pulled my hair back with a headband, I walk downstairs and hear Caleb say, "I'm gonna buy a Ferrari."

"Are you going to save up your allowance?" I ask my son as I switch out my Dior handbag for a smaller crossbody bag that will be more suitable for helping someone move.

"I'm going to buy it when I'm grown up and making my own money," Caleb clarifies.

"Ah, I see. Sounds like a solid plan. Are you ready to go meet some of Drew's cousins?"

"Heck yeah. And I can move boxes. I'm strong enough."

"Well, then let's go."

COMPOUND IS a suitable word for it. I don't know what I was expecting the homes to look like, but I wasn't expecting the modern, lovely homes with manicured lawns and a gorgeous pool between them. There's also a cornhole setup, since the weather's been cooperating lately.

"This is nice," I say to Drew's cousin, Haley. There are so many people bustling about, and I've been introduced, but names are already slipping away from me. Haley, however, has stuck with me. "Do you love living here?"

"*Love* it," she confirms. "Come on, I'll show you our Zen she shed."

"Ah, yes, Drew mentioned this."

"He mocked it," Haley returns, not sounding offended in the least. "But he's a guy; he just doesn't get it."

Haley leads me to the small guesthouse tucked into the backyard and opens the door for me. Inside is a wonderful space, so calm and lovely.

"It's a library," I murmur, taking in the bookshelves, "a yoga studio, and a meditation space?"

"Pretty much. We packed quite the punch in here." Haley props her hands on her narrow hips and smiles as she looks around the room. "My mom used to have a photography studio in here back in the day."

"So, your mom is Natalie?"

"Yeah. She used to be a boudoir photographer, and she had a bed in here, lots of costumes, all kinds of stuff."

"Does she still do that?"

"Not officially, but she still has all her equipment. In fact, my dad bought her a fancy new camera for Christmas last year." Haley looks at me with a raised eyebrow. "Are you thinking of a sexy gift for Drew?"

"Maybe. Christmas is coming up, after all."

"I think that's pretty damn sweet. She'd probably love to do it for you. I'll give you her number."

"Thank you. I'll take you up on that. I hope Caleb isn't driving everyone nuts inside."

"He's a cute kid," Haley replies as we step out of the

she shed and walk toward the house. "He was all gung ho to help."

"I wish he was that eager to help at home." I grin and follow Haley into the kitchen through the back door. Caleb is sitting at the island, eating chips and salsa with three women. He glances my way with a grin.

"Hey, Mom. I'm having a snack with the ladies."

"I see that."

Lucy laughs as she refills the bowl of chips. "London, have you met Abby and Erin?"

"I think so. I have to admit, I'm *very* good with faces and names, but you all are giving even *me* a run for my money here when it comes to remembering who's who."

"We should walk around with a spreadsheet," Erin replies with a laugh. "There are a lot of us. But, with time, you'll learn. Don't worry. Oh, here comes Liv and Vaughn."

I turn to the door and see a gorgeous brunette and the man who's starred in all of my sexual fantasies for the past decade.

"Vaughn *Barrymore?*" I ask, in shock.

The man in question shoots me a sinful smile and walks over to shake my hand. "Guilty. And you are?"

"Shocked." When everyone laughs, I join them and shake my head. "Excuse me, that was rude. I'm London Ambrose, and this is my son, Caleb."

"Ah, the famous London and Caleb," Vaughn says as

he reaches out to shake my son's hand. "We've all heard a lot about you."

"It's so nice to meet you," Liv adds. "I hear you're joining us in Montana?"

I cringe and look down at my son, whose eyes have just grown wide in excitement. I haven't had the chance to talk to him about that yet.

"We're going to *Montana*?"

"Oops," Liv says. "Sorry."

"We're going to talk about this later, buddy, okay?"

"I need to buy skis," he says, already planning the trip of a lifetime. "And I need a new coat. Mine isn't warm enough."

"Caleb." My voice is firm, making my kid frown, so I sigh and move over next to him and brush my hand over his hair. "Buddy, you can't go on this one. Your behavior last night was *horrible*. You haven't earned a ski trip, and you're grounded."

"But *you* get to go?" he demands.

"Yeah. I get to go because I'm the mom, and I'm not grounded. But you're going to stay with Caleb's mom and dad."

"Jealous," Lucy announces. "Aunt Brynna and Uncle Caleb are the *best*. I loved staying at their house the most when I was your age."

"Why?" Caleb asks, and from the look on his face, I'd say he doesn't quite believe her.

"First of all," Abby cuts in, "Brynna makes the best chicken wings *ever*. She always makes a spread for us."

"And Uncle Caleb is so chill. He loves to hang with us and play games or watch movies. Sometimes, he'd take us out to the movies." Lucy nods thoughtfully. "If I had to stay back, that's where I'd want to stay, hands down."

"You all can say that because you get to go to Montana," Caleb sulks.

"Next time," I say to my son and kiss his head. "Maybe for spring break, we can go to Montana. There might not be skiing, but I'm sure there will be plenty of other things to do."

"Okay," Caleb says. "I'm gonna go find the guys and see if they need help lifting something."

He flexes his little muscles and then hurries off, making us laugh.

"Maybe I should go with him." Vaughn flexes his own muscles, and this time, my stomach does the cha-cha. "Just in case they need my muscles."

He follows Caleb, and I can't help but let out a sigh. "Olivia, I'm totally smitten with Drew, but I'm not above admitting that your husband is just...yum."

"He's totally yum," she agrees with a laugh. "No offense taken. Sorry about the Montana slip."

"Oh, don't worry. I just hadn't had time to mention it to him. But I'm really excited to go with you. Thanks for including me."

"I'm so excited I might not come back to Seattle," Erin announces and pops a chip into her mouth.

CHAPTER 13

DREW

"*W*hat's London up to this evening?" Liam takes a pull off his beer. He picked up our cousin, Hudson, and me and brought us over to Keaton's garage so we could hang out and watch Keaton work on a new project while we drink beer and shoot the shit.

It's not a bad way to spend an evening, and we try to do it at least once a month.

"She and Caleb are having mom and kid date night." I watch Keaton grab an Allen wrench and then bury his head in the business end of a 1960-something Corvette. "Is Sidney in Nashville recording?"

Keaton's wife is a country music superstar, and they split their time between Seattle and Nashville. I'd heard that Sid was recording this week, but Keaton shakes his head.

"She's inside, writing songs over Zoom with a collaborator. We'll head to Nashville after Montana."

"So, are you really serious about this London chick?" Hudson, sitting on a tall bench with his feet swinging back and forth, asks. "Don't get me wrong, from what I've seen, she's hot, but she's a *mom*."

"And?"

Hudson frowns. "She's a mom. It feels like a lot to take on, you know? Not bad, just a lot."

"They're a package deal, and that's the way it should be. You guys know that my mom had the girls when she met my dad. That worked out for them."

They nod, and Liam lets out a breath. I eye him warily.

"Just say what you have to say."

"Okay," Liam says, and his face is completely serious, which isn't always typical of my best friend. He's usually the jokester of the family. "Drew, it wasn't all that long ago that you mentioned to us that you didn't have any plans to have any kids. Sure, that could have just been talk, but you sounded pretty serious about it."

"At the time, I had made up my mind. I guess I couldn't see myself having kids because I hadn't met anyone worth having them with before. And I hadn't met Caleb. He's a good kid."

"Is he?" Keaton asks, wiping his hands on a rag as he snatches up a beer and walks over to join us. "We heard about the shit he pulled on you guys the other night. Not cool, man."

"He was great at the compound," Hudson puts in. "Helpful and funny. He wanted to arm wrestle me. I mean, I won, of course."

I snort at Hud and take a pull off my beer. "Of course, you did. Look, I hear your concerns, and I get it. If it was any one of you, I'd be saying the same. What he pulled was absolute bullshit and made him seem like a spoiled brat. He's being punished for it. London and Quinn were both surprised and hurt by it, which tells me this isn't normal for him."

"He's testing you," Keaton says.

"Pushing buttons," Liam agrees, nodding. "Trying to see how far he can push you."

"He's already pulled the *'you're not my dad'* line, so we got that out of the way." I push my hand through my hair. "I'm taking it one day at a time. That's all I can do. I have to try because I'm completely in love with London, and aside from what happened the other night, Caleb's been great. I need to feed that relationship a bit because I plan to stick around."

"Do the guys at work give you shit for fucking the boss?" Liam asks.

"I don't think most of them know. We don't do the PDA thing at work, and we haven't exactly announced the relationship. As time goes on, yeah, they'll flip me some shit. Or just ask a lot of questions. I don't mind."

"Wow, you're in love." Liam grins at me. "Good for you. If the kid gets out of hand again, all of us guys will show up and intimidate him."

"I don't think he'll pull that stunt again. He's pretty mad that he's missing out on the ski trip because he was a punk."

"You might be calling us in for help when he's a teenager," Hudson reminds me, and I feel the blood drain out of my face.

"Teenager." I swallow hard. "Shit, that's not far away. Okay, enough of this talk. Are you two seeing anyone?"

"Fuck no," Hudson says, shaking his head. "I'm busy."

"We're all busy," Keaton reminds him with a smirk. "No one is too busy if it's the right girl."

"*I'm* too busy for a woman," Hudson clarifies.

"Same goes," Liam agrees. "I'm at the firehouse more than I'm home. Plus, women think they want to date a firefighter because, let's be honest, we're hot as hell, but when the reality of long hours and dangerous work sets in, they split."

I don't say it in front of the others, but Liam catches my gaze and then quickly looks away, reading my mind.

He's not interested in dating because he's not over *her*.

And I can't blame him for that. If something ever happened and I couldn't be with London, I wouldn't get over it easily, either.

"We leave on Thursday," Hudson says, reminding us. "I have to get some shit together. I don't own skis."

"You don't have to own skis," I tell him. "You can rent them."

"Nah, I should get some. It'll give me a reason to go more often around here."

"I thought you were too busy for extra shit," Liam says.

Hudson shrugs. "Skis aren't nearly as demanding as women."

"How many days are you going to be gone?"

I'm hanging out with Caleb while his mom finishes packing her things. We have to be at the airport in two hours, and we have to drop off Caleb at my parents' house on the way. At least with the private jet, they won't leave without us.

"I'm pretty sure your mom already talked to you about this, but we're going to be gone for four days. We come back Sunday night. Do you want us to pick you up that night, no matter how late it is, or would it be okay if we get you Monday morning?"

Caleb looks surprised that he's being given a choice, and then he purses his lips as he thinks it over.

"I think I want you to get me Sunday night so I can hear all about it."

"Okay. I'll call you that night to make sure you haven't changed your mind."

He nods thoughtfully.

"Caleb, I need to tell you, it's *so* important that you don't try to pull something on my parents like you did on Quinn. On *anyone*, actually. I'm trusting you to be respectful and to remember that you're a guest in their home. Your mom and I can't just hop in the car and get back super-fast if something were to happen like it did the other night. Of course, if there's a true emergency, we'll move heaven and earth to get to you, but you can't cry wolf again."

"Cry wolf?"

"Haven't you heard the story of the boy who cried wolf?"

He shakes his head, his eyes wide and on mine, as I relay the story to him. "So, in the end, he lost his sheep and his own life because he'd lied so much in the past."

"So, if I do it again, and if I lie and you come home, you won't trust that if something bad really *did* happen, that it was real and I could be in danger."

"Exactly, kiddo. That's exactly my point. So, we need to be able to trust that it won't happen again. It's really important."

"I won't." He shakes his head slowly, finally understanding the gravity of the situation. "I won't do it again. Honest. Even though I can't go, I really do hope you have fun and like it a lot so you want to go back and take me with you."

"That's a good attitude. We'll call it a scouting mission."

"Yeah." He sighs, rubbing his nose. "I guess it's okay that you're with my mom."

"I'm glad you think so. Is it okay that I'm with you, too?"

That makes his lips tip up in a grin. "Yeah. You're pretty okay."

"I think you're pretty okay, too." I kiss the top of his head just as London hurries down the stairs and into the kitchen.

"Okay, we're both packed, and I have your PlayStation *and* the Nintendo packed up, as well. Snacks. I'll pack you some snacks."

"Trust me," I interrupt and snag her arm as she tries to whiz past me. "They have lots of snacks, and there's a grocery store down the street in case Caleb wants *different* snacks. I'm sure you've already packed everything but the kitchen sink. We're good to go."

"Yeah, we're good to go," Caleb echoes and hops off his stool. "Let's do this!"

London grins at me. "He wasn't this excited a few hours ago."

"We came to an understanding."

She nods and boosts herself up onto her toes to kiss me lightly. "Uh-huh, an understanding. And what do we understand?"

"That we're coming back for him, and he's not being left out." I shrug into my jacket and pick up both suitcases. "Will you grab the game bag?"

"Yeah." Her eyes look all soft and dewy as she grabs

the bag. "Have I mentioned that you're handy to have around?"

"Nope, and it was starting to hurt my feelings."

"I CAN'T WAIT to go skiing," Stella announces when we're just a few minutes from landing in Montana. She's bouncing in her seat, watching the mountains pass us by.

London's hand is in mine. She gets along so well with my cousins, and that's a big relief. These people are my circle, and if the woman I love didn't fit in, things just wouldn't work out.

But she does. She and Stella have been comparing luggage and shoes since we got on the plane. Olivia joined in, and the three of them have decided to take a trip to New York to visit the boutique that London owns.

This plane is big, and all the cousins are spread out in groups, chatting, laughing, and being silly. Even the youngest two, Finn and Emma, came along since they're officially adults now.

Add in the spouses, and it's a full plane, and I know it's going to be a damn good time.

"Have you ever been skiing, London?" Vaughn asks as we begin our descent.

"Several times," she replies with a nod. "I'm no master at it, but I can take on the bunny hill without killing myself. Probably. You?"

"Yes." He grins at her and wraps his arm around his wife. "The faster the run, the better. But Liv might be on the bunny hill with you."

"I don't want to break my arm," she reminds him. "I have to use this arm to make your costumes, remember? Also, isn't there a clause in your contract that you can't participate in any life-threatening activities?"

"Probably," he says with a shrug.

The first thing we do once we land is climb into the four vans waiting for us and then set off to get settled into the resort.

"All of these condos are privately owned," Stella informs us, "but they're in what they call the *rental pool.*"

"It's seriously beautiful up here," Lucy says, her eyes wide as she gazes around at the snow-covered trees. "Erin, isn't it amazing?"

But Erin isn't speaking. She's just watching, her pretty face stone-cold sober as she takes everything in.

"Hey, you okay, kiddo?" I ask her, concerned. Erin always has something to say.

"Yeah." She swallows hard and then offers me a fake smile. "Guys, I'm going to bow out of skiing this afternoon. I want to walk around town and soak everything in."

"I'll go with you," Lucy says, jumping at the chance. "This little town is just too cute. You don't mind if I tag along, do you?"

"No, let's do it," Erin says.

We're dropped off at the resort and then break off to find our condos. Mine and London's is on the third floor, in the corner. I key in the code to the door, and we walk inside. London immediately takes off for the floor-to-ceiling windows that give us an incredible view of the mountains.

"Holy shit," she murmurs as she wraps her arms around herself, looking out at a literal winter wonderland. The evergreen trees are heavy with fresh, white snow, and the mountains, including the ski resort we're currently standing on, are all just... "Drew, this is *spectacular.*"

"This unit is for sale," I say casually and wrap my arms around her from behind, kiss her neck, and breathe her in. "But it's a bit more of a commute from Seattle."

"Less than an hour," she murmurs. "By plane."

"True."

I kiss her neck again and feel her melt against me. Every damn time I pull her against me, it's as if she was made just for me. She fits perfectly in every way.

"I'm a little worried about Caleb," she admits and turns in my arms to wrap herself around me in a fierce hug. "And maybe feeling guilty."

"I'm no expert in these things, but that's probably normal." I tip her chin up so I can look down into her eyes. "Let's call him."

"Really?"

"Sure." I pull my phone out of my back pocket and dial my mom's number. She answers on the third ring. "Hey, Mom. We made it safe and sound. Everyone's getting settled into their condos."

"Oh, that's great! Is London with you right now?"

"I'm here," London replies, immediately worried. "What's wrong?"

"Nothing at all, honey. I'm just wondering if Caleb is allergic to anything. Can I give him peanut butter?"

My girl's shoulders fall in relief. "No, he's not allergic to anything that I'm aware of. He loves peanut butter and jelly."

"Perfect, thanks."

"Is Caleb there? Can I talk to him?"

"Sure, of course. He's out back with *Old* Caleb"—she smirks at that—"helping to cut some wood for a fire pit. We're going to make s'mores later."

"Oh, don't interrupt them. I just wanted to make sure he's being good and that everything is okay."

"London, I want you to listen to me very carefully, okay?"

"I'm listening."

I lean in to kiss her forehead. If my mom doesn't stop her jabbering in about two-point-seven seconds, I might toss the phone out the window.

"Your son is excited to be here with us. We have plenty of activities planned for him, and he's happy and healthy. Don't do the mom guilt thing, okay? I know it's instinctual. I can't even count the number of times I felt so guilty for leaving my kids behind, but he's great. There's been no attitude at all out of him, and I have your number if there are any problems. Now, go have fun."

"Yes, ma'am," London replies with a grin. "Thanks for that. I needed it. I'll call before bedtime each day, but otherwise, I'll restrain myself."

"We're here. Call anytime. Have fun, you two."

"Thanks, Mom. Love you."

I end the call, toss my phone onto the nearby couch, and then turn back to London. "See? Everything at home is just fine."

"I feel better," she admits and leans into me once more. "Now, I feel like I can relax. Also? Your mom is the best. I wish I had a mom that gave good advice like that."

"Do you know what I *don't* want to talk about?"

"What?"

"My mom."

She laughs and reaches up to cup my face in her hand. "Okay, we don't have to talk about your mom. Let's get settled and find something to eat. I'm hungry."

"Good plan. Let's scout out this place. It has six bedrooms."

"*Six* bedrooms?" London echoes with a laugh. "That's a lot of space for just two people."

We scout out all of them, and I decide right here and now that I'll make love to her in every bed in the place. I'll tip housekeeping extra well.

It'll be damn worth it.

"These windows," she breathes when we reach the main suite upstairs. The windows match the ones in the living area, giving us a spectacular view of the mountains. "I could just sit here for hours and watch the snow. Look! It's starting to fall now."

Flakes fall lazily outside, and it makes me grin. "There's a hot tub on that balcony. We could sit out there while it snows. Naked."

Her eyes narrow on me. "As long as it's a *private* balcony."

I walk to her slowly. "I don't give a shit who sees, but yes, it's private."

"I give a shit," she responds. "I don't need my tits on the front of a tabloid."

"Right." I shake my head and frown. "Why do I sometimes forget that you're *you*? When we're together, you're London, the woman I can't get enough of, and it sometimes slips my mind that you're London *Ambrose*. One of the most recognizable people in the world."

"Because when I'm with you, I *am* just me, Drew. I don't have to try. I don't have to be *on*. It's actually really refreshing and one of the things that I love about being with you."

She lifts an eyebrow and tugs my shirt out of my jeans, pushing her hand under it and over my skin while humming in her throat.

"I love your warm skin," she murmurs and tickles

my stomach with her fingertips. "Your abs are *hot*, Drew."

"I'm glad you approve." Unable to hold back any longer, I guide her backward until she's pressed against the wall, and I squat before her, tuck my finger in the waistband of her leggings, and pull them down, over her hips and legs. She braces herself on my shoulders as I tug them off her feet and toss them aside.

As I stand, I pull her sweater up and over her head, discarding it with her leggings. With the flick of my fingers, her bra is gone, and my mouth is fastened to her nipple as my hand journeys down her torso and between her legs, where I find her already slick and ready for me.

"Get it off," she says, suddenly in a rush, tugging at my own clothes. "Take them all off, *now*."

Happy to oblige, I strip out of my jeans and shirt and my underwear and socks, and then I boost her up against the wall, and she greedily wraps her arms and legs around me as I push inside of her heat and begin to pound her. Her fingers dive into my hair and fist there, tugging almost painfully as I ram myself into her, over and over again, watching her eyes, so bright with lust, go glassy as her orgasm makes its way through her. She contracts around me, massaging me in the most delicious way until I have no choice but to follow her over.

We're slick with sweat when I lower her to the floor

and brace myself on my hands on either side of her head, breathing hard. Breathing *her* in.

"Four days," I say around my heavy breaths. "I plan to do this for four days."

"Good plan." She pats my shoulder, but her hand slides off from the sweat. "We need a shower before we're fit for mixed company."

"Good idea."

With renewed energy, I toss her over my shoulder and slap her ass as I stomp into the bathroom. She lets out a yelp and then a loud laugh.

"I'm capable of walking, you know, you big caveman."

"This way, I have you right where I want you."

CHAPTER 14

LONDON

I didn't think I was a fan of shower sex.

Boy, did Drew prove me wrong.

Twice.

"You know, the thought of having sex in the shower has always intimidated me." I press my hand to my wet, naked chest, trying to catch my breath as I lean against the tile of the enormous shower. We could easily host a party of ten in this space.

"Why?" He's leaning with his hands pressed to the wall over me, shielding me from some of the shower spray.

"I don't know. It just did."

"Was this the first time you've had sex in a shower?"

"Well, yeah."

He blinks down at me, and then a slow, satisfied grin spreads over his stupidly handsome face. "I like that. I like that a lot."

I smirk and then duck out from under him and get to work cleaning myself up.

"We have to meet some of the others in thirty minutes for lunch. If I don't get moving, we'll be late. I *hate* being late."

"We're on vacation," he replies. "I don't think it's possible to be late for anything on vacation. No one is in a hurry."

I don't bother to wash my hair, but I do wash my face, resigned to the knowledge that I'll have to make quick work putting on a new face of makeup.

When I'm all clean, I hop out of the shower and grab a towel, dry off some, and then wrap it around me as I search for my makeup bag.

And then I hang my head in my hand when I realize that I left it on my vanity back at the house.

"Shit."

"What's wrong?"

"I forgot to grab my makeup bag. Damn it."

"You don't need makeup."

"I do need moisturizer and at least some mascara. I wonder if there's a Sephora in this town. Or a drugstore, at least."

"There has to be a drugstore," he replies and pulls up his phone to check. "Yep. Less than a mile away. I can walk it."

"Not in this cold."

"I have a coat, London. Here, order what you want

on the app, and I'll go get it. It won't take me more than thirty minutes."

"Are you sure?"

"Of course."

Relieved, I put the items I need into the cart, along with a snack or two, and hand it back to Drew.

"Hold on, I'll grab my card."

"I've got this," he says, shaking his head as he kisses me on the cheek. "Be back in a few."

And then he's gone, rushing off to pull on some clothes. I hear the front door close behind him and then stare at myself in the mirror.

"What did I do to deserve him?"

The woman staring back at me looks...*happy*. Dewy skin still flushed from the warm shower and a few rounds of incredible, mind-blowing sex. Eyes bright and full of joy. And that smile? I don't remember the last time I saw a smile like that on myself that I didn't have to force.

It was long before Drew, that's for sure.

"He's good for me," I decide as I walk into the closet to get dressed. I reach for skinny jeans and another sweater, pull on some socks, and then return to the bathroom to brush my hair and teeth.

Life has never been better. My kid is happy and healthy. My businesses are all thriving.

And I'm completely head over heels in love with the sexiest man on the planet. His body is to *die* for. I don't think there's an ounce of fat on him. He's sculpted, and his ass is just so...squeezable. Maybe even biteable. Yeah, I definitely want to bite him.

I honestly can't get enough of him.

But it's more than the physical. Sure, he looks like he was sculpted out of marble, but he's just so damn nice. But not too nice.

"Maybe nice isn't the right word," I mumble as I finish unpacking my suitcase and fold my sweaters, setting them on the shelf in the closet. "He's *kind*. Yes, that's it, he's kind."

I nod, happy with that description.

I absolutely *love* how bossy he is in the bedroom. He's happy to simply take over, putting me where he wants me and telling me what he needs from me. I don't have to be in charge, and for someone who has to be in control of literally everything in her universe, having Drew simply take the reins is a really great break from reality.

I hear the door open, and Drew hurries into the bedroom, covered in snow and panting from the exertion of walking so fast.

"That was more like twenty minutes," I inform him as he passes me the bag. He shakes his head, sending snow tumbling onto the floor around him, making me laugh.

"I hurried." He kisses me, and his nose is cold. "My girl doesn't like to be late."

"Thank you. Oh, you got me peanut butter cups. You're the best."

"You forgot to add them to your list. I know they're your favorite."

I blink at him and feel tears threaten.

"What did I do wrong?"

"Nothing." I shake my head and hug him close, not minding in the least that he's wet and cold. "You're so thoughtful."

"And here I thought you were still emotional from all the crazy-good sex."

I chuckle and look up at him, moved by the gentle way he smiles down at me.

"I love you, Drew."

He doesn't lose that smile. It doesn't slip one bit. He brushes my hair off my cheek and leans down to cover my mouth with his.

"I love you, too," he says. "And I plan to bring you chocolate more often, if this is the reaction I get."

I laugh and pull back, rifle through the plastic bag until I find the moisturizer and mascara, and then hurry into the bathroom to finish getting ready.

"Is everyone coming to lunch?" I call out to him.

"No, some people were in a hurry to get onto the ski hill," he replies. I can hear him changing his clothes. "We're going with my sisters, their guys, and Ike and Sophie."

"Cool." With one last brush of the mascara wand, I return to the bedroom and catch Drew tugging on a dry shirt.

Those abs get me every single time.

"I'm ready."

"Me, too." He looks up at me, and his eyes turn hot.

"We don't have time for another roll on the bed," I inform him, reading his expression perfectly.

"Let's go get this over with so I can get you back here," he replies.

~

"I LIKE HER," Josie decides, watching me from across the table as she eats a chicken wing. "She can stay. In fact, I might like you more than I like him."

"Hey," Drew says with a frown. "You're my *sister*."

"Yeah, well, you're kind of annoying most of the time," Maddie, the other twin, reminds him. "I hope we get to meet Caleb soon. Mom and Dad said he's the cutest ever."

"He's pretty great," I agree with a big smile. "We'll have you all over for dinner soon. I'm also planning on hosting a holiday party, and I hope everyone will come."

"The *whole* family?" Brax asks, blinking in surprise. "That's a *lot* of people."

"It's a big house," I reply with a smile. "We can make it work. Now, how did you guys all meet? You, too, Ike and Sophie. I want to know everything."

"Brax and I have been on and off again since high school," Josie says, smiling at her husband. "We were off again, and then I heard him telling lies on the radio, and he landed in my ER."

"She was pining for me," Brax replies, grinning at his wife.

"In your dreams." Josie pats Brax's cheek, making him laugh.

"That's sweet," I say with a sigh and turn to Maddie and Dylan. "What about you two?"

"Airplane," Dylan says. "We were both headed to Iceland for Christmas. She's a workaholic, and I told her to just enjoy being in first class. And I might have taken her to the restroom to show her how."

"*Maddie*," Sophie breathes. "You didn't tell us that you joined the mile-high club."

"Dude," Drew says, glaring at Dylan. "That's my *sister*."

"You don't even want to know what we've done since then," Dylan responds with a wink.

"He's bossy," Maddie adds but smiles at her husband with adoration. "I ended up spending more time with Dylan than the rest of the family on that trip. I thought it was just vacation sex."

"Turns out," Dylan adds, "it was the rest-of-our-lives sex."

"That should go on a greeting card," Sophie decides with a laugh. "Okay, our turn. Ike ran into me at a park."

I turn to Ike in surprise. "You hit on her in a park?"

"No, I literally crashed into her. We were both

jogging, and I didn't see her. Laid her out flat." He looks very proud of himself.

"My ass still hurts from that," Sophie mutters with a wince. "Then, I saw him later that day at my uncle Will's place. I'm happy to report that he's never assaulted me since."

I can't help but laugh at that. "Good to hear. Ike's a big guy. He could do some damage."

"Don't I know it," Sophie replies. "He's honestly the best. I'm really lucky that he crashed into me."

"Aww, babe. That's the sweetest thing you've ever said about me." Ike kisses her hard on the mouth, then turns to Drew and me. "We know how you two met."

"Office romances are always so romantic," Maddie says, reaching for another chicken wing. "Do you sneak off to have sex in your office every chance you get?"

I press my lips together but can't contain the laughter. "No, not yet."

"Oh, honey," Sophie reaches out and covers my hand with her own. "Then you're doing it wrong."

"I don't think that I want to know what's going on in my boss's office," Ike says thoughtfully.

"Yes, exactly," I agree, pointing at Ike. "That horrible woman who owned the team before us disrespected that office for years. She sexually harassed employees—"

My eyes grow wide when I realize I just said that out loud, and I clap my hand over my mouth.

"You can't repeat that," I insist immediately, waving

my hands in front of my face. "That's privileged information, and it can't go any further. Shit, I can't believe I just said that."

I rub my fingers into my forehead in agitation and feel someone reach out and touch my arm.

"We're in the cone of silence," Sophie hurries to assure me. "Honest, our family is excellent at keeping secrets. You don't have to worry."

I sigh in relief and then take a long drink of water, not proud of the way my hand shakes around the glass.

"Her behavior, her ethics, and just everything about her, really, was awful." I grin at Drew and take his hand, linking our fingers for support. "So, as much as I'd love to lock the door and have as much fun with Drew as possible, I hesitate to do it."

"You're not her," Maddie reminds me emphatically. "You're not that horrible woman."

"And everyone knows it," Ike adds, leaning toward me. "You already have the respect of the team and the staff, London. No one compares you to that bitch. We're glad that you and Rome bought the team."

"That means a lot to me. Thank you, Ike." I clear my throat, and Drew releases my hand to rub my back in circles over my shoulder blades. "I have a thing about being professional. I've worked hard to get where I am in a lot of business arenas, and I don't want to blemish my reputation, I guess you could say. *Not* that being with Drew in any way tarnishes my image. That's not what I mean at all."

I turn to look at him and see so much love there that it takes my breath away.

"I honestly don't care who in the world knows that you and I are together. I just don't think it's appropriate to have sex while at work. I fired my last assistant for doing exactly that. I don't want to come off as a hypocrite."

"Not that you have to explain yourself," Sophie says with a wink. "But I can understand that."

"Still," Maddie insists. "Stolen looks, touches, glances while you pass each other in the hallways. That's kind of hot."

"You know," Dylan says, eyeing his wife, "I'm beginning to wonder if I need to worry about who *you're* flirting with at work."

Maddie rolls her eyes. "Who has time to flirt? Besides, I'm perfectly taken, and happy to keep it that way."

"Right answer," Dylan says and kisses her lips quickly. "Okay, friends, I'm ready to hit the slopes. Maddie?"

"I might die, but I'm ready to go."

I'm shocked when Josie and Brax insist on paying the bill, and then we make our way out of the restaurant.

"Where do we rent skis?" Josie asks.

"You're not renting skis at all," Brax informs his wife. "You have precious cargo, babe."

"I can totally ski," Josie objects. "I asked my doctor and everything."

"I don't give a shit if you asked the King of England, it's a no for me."

Josie narrows her eyes on her husband, but Maddie speaks up. "We can go to the spa. Drink hot chocolate by the fire. Personally, I'm going to *read*. There's a ton we can do, Jose."

"Sorry, I'm out, too," Ike says. "Not because I'm pregnant. My contract says that I can't do this during the season, and I'm literally here with my boss. I have some work to do anyway."

"I'm honestly fine staying with you," Sophie offers. "I don't want you to be alone."

"Nah, go play. I have to diagram plays for next week. Then, we'll have our own party." Ike winks at Soph, then hurries off toward his condo.

"You heard the man," Drew says. "Let's go play."

"I MIGHT BE PARALYZED by the morning," I announce as I wobble my way back into the condo. We spent all afternoon on the slopes, and I swear I fell more than I was on my feet. "I think I've lost all feeling in six of my toes."

"I hope that's six toes on two different feet and not six all on one foot."

I snort and kick my way out of my snow boots, then

pad into the living room, turn on the gas fireplace, and sit in front of it, hoping to thaw out.

"I didn't realize that you're so good at skiing."

"I'm athletic," he says with a shrug. "It's no big deal."

This is the perfect opportunity to ask him questions.

"There are some things I want to know."

Drew raises an eyebrow as he pours two glasses of red wine, passes one to me, and sits across from me on an ottoman, watching me carefully. "Ask me anything. I'm an open book."

I sip the wine and sigh happily, finally feeling warm from the inside out.

"Tell me why you're no longer a quarterback."

A brief frown pulls his eyebrows together as he looks down into his glass, gathering his thoughts. Just when I'm beginning to wonder if I should have kept my big mouth shut, Drew sighs and looks up at me with sad blue eyes that hit me square in the heart.

"I got hit." He takes a sip of his wine, as if it will give him the courage to continue. "Junior year of college. Fourth quarter. Concussion."

I close my eyes and nod slowly.

"It wasn't the first. No, if it had been the first, I might have been able to stretch out the career some, but it was the fifth. And it was the worst. I was dizzy for a year. I still get headaches. I was convinced that I could go back to it, but that was wishful thinking. Every doctor—and I saw many, looking for the opinion that I wanted, trust me—said the same thing. No more football. If I got hit like that again, it could kill me. Or worse."

He takes a deep breath and drinks his wine. He's looking out the dark windows, as if he's watching a movie of that time run through his mind.

I shouldn't have asked. This is obviously a painful subject, and I hate seeing that look on his impossibly handsome face.

"Drew, it's okay. You don't have to tell me any more."

"It's fine." He sets his glass aside and wipes his hands down his face. "It's okay. I don't mind talking about it."

"Liar."

His lips twitch into a small smile. "Okay, it's not my favorite subject, but I'll talk about anything at all with you, babe. I decided, after quite a long stretch of sulking, to go into coaching. And it's done well for me."

"You're healthy now?"

"I'm as good as I'm going to get, and I'm lucky. Aside from the headaches, there don't seem to be any long-term effects, and I'm checked once a year to be sure."

"But if you got another concussion, it could be catastrophic."

"That's true."

Fear shoots through me as I think about the way he hurled himself down that mountain today.

CHAPTER 15

DREW

I didn't mean to scare her. I can see by the look in those beautiful eyes that she's worried, and that's the last thing I want.

"Seriously, I'm fine."

"Okay. I know you're an adult, and you're going to live your life, but, Drew, please, *please* be careful."

"I'm always careful," I reply and tug her to her feet so I can hug her close. I love it when she wraps her arms around me and rests her cheek on my chest, cuddled in. "Trust me, head injuries are my least favorite thing in the world. I won't do anything stupid."

She shivers, and I know it's not from the cold. "I just found you." Her words are soft against my chest.

"Come on. It's time for a diversion." I reach behind me and take her hands in mine, walking backward toward our bedroom. "I'm going to run you a hot bath and bring in some goodies for you to munch on while you soak and relax."

"You're not going to soak with me?"

"Nope, this is all for you." I kiss her nose and lead her to the bathroom, where just hours earlier I fucked her out of her mind in the shower. Immediately, I start the water in the tub.

"I'll be right back," London promises, turning to walk into the closet.

While she's gone, I light a candle and set it on the tray that spans the width of the soaking tub. I sprinkle oil into the water to make it fragrant and relaxing, and when I turn around, I see that London has returned.

Naked.

Seeing her like this never fails to knock me on my ass.

"You're so fucking beautiful."

Her lips curve as she steps closer to me. "I'm glad you think so. Where do you want me?"

On my cock. Riding me hard and fast.

I clear my throat. "In the water."

She steps into the tub and sinks down into the water, leans back, and sighs deeply. "Oh, this is *nice.*"

"You soak. I'll be back."

"I have no issue with that."

I can't help but pause for just a moment, taking her in before I pad out to the kitchen and load a plate with some of the peanut butter cups, cashews, grapes, and cheese. After refilling her wineglass, I return to the bathroom and see that she's pushing her hand in and out of the water, watching it run between her fingers.

"Are you bored?" I ask her with a laugh.

"No, just thinking." Her eyes widen when she sees the spread on the plate. She pops a grape into her mouth. "Wow, thanks."

"You just enjoy."

"Where are you going?"

"I was just going to give you some time alone."

Her brow creases. "I don't want to be alone. I'll be alone all the time after we get back to Seattle and we can't spend the nights together anymore. I want you to stay."

"You have a good point." There's a small bench tucked under the vanity, so I grab that, set it by the tub, and sit.

"Have some food," she offers. "I can't eat it all."

The water laps tantalizingly over her breasts and shoulders. Sitting here in the candlelight, I'm not sure if she's ever been more beautiful.

Then again, I think that every day.

"Have you heard any more from your dad?" I ask.

"Not since you told him to mind his own business." She grins over at me. "You know, I don't think anyone has ever spoken to him like that in his life. It was marvelous."

"It was necessary." And I know that once I get back home, I'll have to set up a meeting with him so I can declare my intent to marry his daughter. "I'm glad that he's backed off."

"You know, it was the weirdest thing." She sips her wine thoughtfully. "He's never taken much of an interest in my personal life in the past. Even when I was pregnant with Caleb, he didn't really care. Obviously, he didn't like Caleb's father because he didn't come from a good family, and he was poor as fuck, but he didn't try to talk me out of anything. Well, he didn't try *hard*, anyway."

I nod, listening.

"So, for him to suddenly decide to try to set me up with one of his single, rich friends is just strange. It's not like we need to align our rich family with another to carry on the family name, or something stupid like that."

"Maybe *he* was bored," I suggest.

"Could be. I don't think my dad is a very happy person. He's always flitting from one idea to the next, now that he's semi-retired. Anyway, it's been nice to have him back off."

She chews happily on a peanut butter cup and leans back in the water, closing her eyes in contentment. Now, the water slides over her nipples, just barely revealing them at the surface, and I can't resist reaching over to gently glide my fingertips over one of them.

London doesn't open her eyes, but she hums happily in her throat.

As London bows her back, I lean forward and pull a nipple into my mouth, sucking gently while my hand roams under the water, down her belly, to her core.

She pulls her knees up as she gasps, but she doesn't tell me to stop. Her hand dives into my hair and fists there, as if holding me right where I am, and I push my fingers through her folds, loving how slick she is, despite being in the bath.

"Shit, Drew," she whispers. I pull up so I can watch her flushed face. She bites her lower lip, and when I push a finger inside of her, she moans.

"You're the sexiest woman I've ever seen in my life." I lean over to kiss her cheek and down to her ear. "Your body was made for me. Look at how beautifully you respond to my touch."

She whimpers, and I push another finger inside of her while pressing my thumb to her hard clit. She gasps, arches her head back, and opens wider for me.

"That's right, give it to me."

"Holy shit," she mutters as her body begins to tighten, and then her pussy is squeezing around my fingers as she succumbs to her orgasm.

"There you go," I croon. "You're amazing, baby."

She's catching her breath, and her eyes are open now, shining with lust as she watches me.

"I told you I was going to take advantage of these four days," I remind her.

"Thank God you're good at keeping promises."

"NO WONDER ERIN hasn't skied much," London says as we stroll along what's called Central Avenue in Bitterroot Valley. "This town is just too cute."

We decided to forgo the ski hill today, and instead, we made love all morning before finally getting around to leaving the condo to explore the little resort town in search of food and to check it all out.

"And they have good pizza," I add. "That Old Town Pizza joint was legit."

"You ate an entire large all by yourself."

I kiss her temple. "You made me work up an appetite this morning."

"Sure, it was all my fault." She sticks out her lower lip in a pout. It's been fun to be out with her today. She's more carefree and a little silly.

"I'd say it was a joint effort," I reply with a laugh.

"Oh, look, cowboy hats. I want to try one on." London drags me into a hat and boot shop, and she waves at the person who welcomed us in. She reaches for a brown hat and sets it on her head. "What do you think? Do I look like a cowboy?"

"Hmm." I narrow my eyes, thinking it over. The truth is, she looks ridiculous. She makes a beeline for a mirror to check herself out.

"Nah, I'm not a cowboy. Here, you try." She removes the hat and sets it on my head, then steps back to take stock, her hands on her hips and her head cocked to the side. "Is there anything in the world that you're *not* sexy in?"

"I probably wouldn't do well in a clown costume," I reply, rubbing my chin as I think it over. "But I can't think of anything else, now that you ask."

"It's good that you're humble," she decides as I take off the hat and set it back on the shelf. "So incredibly modest."

"It's not easy," I agree and laugh when she narrows her eyes at me. "Come on. I want to find something for my parents as a thank-you for keeping Caleb."

"Oh, that's an excellent idea," London says as we step back out into the snow. "Also, off topic, but have you noticed that Bitterroot Valley looks like it belongs in a Hallmark Christmas movie?"

"I noticed," I reply with a nod. "I'm glad we came when they have all the lights up and stuff. It's cute."

"It's *gorgeous*," she insists. "How much is the condo we're in going for?"

"Fifteen million."

She doesn't bat an eye. "Seems steep, but for a little resort town like this, it doesn't surprise me."

"You're not thinking of buying it, are you?"

She looks up at me. "Why not? You said it your-self, it's a great town. The skiing is excellent, and you can ski in and out of the condo. Not to mention, I might be a little sentimental when it comes to that unit now. We've already made a lot of good memories there."

I brush my fingers under her hair and rest my hand on the back of her neck as we walk down the block.

"Those are good points."

"And Caleb would go crazy for it. I don't know... It might be high on my list."

"You can't just buy every place we visit where we've had some excellent sex, London. You'll end up owning most of North America."

"And maybe some of Europe," she adds, and then lets out a loud laugh. "Okay, I'm not *that* sentimental. I'll have to think about it. Oh, look, an art studio."

We cross the street, making a beeline for a place called Bitterroot Gallery.

"Maybe we'll find a piece for your parents in here," London says as I hold the door open for her. "Also, I have a question for you."

"Shoot." I eye a bronze sculpture of a buffalo. "Ask anything."

"Does it make you uncomfortable that I can buy a fifteen-million-dollar condo on a whim?"

She's not looking my way at all. Instead, she's focused on staring at a rack of postcards.

"No. Not at all." She looks up at me in surprise. "I make good money of my own, and while it's not on the same scale, it doesn't bother me in the least, babe. I grew up around a lot of wealth. My parents are *not* wealthy. Several of the aunts and uncles aren't, actually. But the majority are, and it's never really been an issue for anyone. We don't compete in that way. The way I was raised, we celebrate everyone's accomplishments, whether that's in business, art, or hell, building a new house. Whatever that looks like. If you want the condo and can afford it, buy the condo. We'll use it."

"I would love it if *everyone* felt comfortable using it," she admits softly.

"If you put that out into the universe, my family will take you up on it. Why do you ask?"

I step forward, cup her cheek, and kiss her forehead.

"Because a *lot* of men are insecure assholes if the woman they're with makes more money than they do."

"Yeah, that's not me. You're a badass. You work your butt off, and I'm proud of you. I'd be proud of you no matter how much money you make. You just need to know two things. First, I'm not with you because of the wealth. And second, I don't want anything from you except *you*."

"Boy, you're swoony," she says with a sigh. "And I already knew those two things. It's why I'm still with you. If I thought differently, we never would have happened."

"Great, that's settled, then. Hey, what about this painting?"

I walk over and point to a smaller piece. It's a painting of the mountains, with some horses grazing inside a white fence.

"The sky is so beautiful," London says, admiring the piece. "Yes, let's do it."

"I CAN'T BELIEVE I ran into you guys." Erin grins hugely after hugging both London and me. We've spent the day wandering through just about every shop in town, and when we were leaving the last one, we almost smacked right into Erin. "What are you doing now?"

"Actually, I think I'm hungry again," London says with a laugh. "But I'm not sure what we should grab."

"I know," Erin announces. "Are you in the mood for barbecue? Because there is the *best* place just down the street."

"I'm down for that," I agree, and the three of us set off walking. Just as she said, there's a place called Rocky Mountain Smokehouse at the end of the street, and from the delicious aromas coming from inside, I'd say it's a winner. "You'd better join us, Erin."

"Oh, I'm definitely in. I'm *starving*."

We're led to a booth by the windows, and Erin slides in across from London and me, accepts the menu, and hums happily under her breath while she peruses the options.

This is the perkiest I've seen my cousin in *years*.

"What have you been up to, Erin?" London asks as she sets her menu aside, obviously ready to order. "We haven't seen much of you lately."

"I know. I'm sorry that I haven't been hanging with the fam much, but I just *had* to soak in this town. It's adorable." She sets her own menu aside just as the waitress walks over to take our order. "I want the three-meat platter, with a half-rack of ribs, the roasted chicken, and brisket. No beans, please."

I blink at her and then laugh. "You definitely have your father's appetite. I'll actually have the same, but I want the beans."

London orders a full rack of ribs, with all the sides, and then we're left alone once more.

"We're obviously all hungry," London says with a grin. "So, what have you learned about Bitterroot Valley, Erin?"

My cousin bites her lip and looks up at me, then over at London. "I think it feels like home, to be honest."

I narrow my eyes on her, and she hurries to continue.

"Drew, I told you not long ago that I want out of Seattle. I love my family, especially my dad, but living in his shadow is *hard*. I would never say that to him, of course. It would just hurt his feelings, and I can't do that. But it doesn't make it less true. I hated college, and I don't know what I want to do for a living, but I do know that it's not in Seattle. I want a small town, where no one cares who my parents are or who my uncles are or who my cousins are married to."

"It's a lot," I agree with a nod. "Our family isn't easy. It's fun, but it's not easy."

"I can respect what you're saying, Erin," London says. "My dad is bigger than life, too, and it wasn't a

aside for you by your parents so you would never have to struggle."

"Maybe the struggle makes it more worth it." Erin shrugs a shoulder, and her eyes light up when our meal is served. "Holy shit, this is some *food*. My dad would love this place. I'll have to bring him here when he comes to visit me."

"He'll be here by next weekend, trying to haul you back home, after he finds out that you've decided to move here."

"He can try," Erin says, not looking concerned in the least. "I don't think I've ever felt more at home than I do here, and I'm not leaving on Sunday with the rest of you."

I take a deep breath and let it out slowly. "Well, if you decide that this isn't right for you, you can always come home. That's the perk of having a gigantic family who would do anything for you."

"I know." Her eyes fill with tears as she looks up at me. "I know, Drew. That's the only reason I have the guts to try in the first place."

I blow out another breath and then dig into my own meal before it goes cold. "Well, great. Your dad's gonna kill me."

She grins. "No, he won't. I mean, he probably won't."

CHAPTER 16

LONDON

"*S*idney, you *need* this!" Emma, who I've learned is the youngest of the cousins at nineteen, waves a scarf in the air as she hurries over to Sidney Sterling. I recognized Sidney right off the bat because I'm more than a little obsessed with her music.

She's the hottest thing in Nashville right now.

And, she just happens to be married to Drew's cousin, Keaton.

The number of celebrities in this family is jaw-dropping. All the girls decided that today, our last day in town, was the perfect day to spend shopping in Bitterroot Valley, while the guys wanted one more day on the slopes.

Shopping is keeping me from obsessing about Drew getting hurt.

"It'll be perfect to wear on stage while you sing

'Little Miss,'" Emma continues. "It's country, but it has an edge to it, you know?"

"I think you're right," Sid responds with a grin. "Sold. Why don't I just hire you to outfit my whole stage look? You're way better at it than me."

Emma preens under the praise. She's dressed stylishly in jeans and a white, cut-off sweater that shows her flat stomach. A long, brown jacket completes the look, along with matching boots.

She's stunning.

"You're seriously good at the fashion thing," Stella says to Emma. "You should change majors to fashion design."

"Right." Emma rolls her eyes and moves on to a rack of sweaters. "My dad is convinced that I'll be taking over the family business."

"And what is the family business?" I ask, completely in the dark.

"Wine," Olivia says with a wink. "Uncle Dominic owns Cuppa da Vita winery."

"I love their wine." I turn to Emma, impressed. "That's pretty cool."

"Sure, it's fine." Emma shrugs. "But it's not exactly my *passion*."

"Tell your dad that," Sidney suggests. "He's not a mind reader, Em. And I may not know him well, but he's not unreasonable."

"No, he's just annoying," Emma mutters. "Anyway,

let's not talk about this anymore because it's totally a bummer."

"I'm buying this scarf," Sidney says, setting off for the cashier.

"I want to go to that shop next door," Lucy announces. "The name of it is so cute. *A Pocket Full of Polly.*"

"I'll meet you over there," Sidney says with a wave, and we all head over to the other shop. Most of us have stuck together. Drew's sisters, along with Sophie and Haley, are down the street at a pet shop, and promised to catch up with us. They wanted some things for Sophie's dog.

"I'm really impressed by all the cool shops in this town," Zoey, Erin's younger sister, says. "I mean, it's a *tiny* place, but the shops are on point. The food's been good, too."

"I agree." I smile at Zoey, and I can't help but wonder if she knows that her sister isn't coming back to Seattle with us tomorrow.

It's certainly not my place to say anything.

"Oh, this is *adorable*," Olivia announces as we make our way inside the dress shop.

And she's not wrong.

The clothes are stylish, while also keeping in the western/cowboy theme. It's not cheesy at all, and I already see some things that I'd like to try on.

"Hi, everyone." A beautiful woman, so petite and

small, with flaming red hair and the prettiest blue eyes, approaches us. "I'm Polly."

"The owner," I guess, and smile when Polly nods. "This shop is fabulous, and I just stepped inside. I already love it."

"Thanks." Polly smiles widely. "I have hot apple cider and cookies over on that table. Please, feel free to help yourselves while you shop."

"Clever," I murmur, taking mental notes. It smells homey and inviting in here, and I can't resist leaving the others to shop while I approach the owner to chat business. "I just wanted to tell you that I really do love this space. How long have you owned it?"

"About four years," she replies with a smile.

"The name is brilliant."

"I worried that it was too, I don't know, corny at first, but people don't forget it. I'm so small, and when I was growing up, I was called things like Polly Pocket, or the parents of my friends would say they could just put me in their pocket. I decided to make that work to my advantage."

"Good for you. I'm a co-owner of a boutique in New York, and I know a good business model when I see one. You have a good one here."

"I can't tell you how much I appreciate that. I want to start branching out into shoes and other accessories, but I haven't found the right vendors for me."

"Oh, I can absolutely hook you up." I pull a card out

of my purse and pass it to the other woman. "Please, shoot me an email, and we'll send over some suggestions for you."

"Thanks, I'll do that." She glances down at the card and then visibly pales. "You-you're London Ambrose"

"Yes, ma'am."

"I'm sorry. I didn't recognize you."

"There's no need to be sorry." I smile at her, hoping that she doesn't want to end the conversation just because of my famous name. "Businesswomen have to look out for each other."

The smile returns to her face, and she nods twice. "You're right, we do. Are you all visiting?"

"Yes, they're all cousins, and I'm dating another of their cousins." I laugh and eye the apple cider. "So, it's been a family vacation. We're staying up at the ski resort."

"Well, welcome to Bitterroot Valley. If you guys need to try on anything or have any questions, I'll be wandering around."

"I already need to try stuff on," Lucy calls out from across the boutique. "I think we might clean you out today, Polly."

"That's not a bad problem to have," Polly replies with a laugh.

We spend two hours in the adorable store. The other girls join us, and we do end up buying at least one of everything that Polly offers. By the time we're ready to go, we decide we need a pick-me-up.

"Coffee," Erin says with a grin. "There's an awesome coffee shop just around the corner called Bitterroot Valley Coffee Co. They have the *best* lattes."

"Sold," Olivia says. "I need to refuel after that awesome shopping spree. I know my clothes, and what Polly offers is excellent quality."

"Also super cute," Stella agrees. "If I lived here, I'd shop there all the time."

I glance at Erin and see her smile happily. She really *does* love it here.

The coffee shop is quiet when we walk inside, and I'll admit, it smells divine.

"This is exactly what I needed," Lucy comments, taking in a deep breath. "Do you roast your own beans?"

"We do," the woman behind the counter replies with a smile. Her nametag reads Millie. "You can buy beans to grind at home, or we can grind them for you. We also make the little pod things. Or you can just take a cup to go."

"I want a cup to go *and* a bag of beans," Sophie decides, and several of the others nod in agreement.

We're happy to wait for our orders and peruse the small gift shop while we do. I'm admiring some locally handmade mugs when I hear Erin approach Millie and ask in a low voice, "Are you hiring, by any chance?"

Millie nods and tells Erin to apply online.

Amazingly, no one else heard the exchange. Erin glances my way and winks. I have to admit, I'm happy for her. I hope it all works out just the way she wants it to.

"I think Vaughn and I are going to order dinner in tonight," Olivia says as we begin to make our way back to the condos. "I don't mean to be antisocial, but I kind of want to relax. It's been a busy few days."

"You know, Gray and I were thinking the same thing," Stella says. "A quiet night in with some snowy sexy time sounds pretty great."

I grin, silently agreeing. I love Drew's cousins. They're smart and funny and so welcoming. I haven't felt like a practical stranger even once the entire time we've been here.

But I can't help but agree with them. A quiet night in does sound really good.

"London, my mom mentioned that she's going to have a photo session with you," Olivia says as she sips her coffee.

"Yes, and I'm *so* excited. She had all kinds of fun ideas when we were on the phone, and I can't wait to see what she has for me when I get there. I don't always love having my photo taken, but I think it'll be a fun gift for Drew."

"He'll lose his shit. Speaking of men, there are a few of our guys now," Sidney says, pointing down the block. Keaton, Drew, Liam, and Ike are talking with some people on the sidewalk. They're smiling and nodding, and Ike is signing something for a woman who's jumping up and down.

"Uh-oh, Soph," Erin says, "better go stake your claim. She's a little overzealous."

But I'm not watching Ike with the excited fan. I'm watching the way Drew is smiling at her friend, listening intently, and then laughing at her joke. She tucks her hair behind her ear flirtatiously, and Drew looks her up and down, getting an eyeful.

Blondie giggles at something he says and leans against him, pressing those tits of hers against him, and *he doesn't pull away.*

And I see red.

I can't say that I've ever felt jealous in my life, but in this moment, I want to scratch that woman's eyes out.

Of course, I've been trained better than that.

I hang back and wait for Drew to see me. It takes him a few minutes because he's too wrapped up in what the blonde is saying, but when he does, he blinks in surprise and disentangles himself from the woman, who narrows her eyes menacingly at me as he turns his back to her.

I simply raise an eyebrow and stare at her coldly until she walks away.

"Hey," Drew says and leans down to kiss me, but I turn my face, and his lips land on my cheek. He frowns down at me. "What's wrong?"

"I think I'd like to stay in tonight," I reply. I can hear the ice in my voice, and I don't care. This isn't the time or place to have a fight, in the middle of town and in front of most of his family. "Let's order dinner in."

"Okay, that's fine with me." He narrows his eyes, then takes my elbow in his hand and turns to the others. "Have a good night, guys. We'll see you tomorrow."

The cousins wave and bid us goodnight, and we set off walking to the condo.

"What the fuck is going on?" he asks again.

"I'm not going to talk about this in front of an audience," I reply tightly. I want to pull my arm out of his grasp, but that's petty. I don't like feeling unsure and insecure. It's the *worst*. But seeing another woman sidled up to my man, and he does nothing at all to push her away is ten times worse.

I'm so damn mad.

It's getting dark. The sun has already set, and the last of the light is fading. By the time we reach the condo, it's completely dark outside, and I don't bother to turn on any lights as I march into the living room and flip on the fireplace to get warm. I shed my coat and boots, tossing them aside.

"Okay," Drew says, sounding completely calm. "We're alone. Why are you mad, London?"

I turn and look at him, standing on the other side of the room, his arms crossed and looking so fucking beautiful it steals my breath away.

I'm so in love with him, and just the *thought* of him looking at someone else has my heart breaking into pieces.

"I think that maybe we're more different than I

thought." My words come out slowly, as if I have to push them over the lump in my throat.

"What are you talking about?"

"I *saw* you," I reply, unable to hold the frustration or anger back any longer. "I saw the way you were looking at that woman and smiling at her. You smile at *me* like that, and I've just learned that it isn't because I'm special in any way. Apparently, you look at anyone you want to fuck like that. And then she pressed herself up against you, all cozy like, and you did *nothing*. You didn't push her away. You didn't tell her no. You just let her do it."

"You've got to be kidding me."

"Don't do that." I point at him and round the couch, pissed off now. "I don't even *think* of anyone else besides you. You completely consume me, so imagine my surprise when I saw you with her, flirting and smiling. Imagine if the tables were turned, Drew. Or maybe it wouldn't piss you off. Maybe I've misunderstood what we're doing here, and if that's the case, fine. I have options, too, you know. I have a whole phone full of eligible bachelors' phone numbers that I can use."

His eyes narrow, and his hands fist in anger, but I raise my chin defiantly.

"What would you have had me do?" he demands. "Be an asshole to them? They recognized Ike and wanted to talk to him, so we humored them. It was *nothing*."

"It didn't look like nothing."

With the anger drained out of me and nothing but hurt remaining, I turn to look out the window, staring out into the dark.

I can see his reflection as he walks up behind me. At first, he doesn't touch me at all; he just watches me.

"It was *nothing*," he repeats, his voice calm now, and even hushed in the darkness.

"I've realized recently—maybe in that moment when I watched you with her and you didn't know I could see you—that I've never really loved any man the way that I've fallen in love with you." I'm so glad he's behind me and can't see my face because when I close my eyes, tears track down my cheeks. "And that means that no one can hurt me the way that you can. Even if that's a simple, careless look at another woman's tits. It was enough to stab me in the heart. But when she touched you, and you let her? I don't want to relive it."

He sighs and moves toward me. I can feel him just inches from me, but he still doesn't touch me.

"And it made me wonder," I continue after taking a breath, "if this is one-sided, because I don't think that I would ever do that to you. No, I *know* that I wouldn't. Because I would never want to hurt you like that."

His arms come around me now, around my own arms, and he hugs me tightly from behind. I want to lean back against him, but I'm too hurt to give in.

"I'm going to tell you this," he says into my ear as his hold on me tightens, "as many times as you need to hear it, because it's the God's truth, and I've never lied to you, London. There is no one in this world that I want besides you. I didn't know that I was looking at her in any kind of way. I was being polite while Ike spoke with fans; that's all it was from my side. And when she leaned in, I don't know, it was so insignificant—*she* was insignificant—that I just didn't care."

I swallow hard and lift my arms so his hands can drift down to my stomach. He pulls my sweater up and over my head so his hands can wander over my skin.

"You're all I fucking think about," he says, his voice growing rougher. He pushes against me, and I can feel his hard cock strain against me through his jeans. "*You* do this to me. No one else. I don't feel like I want to move heaven and earth for anyone but you."

I'm melting against him now, completely hypnotized by his touch, by his words, and by the fierceness in his voice. He *means* what he's saying, and I realize that I might have overreacted in the moment.

He takes my hands and props them on the glass and pulls my hips back. He unfastens my jeans and wrangles them down my legs, and when I'm naked from the waist down, he urges my legs apart. His hands travel up the inside of my thighs, and then he's touching me, and I cry out, unable to help myself.

I move to turn around, but he stands and quickly replaces my hands on the glass, tipping my face toward him.

"I'm going to show you," he murmurs against my lips. "Unless you don't want me to touch you. If that's the case, just say so."

"I always want you to touch me."

His lips twitch into a small smile as he kisses me, and then he bites my lower lip before he moves behind me once more. I hear him shed his own clothes, still seeing his dark reflection in the glass. We're completely exposed here. If it weren't dark, someone on the mountain might see us.

His hands are *everywhere.* Moving over my breasts, down my thighs, and then back up between my legs, where he worries his fingertips over my clit.

"You," he says, "are *mine.* Every bit of you, London Ambrose. This"—his fingers slide inside of me—"is mine."

His fingers move quickly, working me up into a frenzy before he pulls them out, and with his eyes on mine in the glass, he cups my chin in one hand and offers the fingers of the other to my lips. I don't hesitate to open my mouth, and I can taste myself on him.

"Mine," he whispers again, and slides easily inside of me, making me moan around his fingers. "But that works both ways, baby. I'm *yours.*"

He pulls out and then pushes in again, then stops, seated fully.

"I belong to you in ways that I can't even fucking describe. Do you know what I was thinking when I looked at her?"

I narrow my eyes, and he has the audacity to *laugh.*

"I was thinking about how I wanted to do exactly this to you tonight. I was wondering when we could get away from them so I could see *you* because I hadn't been near you in hours, and I was craving you."

I sigh at his words, and he begins to move. His hands come down to my hips, and I lean against the glass as he thrusts harder and harder, as though he's hammering the point into me how completely and fully I belong to him.

And vice versa.

"You." He bites my shoulder. "Are." He kisses right between my shoulder blades. "Mine."

I can't suppress the orgasm any more than I can stop the snow from falling outside. It washes over me, completely overwhelming me, and I feel Drew follow me over the edge into his own orgasm.

Finally, he turns me in his arms and kisses the hell out of me before lifting me and sitting on the couch, cradling me in his strong arms.

"You're the only thing that matters," he assures me, brushing my hair off my cheek. "I promise you that."

"Same." I brace his face between my hands, my wounded heart healing and feeling so much love for him it staggers me. "It's overwhelming and big, and I've never been jealous a day in my life, Drew."

"I guess there's a first time for everything." He kisses my forehead. "But you *never* have to worry or wonder what I'm feeling. I love you. It's as simple and as terrifying as that."

I can't help but chuckle at that because that's exactly how it feels.

Completely terrifying.

～

"WHAT DO YOU *MEAN*, you're not leaving with us?" Stella, her hands on her hips, stares at Erin in shock and dismay. "Of course, you're coming home. You don't live here."

"I do now," Erin replies and smiles bravely. "I'm *so* happy here, you guys. I love it, and I think that this is where I'm supposed to put down roots and make my home. I don't enjoy the city. I don't have stuff figured out there like all of you do."

Hudson shakes his head and then hurries over and scoops Erin into his arms, hugging her tightly.

"What are we supposed to do without you?" he asks, obviously perilously close to tears. "You're my best friend, E. You can't just leave me."

"Dude," she says as she pulls back and pats Hudson's cheek. "I'm just in Montana, not Egypt or something. We'll have visits. I have a phone. It's going to be okay."

"Your dad is going to kill us all," Vaughn says thoughtfully. "You'll be responsible for a mass homicide."

"He won't do that," Erin says with a laugh and then

turns to her sister. Zoey's not crying or showing any kind of emotion at all. "Love you."

"Right." Zoey turns on her heel and walks up the stairs, into the plane, and Erin winces.

"She's hurt," Olivia says, walking over to hug Erin. "So I'll hug you twice, once for her. You make sure you call us all the time, and if you ever need *anything* at all, we're only a phone call away. Seriously, *anything*."

"I know. Thank you."

Everyone takes turns hugging Erin, murmuring words of encouragement and wisdom, before we all climb onto the plane to head home. Erin's eyes shine with unshed tears as she watches us all through the windows. She waves and steps back, walking to the edge of the tarmac, and she waits there until the plane takes off, smiling and waving.

"What is she thinking?" Liam asks. "And how did we just *leave* her here?"

"She's an adult," Stella says with a sigh, watching out the window with worried eyes. "But man, am I going to miss her."

"We had s'mores *every night*," Caleb says, bouncing on his toes with eagerness to tell me everything that's happened while we were gone. "Old Caleb made a big fire in the backyard, and Brynna bought all the stuff, and we ate a ton of them."

"The kid can pack the food away," Drew's dad says with a grin.

"Thank you so much." I hug my son to my side as I thank Drew's parents profusely. "Are you sure you won't let me pay you?"

"Absolutely not," Brynna says, shaking her head. "It was our pleasure. Maybe we can do it again really soon."

"Next weekend!" Caleb exclaims, obviously ready to spend more time with the older couple.

"Sometime," I agree with a wink for my kid. "Have *you* thanked them?"

"More than once," Brynna confirms. "He's quite the little gentleman."

"Well, we brought you a gift," Drew says as he runs back down to the car to fetch the painting.

"You didn't have to do that," *Old* Caleb says, shaking his head. "It was fun to have a partner in crime around for a few days."

Drew returns with the painting, covered with brown paper, and Brynna unwraps it, then gasps in excitement.

"Oh, this is *beautiful.* Is it this pretty in person up there?"

"As lovely as this painting is, I'd say it's prettier in real life." I nod when Brynna looks at me in surprise. "You'll have to go sometime."

"I think you're right," *Old* Caleb says, and looks down at his wife. "Maybe for our anniversary."

"We should *all* go next time," my Caleb adds. "It's only fair."

"We'll talk about that," I reply.

"That means no," Caleb says with a sigh. "Thanks, guys. It was fun!"

And with that, he takes off for the car, making me wince.

"Clearly, we need to work on some manners."

"Not at all," Brynna assures me and pulls me in for a hug. "He's great. It's late, and he wants to get home. I can't blame him."

She pulls back and opens her arms for her son.

"London, I'd like to get together for lunch sometime so you can tell me more about your trip."

"I'd love that. I'll check my calendar and give you a call."

"Perfect." Brynna takes her husband's hand in hers. "Have a good night, you two."

"Thank you," Drew says again, and a few moments later, we're back in the car and headed toward home.

"Did you really have fun?" I ask Caleb, turning around so I can see his face. His eyelids are heavy. He'll be asleep before we hit the freeway.

"The best. Is this what it's like to have grandparents?"

I blink but do my best to keep my face neutral. "I guess so."

"It's pretty cool."

As Caleb drifts off to sleep, I turn in my seat, and Drew takes my hand, kissing it.

"You okay?" he asks.

"Yeah." I swallow, feeling sad and angry that my parents have *never* done for my son what Drew's parents were able to do in just one weekend. "Yeah, I'm fine."

CHAPTER 17

DREW

*I*t's been two days since we've been back from Montana, and I've only spent a handful of minutes with London here and there.

I miss the hell out of her.

So, with a couple-hour break from training my guys, I head up to her office, hoping to catch her at a good time so I can lock that door and kiss the fuck out of her.

I don't like that she felt uneasy or insecure about where she stands with me, even for a second. It won't ever happen again.

I'm surprised that Lucy isn't at her desk when I arrive at London's office, but London's door is open, and I can hear voices inside.

I knock on the door frame, and London smiles when she looks over at me.

"Sorry to interrupt."

"You're not. Come on in. Lucy and I were just going over a couple of things."

"You might want to keep an eye out," Lucy warns me, looking over my shoulder and toward the door behind me. "Uncle Will is on the warpath."

I wince as I shove my hands into my pockets. "I take it Erin finally called him and Aunt Meg?"

"Yep, and from what I hear, it didn't go over well."

"Great." I rock back on my heels and sigh. "What are you two ladies up to this afternoon?"

"I'm buried in work." Lucy wiggles her eyebrows and does a little shimmy. "It's fabulous. I'll get those emails sent out right away, London."

"Thanks, Lucy. Feel free to take off early today if you want. I'm leaving in about an hour to get Caleb from school."

Lucy nods and moves to walk out of the office but stops short and frowns. I turn to follow her gaze and see my uncle, looking good and pissed, stomping our way.

"Shit," Lucy whispers.

"Hi, Uncle Will."

"What in the actual *fuck*?" Will demands, propping his hands on his hips. "You left my kid in *Montana*, of all places."

"Well, I—"

"And no one bothered to call and tell me. To give me a heads-up. No, it wasn't until this morning that Erin called us to tell us that she stayed."

"Listen, we—"

"Now, she's alone in a town that none of us knows, and I don't have even one fucking contact there that she can call if she needs help. So, I'm going to need you to explain to me why in the hell you thought that was a good idea."

"Whoa." I hold my hands up in surrender. "Slow down. First of all, she's an adult."

Will's eyes narrow into slits, and if I'm not mistaken, he *growls.*

"Like it or not, she is. Secondly, this wasn't a shock to me. She'd told me a while ago that she wasn't happy in Seattle and that she wanted something smaller, something slower paced."

"Then she should have come to me and talked to me so I could help her make an informed decision."

"No," Lucy says, shaking her head. "Uncle Will, she's not a baby. She's not even a teenager. She's a grown woman, and she knows what she wants. You should have seen her face in Bitterroot Valley. She smiled *all the time.* She didn't even go skiing with us because she wanted to soak in the town. She couldn't get enough of it. By the time we left, she knew every inch of that place like the back of her hand."

"It's true," London offers, her voice gentle. "She is *so* happy there, Will."

"She won't take any money," he says, pushing his hands through his hair as he paces London's office. "I looked at real estate there. How in the *hell* is she

243

supposed to be able to afford to live there if she won't let me help her?"

"She said she has some money saved," I reply, trying to sound reasonable. "She'll get a job, and she'll work for a living like the rest of us. She's a smart woman. And she knows that if she decides that she made the wrong choice, she can always come home."

"All that money, and she won't fucking touch it," he mutters, clearly disgusted. "She's too much like her mother, that's for sure. I had the same problem with her when I first married her. Too damn stubborn to take any help."

"I'm pretty sure, according to family lore, you bullied her into letting you help her."

Will turns to me and glares.

"That's beside the fucking point."

"Right. Sorry." I nod and then sigh. "She's happy. Like, *really* happy. Let her try this, Will. There's not really much you can do about it anyway. And she'll have more respect for you if *you* respect the way she feels and support her. At least she knows that you're there if she needs you."

"Why do you sound like your aunt?" he demands and then blows out a breath. "I'm so mad at her for keeping this from me. I want to fly out there and shake some sense into her."

"Yeah, 'cause that'll help," Lucy says, rolling her eyes. "None of us are children anymore, Uncle Will. No matter how much you wish we were."

"You're our kids," he says with a shrug. "We will always worry about you."

"It wasn't my responsibility to make her come back." I shrug when he turns his gaze to me. "It just wasn't. But she's smart, and it sounds like she has a plan. Let her work her plan and be happy."

He sighs, as if the wind has just been let out of his sails. But he doesn't say a word as he walks out of the office.

He doesn't even walk into his own office.

He just leaves.

"That sucks," Lucy says. "All of our parents are so overprotective."

"He'll get over it." I shrug again and watch him disappear into the elevator, then turn back to London. "But he might not come back today."

"I figured."

"I'm going back to work," Lucy announces and leaves the office, closing the door behind her, and I make my way around London's desk, pull her into my arms, and sink into her.

She moans in that way she does that makes me want to devour her as she wraps her arms around my neck and holds on.

Finally, I pull back and kiss her nose. "Been missing you lately."

"Yeah?" She rubs her fingers through the back of my hair. "That's nice to hear because I've missed you, too. I got used to sleeping with you at night. Now, no one is snoring next to me."

"I don't snore."

"Sure, you do. It's okay. I kind of like it."

I kiss her again, another long, slow kiss that makes me want to take it much, much further, right here on her desk. But I remember what she said in Montana about remaining professional, and I pull back.

"Do you have plans for tonight?" I ask her.

"I promised Caleb that he and I would go on a date to the movies." She winces and bites her lower lip. "It always sounds like a good idea at the time, until I have to keep the promise. But you're more than welcome to come over after. We're going to a matinee after school so we don't get home too late."

"I might do that. I have plenty of work tonight to keep me busy, though."

She nods. "Yeah, I'm still catching up from being gone, too. But seriously, come over later. We can work together."

I nod and kiss her forehead before pulling away. "I'll do that. Have fun at the movies."

I *LOVED* this condo when I bought it just a few short months ago. Now, it's too quiet and too lonely.

Being without London and Caleb sucks. I respect London's decision to not sleep together when Caleb is in the house, but I want to be with *both* of them.

She texted a little while ago to let me know that their date turned into dinner out, as well, and she would text me when they got home.

It's almost eight now. I should just stay in and see her tomorrow at work.

But I want her. Any way I can get her.

My phone pings, and I see that it's from London.

London: We're home! Finally. I'm so sorry it's later than I thought, but feel free to come over any time.

Without responding, I grab my jacket, keys, and my laptop and hurry down to my car. I like that her place is less than thirty minutes from mine, and before long, I'm waving at the security guard at the gate and driving down her long driveway to the house that's lit up.

I raise my eyebrows in surprise. Not only are the lights on, but someone came and hung holiday lights on all the trees and the house. Wreaths hang in every window.

She finally got her decorations.

With a grin, I walk to the front door and knock, and just a few seconds later, I hear Caleb ask, "Who is it?"

"Santa Claus," I reply.

"Oh, boy!" Caleb opens the door and then giggles. "I knew it was you."

"And here I thought I could trick you. Did you and your mom have fun at the movies?"

"Yeah, it was totally awesome. And then we got tacos. I had *four* of them."

"That's a lot of tacos." I hang my coat in the hall

closet and kick off my wet shoes before following Caleb down to the kitchen, where London's filling the dishwasher. The inside of the house is decorated, as well, with lots of lights and bows and garland. I have to admit, it's pretty great. "Hey, beautiful."

"Hi there. How was your evening?"

"It's looking up. I hear there was a taco feast."

"Caleb's going to make me go broke," she confirms, but Caleb just shakes his head.

"We're loaded," he informs me, not concerned in the least as London passes me a bottle of water.

"How do you know?" I ask.

"None of my friends have a house this big," he replies with a quick shrug, making me laugh. "Okay, the deal was that I have to go to bed without a fuss in exchange for date night, so I'm gonna go get ready for bed."

London raises an eyebrow. "Are you sick? Are you sure you're my son and not an imposter?"

"I'm not an imposter."

"Say something that only Caleb knows."

He wrinkles his nose. "I have a mole right on my butt."

The water I just drank sprays out of my mouth in surprise, and that sends Caleb into another fit of giggles.

"It's true," he says, still laughing at me. "Okay, see you later."

He waves and runs up the stairs to his bedroom.

"He's a nut."

London sighs, and the smile on her face fades as she wipes down the countertop.

"What's wrong?"

"Oh, nothing at all." She stops and looks over at me. "I think I'm just tired."

"I'll finish this," I offer. "Go up and take care of him."

"I'll take you up on that." She stops in front of me and passes me the wet rag, then kisses me before walking to the stairs. "Thanks."

I don't mind cleaning up the rest of the kitchen. I even make sure that Caleb's lunch is ready for tomorrow, and then I set out some snacks for London and me to pick on this evening while we work.

But when she comes down thirty minutes later, looking dead on her feet, I put the snacks away and take her hand in mine.

"We're not working tonight," I inform her.

"We're not?"

"No, ma'am. You're exhausted. We're going upstairs, and you're going to get comfortable, and I'll rub your feet for a while."

She doesn't argue. Silently, we climb the stairs and walk down the hall, past Caleb's room, to hers.

London closes the double doors so we have some privacy, and I walk into her bathroom to start her a shower.

"Have you ever noticed that you're always bathing me?" she asks with a sleepy smile.

"It's relaxing," I reply and kiss the top of her head. "Get cozy."

With her in the shower, I toss some pillows onto the couch, along with a blanket, and twenty minutes later, she walks out, looking soft and fresh in a tank and some sweatpants. I lead her to the couch and get her settled in, pull her foot into my lap, and begin to rub.

"I'm sorry," she says, and my gaze whips up to hers. "For what?"

"A lot of things." She wiggles back into the pillows, getting more comfortable. "Mostly, I'm sorry that we can't spend more time together. I really do wish that you could stay here with me."

"London, have you thought about us talking with Caleb? He's a smart kid. We could have an honest conversation with him and see where he's at with the situation."

"You're not wrong." She yawns hugely. "Sorry. I think you're right. We should do that."

"Or, now that I think about it, maybe *I* should do that. Man-to-man."

That brings a sparkle to her eye. "That would probably make him feel really important."

"He *is* important. I'll do that this week."

"I have an idea. Why don't you come over tomorrow night and help us trim the Christmas trees? You can find a moment to talk to him then."

"The sooner the better works for me, because I

don't want to be away from you any longer than I have to be."

Her eyes soften as I switch feet.

"But I'm not just going to ask his permission to stay the night now and then."

Her eyebrow lifts, waiting for me to continue.

"I want to move in permanently, babe. How do you feel about that?"

She blinks slowly, taking some time to think it over, and finally, just when I think she's going to tell me to take a hike, she says, "Yeah. Yeah, I think that's a good idea."

Her eyes are *so* heavy, but they're happy, too.

"One more thing before you fall asleep," I continue. "I want to apologize for the other night."

She frowns and tilts her head to the side in question.

"I don't want you to *ever* think that I would be unfaithful to you. I don't want you to feel uncomfortable. I know we already moved past this, but it's still bothering me, and I want you to know that it won't happen again. I'll be aware of it now, if I'm ever in a similar situation."

"Thanks for that," she says. "I'm not sorry that I got upset. My only regret is that I didn't tell her to take her badly manicured hands off my man."

"That might have been sexy."

She snorts. "It's been so ingrained in me to be polite, to never make a scene. But fuck that. Maybe I should make a scene more often, especially when it comes to something I care about."

"Fine by me. Now, are you going to tell me why you're so tired?"

"My mother called today after I left the office. She's always exhausting. Today, she was crying because her husband has been ignoring her, and she feels lonely." London rolls her eyes. "She only calls me when she needs to be tended to. It's really annoying and zaps the energy right out of me."

"Maybe don't answer the phone."

Her eyes find mine again as I shrug a shoulder. "If she's going to be that way, you're not available. Save the energy."

"You know, that's an excellent idea."

"I HAVE SOMETHING FOR YOU," I inform Caleb the next night. We decided to start trimming the trees in the game room, and Caleb just hung the last ornament on his tree.

"It's not even Christmas," he says with excitement.

"I know, but this is important and goes along with what we're doing." I pass him the small red gift bag with gold tissue paper. "You can open this one now."

It only takes him seconds to pull out the ornament I found for him when London and I were in Montana.

"It's a controller," he says, frowning. "But I can't tell what kind."

"It's the original Nintendo controller, from way back in the day. Even before my time." I laugh when his eyes get really big. "I thought you could add it to your tree."

"This is *awesome*. Thanks, Drew." He runs over and adds the ornament to the tree, and I look over to see London watching me.

"I found it in Montana," I tell her. "Decided he needed it."

"Thank you," she says, her face all soft and gooey. The way to this woman's heart is definitely through her kid. "I have to go make a quick phone call. I'll be back in a few."

"Mom, do you like where I hanged it?"

"Hung it," she corrects him. "And yes, it looks great."

London leaves the room, pulling her phone out of her pocket as she goes, and I decide now is the perfect time to have a talk with Caleb.

"Can I ask you something?"

Caleb looks over at me. "Sure. What's up?"

Why does the kid sound thirty?

"Well, first, I want to tell you that I love your mom a lot."

"Yeah, me, too." He nods. "She's pretty cool."

"But I love you, too, Caleb. Not just your mom."

That has him going quiet and his eyes sobering as he watches me. "You do?"

"Yeah. You're a really great kid, and I like being around you both. So, I wanted to take a minute when it was just you and me to talk to you. Man-to-man."

Caleb raises his chin and sits on the ottoman opposite of me. "Okay."

"How would you feel if I stayed here sometimes? Like, overnight?"

"Why wouldn't you just stay *all* the time?"

I can't help but smile at that question, already feeling a huge relief. "That's a good question. If your mom and I decided that it was a good idea for me to move in here with you guys, would that be okay with you?"

"Yeah, that's fine. But would you sleep in her room? Like how my friend Sam's parents sleep in the same room?"

"Yes, we would."

He frowns. "Would you have a lot of sex?"

I cough, surprised by the question, although I shouldn't be. "That will never be something that you have to worry about. It won't be an issue for you."

Jesus, I hope I'm right about that and he doesn't ever walk in on us the way I walked in on my parents when I was twelve and wanted to poke my eyes out.

"Well, yeah, I mean, if you love us and we love you, we should probably just be together."

I love how he can get to the heart of it so easily.

"I guess that settles it, then, huh?"

"Do you want me to talk to Mom about it?" he offers, patting my arm. "Maybe I can soften her up."

"I don't think it's going to be a bad conversation," I reply. "In fact, I think she'll be pretty happy about it."

CHAPTER 18

LONDON

"*I* think we've made about a billion gingerbread men." Caleb carefully uses the spatula to move the last cookie from the tray to the cooling rack. "What are we making next?"

"What's your favorite?" I ask him.

"Gooey butter cookies." His eyes brighten. "Are we making those today?"

"Yep." I check my watch and wonder where the morning went. It's already close to noon. "But we have to hurry because Uncle Rome will be here soon to get you."

"What's happening with Uncle Rome?" Drew asks as he saunters into the kitchen, carrying his gym bag over his shoulder. His hair is still damp from his shower at the gym. Since he'll be moving in soon, I went ahead and gave him the code to the doors and space in the garage.

Even though he hasn't technically moved in yet, he's been staying here every night since he talked with Caleb last week.

"He takes Caleb on a special guys-only shopping day before Christmas every year."

"So I can get Mom something," Caleb adds and helps me crack an egg into the mixing bowl. "We're making cookies for Mom's party tomorrow night."

"Will you miss this one?" Drew asks as he picks up a gingerbread man and bites off his arm.

"Not now," I reply with a laugh. "How did it go at the gym?"

"It was good. Most of my guys were in today, even though they have a couple of days off before Sunday's game, with Christmas falling on Saturday."

"I want to go to the game," Caleb announces, and my eyes meet Drew's across the island. "I never get to go, and I want to watch the guys play and Drew coach. Can we go, Mom?"

"You know, buddy, we've talked about this before. I don't think it's a good idea."

"Maybe you could just think about it," Caleb suggests just as we hear the front door open and Rome call out that he's here. "Ah, man, I'm gonna miss the gooey butter cookies."

"They'll be here when you get home," I remind him and smile at my brother as he saunters into the kitchen. "Hey. Want some cookies?"

"Always." He nods to Drew and then smiles down at

Caleb. "Hey, have you seen Caleb around here? He's a little kid, much smaller than you."

"Ha ha, it's *me*, Uncle Rome."

"What? You grew ten inches since I saw you last."

Caleb laughs as he runs into the mudroom to fetch his coat and shoes. "I know what I want to get for Mom."

"Don't say it in here," Rome advises, "like you did last year."

"I won't." Caleb hurries over to hug me, does the same to Drew, and then he's running for the front door. "Let's go!"

"That kid never stops moving," Rome says, shaking his head. "Good thing I haven't worked out yet today. We'll be back in a few hours. I'm going to take him to lunch."

"Have fun," I say with a wave and finish setting cookie dough balls on a cookie sheet, then pop them into the oven.

"You weren't kidding the first time you showed me this kitchen," Drew says as he finishes his cookie. "You *do* use the entire island for this project."

"I love spreading out while I bake. Besides, cookies take up a lot of room."

I roll more butter cookies and place them onto the next cookie sheet.

"Maybe we *should* talk about you and Caleb coming to the game on Sunday," Drew says, making me frown. "I'm not trying to be pushy; just hear me out."

"Okay, I'm listening."

"My family has a box. They've owned it for as long as I can remember. Probably long before me. Anyway, some of the parents and cousins come to the games and hang out in the box. You should bring Caleb and hang out there, rather than in the owner's suite. No one would be looking for you in our family suite, and you can relax a little."

"It does sound like a decent compromise," I admit as I set the last ball on a sheet, then turn to the sink and wash my hands. Honestly, I'd really like to watch Drew in action on the field. They don't show him much on the television. More than that, I want to support him and my team.

"I think my parents plan to go," Drew continues. "They usually like to go to the Christmas game when we're at home. Caleb will get a kick out of it. You can even make it one of his holiday presents."

"He would love that," I concede with a sigh as I turn back to Drew. "Okay, we can try it. If the press becomes crazy, I won't take him again."

"My family members are a bunch of pros at avoiding the press," he assures me. "We'll make it work."

The oven signals that it's time to take out the cookies, so I grab a mitt and retrieve the tray, but before I can slide the next one in, Drew stops me.

"Wait on that, will you?"

"Why?"

"Because I don't want to worry about the house burning to the ground while I do this."

He pulls the mitt off my hand and tosses it aside, then frames my face in his hands and kisses the ever-loving hell out of me.

"I don't know if you noticed," he says against my neck as he nibbles his way down, pushing my shirt aside, then simply pulls it over my head and tosses it onto the floor, "but we're all alone. For several hours."

"You know, I did notice that." I giggle and then sigh when he removes my bra and teases the hard nubs with his thumbs. "I suppose the only right thing to do is to take advantage of it."

"You bet your beautiful ass."

He undresses us both, but not quickly. He takes his time, kissing every inch of flesh that he uncovers.

"I don't have to rush," he says, kissing my chest. "I don't have to be quiet. Hell, I don't have to make sure *you're* quiet."

"You've been making sure I'm quiet?" I frown down at him, surprised. "How do you do that?"

"I have ways," he murmurs. "But right here, right now, I can do what I please, and you can be as loud as you fucking want."

"Fun." I laugh when he playfully smacks my ass. "Should we go to a bedroom? We have a few to choose from in this house."

"In a minute." Figuring he'll boost me up onto the

counter, I'm surprised when he leaves me long enough to find the tube of vanilla icing that I used for cookies. "First, we're going to have a little playtime."

With his brow furrowed in concentration, Drew draws a red heart right in the middle of my chest. I raise an eyebrow.

"That might stain, you know."

"It's winter, you'll wear clothes." He smirks and leans in to lick it off. "Mm, delicious."

"My turn." Taking the frosting, I write *D + L*. Before long, we have all kinds of things written on us—initials, symbols, and designs.

Before we can get close to licking it all off, the bag of frosting is empty, and we're kissing, rubbing, and smearing the frosting between us because we can't keep our hands off each other any longer.

"Goddamn, you're fucking sexy," Drew growls, and does boost me up onto the counter. I wrap my legs around his hips and scoot forward, giving him easier access to me.

But he doesn't slide into me.

"Drew, if you don't fuck me *now*, we're going to have a problem."

He raises an eyebrow. "Is that so?"

"Yeah. Come on. I want you."

He drops to his knees, props my legs on his shoulders, and proceeds to lap at me with more gusto than he did the frosting.

"Oh, shit." I lean back on my hands and just about come out of my skin when his teeth rake over my clit just hard enough to make my entire body zing. "Ah, hell, Drew."

He hums, which sends another zing through me. When he pushes a finger inside of me and makes that little *come here* motion, I shatter, right here in my kitchen.

Drew stands now, but I don't give him the chance to slide inside of me. Instead, I push him back, slide off of the counter, and kneel before him, taking his cock into my hand and mouth and mentally high-fiving myself when he growls in surprise and satisfaction.

I suck gently at first, then grow bolder when his hands weave through my hair and he holds on, not guiding me, just holding on as I pleasure him.

"Shit," he mutters and takes a deep breath. "Shit, baby, I'm going to come."

"Mm-hmm." I don't stop. In fact, I move faster, a little harder, and relish in the satisfaction that I made him fall apart as completely as he did me just a few moments ago.

"Jesus Christ, I fucking want you." He sounds almost angry as he pulls me to my feet, spins me to face the counter, and slaps my ass before pushing inside of me. "I *never* stop wanting you."

His hand slides into my hair again, but this time, it's at the base of my neck, and he squeezes his fist, tightening his hold deliciously.

"Fuck, that's hot," I breathe, pushing back against him as his thrusts become harder, more intense, and then we're falling over another edge together. I glance down at myself and laugh breathlessly. The countertop, the floor, and even Drew and I are covered in smeared frosting. "We made one hell of a mess."

"Come on." He slings me over his shoulder and carries me to the bathroom. "I'll clean us up."

"DID YOU SEE HER *CLOSET*?" Jules asks as she and Natalie come down my staircase. "It's the size of Brazil."

"I have to tell you," Brynna says as she joins me and offers me a cocktail, "when you said you wanted to host a holiday girls' night out, I didn't expect it to be this incredible."

"Well, I like to throw parties. I figured this would be a better holiday party than the boring ones I usually throw with all the business executives. I'd much rather hang out with all of you."

"We're a fun bunch," Lucy says with a wink. "The caterer is about to set out the dinner buffet. The bartender just had a family emergency and had to leave, so Stella's stepping in to take over, but aside from that, all is well."

"You're the *best*," I inform her. "Also, this is a party. You're not at work. Relax and have a little fun, why don't you."

Lucy laughs. "Work *is* fun. But I get it. Just holler if you need me."

She rushes off to join some of the others dancing in the game room.

"Hiring her is the best thing I've done in a *long* time. She's amazing."

"Lucy is wonderful," Brynna agrees. "Have you met her mom? Meredith is around here somewhere. There she is, over with Alecia."

"And Alecia is Emma's mom?"

"That's right."

"You have a huge family," I inform Brynna. I couldn't even say, off the top of my head, how many women are here tonight. All the cousins, minus Erin, and all the moms and aunts are here. "I think I need a chart hanging somewhere so I can keep everyone straight."

"You'll learn. It'll just take some time," she assures me. "I hope you don't mind that a few of the girls are playing in your closet."

"I don't mind at all. I'd be playing in there, too. Uh-oh, Meg looks upset."

Meg, blinking back tears, comes wandering over. "Would you please point me in the direction of a bathroom?"

"Of course, I will, but what's wrong?"

"I miss my girl." She swallows hard, and Brynna steps in to wrap her arm around Meg's shoulders. "Erin would *love* this party, and I wish she was here.

Why did she move away from us at Christmas? I have a mind to fly over there and shake some sense into her."

"I have an idea," Brynna says, pulling her phone out of her pocket. "Let's video call her."

Before Meg can reply, the phone is ringing, and Erin's pretty face fills the screen.

"Hi, beautiful niece," Brynna says. "We're having a girls' night at London's place, and we had to call and include you."

"Oh, that's so fun! Is everyone there?"

"Yep, including your mama, who's a little sad without you."

"Oh, baby, you look so happy." Meg wipes at a tear. "How are you?"

"Mom, I'm great. I promise. I'm working at the coffee shop full time, making bank in tips. The people are *so* nice, and I even have a really cute apartment. Seriously, don't worry about me."

"Right. That's like telling me not to breathe," Meg replies but smiles at her daughter. "I'm so happy that you're happy. But I'm allowed to miss you, especially at Christmas."

"I know, and I'm sorry I can't come home, but I'm the newbie at work, so I'm the lowest on the totem pole. You and Dad should come visit sometime."

"Oh, trust me, we will. I'm surprised your dad hasn't already packed us up to go out there. We'll come see you soon."

"Good. Now, how's the food? And the drinks? If London's hosting, I know it's an awesome party."

"Hey, thanks." I poke my head over Meg's shoulder so Erin can see me. "We miss you."

"Aww, this might be the first time I've been a little homesick. Where are all the other girls? Is that London's house? It's so pretty!"

Meg takes off, showing Erin everything and letting all the cousins and aunts have a minute to say hi.

"That was a good idea," I say to Brynna.

"Hey, I'd miss my kids if they decided to move away, too. Speaking of my kids, how are you and Drew doing?"

"We're fantastic." I can't help but smile at the question. "Like, *really* good. Brynna, you raised a really great man."

"I know, and you're welcome." She winks at me. "He really loves Caleb, too. I can tell."

"They get along so well. And Caleb adores Drew. Sometimes I feel like *I'm* the odd man out, and that's really okay with me. I wouldn't want it any other way. It's a big ask to hope that a man will love your kid as much as you do."

"I understand completely," Brynna assures me. "I had the twins when I met my Caleb, or as I've now started calling him, *Old* Caleb. It makes him laugh. Anyway, they took to him right away, and it was huge for me. Honestly, it made me fall in love with him even more."

"Yes, exactly," I agree, nodding my head. "Drew's going to be moving in here at the end of the month."

"And I'm moving into the condo," Lucy informs us as she joins us. "He offered to rent it to me, and I snatched it up. I'll miss the compound, but I won't miss the commute. Listen, I'm sorry to interrupt, but security just called up. There's a woman trying to get through to the house."

"Who is it?"

"Adelaide," Lucy replies with a wince, and I feel my stomach fall. "What should I tell them?"

"Let her through," I reply with a sigh. "And I'll figure out how to get rid of her."

"Who's Adelaide?" Brynna asks.

"My mother, unfortunately. Listen, this could get messy. I apologize in advance. Would you mind quickly letting the others know for me?"

"Of course, I will. I'm sorry, honey. We'll figure this out."

"Thanks."

The doorbell rings, and I hurry over to open the door, seeing that this is going to be messier than I thought.

She's fucking drunk.

"Baby," Mom says and practically falls into my arms. "Oh, my baby. Don't worry, honey, I'm home. I'm home now."

"Uh, Mom, pull yourself together." I manage to

disentangle myself from her and pull back, frowning. "What are you doing?"

"Why, I came to visit, of course. It's Christmas. Oh." She blinks rapidly as she looks around and sees so many people staring at her. "You're having a party. A *holiday* party. How lovely. I'd like a drink."

"I think you've had enough to drink already."

"There's no need to be snide," she hisses at me, baring her teeth. But then, as quickly as it was there, it's gone again, and she's smiling, staggering on her feet. "I'll just put my things in a bedroom and join the fun."

"No."

I'm well aware of the audience we have as my drunk mother rounds on me. "*No?* What do you mean, no? I came to see you."

"You can't stay in my house. Caleb doesn't even know who you are, and I won't have him upset at Christmas. You can stay at a hotel, and I'll fit in a dinner with you this week."

"You were always ungrateful," she snarls. "Ungrateful for everything I did for you. All the sacrifices I made."

"Right. Sure, okay. I hope you didn't let that Uber go."

"You listen to me," she begins, but Lucy hurries over.

"Hello, ma'am. I'm Lucy. Don't you worry at all because I've made a reservation for you at the Four Seasons—a suite, of course—and they're expecting you.

I've also made sure that dinner will be waiting for you in your suite when you get there. We want you to be as comfortable as possible, and we appreciate your understanding that this is a private party that London has been planning for *weeks*. I know you wouldn't want to disrupt that."

"Well, of course not. Did you order me some wine?"

"Oh, yes, a bottle of white and one of red, since I wasn't sure of your preference."

"I'll drink both." Mom winks at Lucy, then glares at me. "At least someone here has the manners to take care of a guest."

She pushes her scarf over her shoulder theatrically and turns to leave through the door that Lucy has already opened.

My assistant escorts my mom to the Uber, and when she returns, I take a deep breath before turning to find all the Montgomery women watching me. But they're not staring out of judgmental, critical eyes. They look *worried*.

"Are you okay, London?" Brynna asks me.

"I'm embarrassed, actually." I offer her a shaky smile. "My mom and I, well, we don't—"

"You don't have to explain," Meg says, shaking her head. "It's none of our business, as long as you're okay. Trust me, I know all about having an asshole for a mom. It sucks."

What did I do to deserve this amazing family that's swooped in and accepted me as one of their own? I'm so overwhelmed by the support it brings tears to my eyes.

"She's gonna blow," Stella says, making me laugh.

"No, I'm not. I'm just grateful. Now, I think I need a drink."

"Oh, that's me," Stella says, clapping her hands. "Don't worry, I'll hook you right up."

CHAPTER 19

DREW

"What the fuck, man?" Hudson scowls at Liam, who just smashed the ping-pong ball in his face.

"Seriously?" I ask and point to Caleb. "There's a kid here. Watch your mouth."

"It's okay," Caleb assures Hudson and takes a swig of his cola. "My mom swears all the time. I've heard it before."

Hudson winks at him and then serves the ball back at Liam.

A bunch of us guys have decided to get together since all the girls are at their holiday girls' night out. We've gathered at Ike and Sophie's place because he has an awesome man cave with not just ping-pong but also arcade games, a pool table, and a full bar.

"I'm surprised you weren't called out tonight," I say to Liam as he misses the ball.

"It's my few days off," he says. "I just finished a four-day shift."

"You were at work for *four days?*" Caleb demands with big eyes.

"Liam's a fireman," I inform him. "He works a lot."

"But you save people's lives." Caleb's voice is hushed and serious as he stares at Liam as if the man was Captain America himself. "That's the coolest."

"I really *am* the coolest," Liam agrees as my dad and Uncle Luke cheer at the pinball machine. It seems like a lot of people to pack into this room, but we don't mind.

Some of the guys are out watching a basketball game in the living room.

We're kind of spread all over the place.

"Looks like you guys are headed for the playoffs," Hudson says as Ike walks into the room.

"We have to win Sunday," Ike reminds him. "Then we'll be in the playoffs."

"I'm trying to talk my mom into letting me go," Caleb says. "She's weird about it."

I smile down at him and ruffle his hair. He's going to be stoked on Christmas morning when we tell him he gets to go.

"Maybe she's just trying to be a good mom," Liam says conversationally.

"She's the best," Caleb agrees. "But sometimes she's too strict."

"Moms do that," Hudson agrees. "Hey, Liam, I forgot to tell you, I ran into Bee the other day."

My eyes fly to Liam, who's suddenly gone very still. "Is that so?"

"Yeah, she looks great. She just opened that new salad place on Alki Beach. I took my mom there last week, and it was really great. I didn't realize she'd opened a restaurant. Did you know?"

"No." He stares down at his paddle, then turns to Caleb. "Hey, buddy, do you want to step in for me? Kick his butt."

"Sure," Caleb says and hurries over to take Liam's paddle. "You're dead meat, Hud."

"Yeah right, kid."

I hurry behind Liam, who's bounding down the stairs and through the house to the back door.

"Where are you going?" I ask him.

"I just need some air," he replies as he walks out to the back deck, leans against the railing, and takes in a long, deep breath of chilly, rainy air. "Fuck, that sucker-punched me."

"I see that." I shove my hands into my pockets, watching him. "Have you seen Bianca at all in the last couple of years?"

"No." He shakes his head and pushes his hand through his hair. "She made it pretty clear that we were done, and I'm not one to harass a woman after she says no."

"But you love her."

"She was done," he repeats. "She always talked about opening up a salad place. She has stomach issues and

273

can't always eat at restaurants. Has to be careful. I'm glad she followed through on that."

"You should go check it out."

He shakes his head.

"You live in the fucking neighborhood, Liam. Go check it out and say hello."

"Listen, I'm fine here, Drew." He doesn't look me in the eye, and I know that he wants to be left alone. "I appreciate you wanting to help, but I've got this."

"Yeah, you've got it, all right." I shake my head as my phone pings with a message. Looking down, I frown.

"Who is it?" he asks.

"Lucy. She's giving me the heads-up that there was some drama with London's mom tonight. She showed up at the house in the middle of the party."

"I take it London and her mom aren't close?"

"No," I say grimly. "They aren't. I hope London's okay. Lucy said they're starting to wrap things up there, so I might go ahead and take Caleb home."

"Hey, I like the kid, man. And his mom. And I like how happy you are with them."

I smile at my best friend and pull him in for a man hug. "Thanks. I like them, too. A lot. They're mine now."

"I know." He nods and offers me a smile. "Don't fuck up like I did."

"No one can fuck up that badly...unless they're you." He barks out a laugh as I make my way back inside to collect my kid so we can go see to his mother.

"He's asleep," London says as she makes her way into the bedroom. While she took Caleb up to bed, I made sure the last couple of aunts got home okay. Uncle Luke came to gather up Natalie and Jules and hauled their drunk asses home.

They were arguing about how many orgasms a woman can have in one night.

I don't want to think about either one of them having any orgasms.

"He had fun," I inform her. "Nothing got out of hand. It was a pretty laid-back guys' night. He might have heard some language, but he assured me that it isn't anything he hasn't heard before."

London laughs and rubs her hands over her face as she sits on the side of the bed. "I'm glad that he had fun. We did, too. I *adore* the women in your family, Drew. They're all just amazing. Your aunt Samantha is married to *Leo Nash.*"

I grin at her. "Yeah, I know."

"It's just crazy to me." She blows out a breath and watches me with tired eyes.

"Want to tell me about the drama?"

One perfect eyebrow lifts. "Who told you?"

"Lucy texted me. Said your mom showed up."

"Yeah." She sighs, leans forward, and just rests her face in her hands. "She showed up. Thought she could just join in on the fun and stay here with me."

"What happened?"

"Before I could do much, Lucy had a suite at the Four Seasons booked, along with dinner in her room because she was *hammered*, and then she escorted her out to the Uber. And it just occurred to me, why was my mother in an *Uber*? Why wasn't she in a black car or a limo?"

"I have no idea. Did she say why she came?"

"She didn't have to. I know why. The new husband is boring her, and she wants attention. She does this about every five years or so. But this time, her timing was *horrible,* and I was so fucking embarrassed, Drew. She was drunk, like I said, and ridiculous. Of course, your family was wonderful, as always. Did you know that your aunt Meg had a horrible mom?"

"Oh, yeah, the stories I've heard are crazy. My uncle Will paid that woman a quarter of a million dollars to make sure she never came back and asked for another dime. She had to sign a contract and everything."

London blinks at me. "Wow. I wonder if that would work with my mom."

"Is that what you want? For her to go away so you never have to deal with her again?"

"Yes, actually. I know that my father isn't the best. I mean, he seriously thought I should be with that asshole, Felix. But you know what? He was around. He looked in on us. He didn't just leave us with the nannies and completely forget about us for months at a time."

"But that's what she did."

"Yeah, it's like once she had kids, she thought that her responsibility to give my dad heirs was over, and she could just go do her own thing. Which is exactly what she did. Finally, he divorced her and cut his losses. He's not the dad of the year, but he's a *dad*. I don't know her. I don't *want* to know her."

"I think you need to tell her that." I move over and squat before her, taking her hands in mine. "She'll yell and cry and carry on, I'm sure, but then you can disassociate yourself and move on with your life, *without* your mother interrupting every few years."

"I'm supposed to arrange to have dinner with her this week," she says, nodding slowly.

"Christmas is just a few days away."

"She has great timing." London's voice is as dry as the Sahara. "And I'm sure that was part of her plan. Come in the middle of Christmas. I'm not giving that to her. Caleb doesn't even know her, and I want him to have a good holiday. She gets dinner, and I'm going to tell her to get lost. But not until after Sunday. We're going to have a fun week together, Drew."

"Agreed. I think that sounds reasonable, and you're right. We're going to have fun this week. Caleb's going to flip his shit when he finds out he gets to go to the game. He was talking about it again tonight."

That brings a small smile to her plump lips. "Good. I talked with Brynna about the game tonight, and she understands my hesitation. She said she'd talk to your dad about it, and they'll make sure we have extra security for the family suite. I offered to have it done, but she said that it would garner attention if I saw to it. If *they* do it, it's no big deal."

"My mom's pretty damn smart."

"I hope this works." She cups my face in her hands. "Because *I* would like to go to the games and watch you work. It's really sexy."

"It's sexy when I yell at professional football players?"

"Yeah, I like it when you're bossy."

I lean in and kiss her, pleased when she sighs against me. "How about if I get a little bossy right now?"

"Yes, please. But first," she pushes back on my chest, "I have a Christmas present for you."

"This *is* my present, sweetheart."

She laughs and disappears into the closet, then returns holding a box wrapped in gold paper with a green bow.

"This is for you."

"It's not Christmas yet."

"Just open it, Drew." She sits on the side of the bed and smiles as I start to rip into the paper.

"It's a book," I say in surprise. But it's not just *any* book. This is a photo album with a brown leather cover embossed with a heart in the center.

And when I open it, I just about swallow my tongue.

"I made an appointment with your aunt Natalie, and she's a freaking *genius.*"

I can't speak as I page through the photos. London's in different sexy lingerie, red and black, and then she's in nothing at all except for a sheet, her short hair a mess, and she's staring at the camera, those gorgeous eyes wide, and she's biting her lower lip.

"This is the sexiest thing anyone's ever given me."

"Oh, thank God," London says and lies back on the bed. "These kinds of gifts can go either way, you know? I admit, it was a fun session. She said she also used to do couples, and I thought it might be a fun thing for us to do together sometime."

"Sorry, babe, I'm not getting sexy in front of my aunt. It feels too creepy to me."

"I'll talk you into it," she says with confidence. "Now, where were we before?"

"Hold that thought." I cross over to the bathroom, and to the drawers that London cleared out for me. I hid her gift in the bottom drawer.

"You didn't have to get me anything," she insists, but her eyes are bright and fixed on the red-papered box in my hand. "Gimme."

With a grin, I pass it to her, and she quickly rips the paper away, then opens the black velvet box and sighs.

"Oh, Drew. These are *gorgeous.*"

"Another something I found in Montana," I reply as London brushes the tip of her finger over the sapphire earrings. "Those sapphires are mined in Montana, and I thought they were pretty."

"They're beautiful." She immediately pulls them out of the box and affixes them to her ears, then rushes over to the mirror to admire them. "You know, I think we should always exchange gifts like this, just the two of us. Make it a new tradition."

The fact that she's thinking of future holidays together, that this is only the first of many, is sexy as fuck.

"I can live with that. You probably couldn't have given that book to me in front of Caleb."

She wrinkles her nose in disgust. "Ew. No. I don't want to damage the poor kid. Now, really, where were we?"

"I believe you requested that I get bossy."

"Oh, yeah." A slow, satisfied smile spreads over those lips. "Let's definitely do that."

"On the bed. Scoot back, and lose the clothes."

Her eyes dilate, and her mouth opens, but she doesn't hesitate to comply. She scrambles out of her holiday dress, and my mouth goes slack when I see that she's in thigh-high stockings.

"Wait," I say. She pauses with her hands at the top of one of the stockings. "You can keep those on. With the shoes."

"That's not a cliché at all."

"There's a reason it's a cliché," I reply as I walk to the door and lock it, then shed my jeans, tug my shirt over my head, and push onto the bed, already hard and ready for her. "Because it's a *thing*."

"Okay, I'll leave them." She leans back against the pillows, wearing her black bra and the garter, and I've never seen anything so fucking *hot.* "Remember, we have to be quiet."

"I won't forget."

And I'll make sure she doesn't forget, either.

"MR. AMBROSE WILL SEE YOU NOW." The young receptionist nods politely to me and then escorts me, over carpet so thick I sink into it, down a long hallway, to an office that sits on the top floor of a high-rise that's coincidentally next door to Uncle Luke's production company.

When I step inside, I'm surprised to see that Rome is here, as well.

I asked for a meeting with London's dad and thought that, because of Christmas being tomorrow, he would want to meet at his home.

I guessed wrong.

"Hello, Drew," Chandler says with a nod. "I hope you don't mind that Rome is joining us."

"Not at all," I reply easily and shake both of their hands. "Thanks for seeing me on such short notice."

"Not at all," Chandler replies again and sits in his

chair, steepling his hands. "How can I help you? I trust everything with our quarterbacks is okay."

"Yes, sir, the team is doing well." I sit across from him and glance over at Rome, who's watching me with a smug grin on his lips. "I wanted to discuss London with you."

"Go on," Chandler replies.

"I'd like to marry your daughter, sir, and I would like your blessing before I propose to her."

"I see." He glances at Rome and then down at his hands. "And if I say no?"

"I'll still ask her." I smile humorlessly. "But my parents raised me to be respectful, and I'd like your blessing before I do."

"I told you the night of the gala that this wouldn't last," he replies after a moment of consideration. "We both know that she came with you that night to shake off Felix."

"Maybe. But that's not the situation now. It hasn't been for a long while."

"No, I can see that. What is it about my daughter that you think you've fallen in love with?"

I sit back and take a deep breath. "I hope you have some time on your hands for this answer. London is smart. She has a sharp intellect and a quick wit, and because of those qualities, along with compassion and passion, she's been successful in her businesses. *All* of her businesses. She loves working and building something to be proud of. She's so fucking funny. She makes me laugh all the time, and you know what? She's not afraid to stick up for herself, to stand up for what's right."

I shake my head, thinking of how she called me out in Montana.

"She's brave. And she wants to belong to something great. She wants a *close* family, but she's too shy to ask for one. London's loyal, Mr. Ambrose. Sometimes I wonder if she's loyal to a fault, but I don't think so. She loves you."

That makes him blink in surprise.

"She talks about you often, and I think she's proud of you. Of both of you. But what I love most about London is what an absolutely amazing mom she is. Caleb is lucky to have a mother so dedicated to him. She doesn't do it out of responsibility. She does it because she *enjoys* being a mom. She loves being with her son, and that's something that I both respect and love about her. The three of us have a great time together. I love them both very much.

"You don't have to worry. I'll be happy to sign a prenup or whatever it is you want me to sign. I don't give a shit about the money. As you know, I come from a wealthy, influential family. Not to mention, I do just fine for myself. I want *her*. All of her and Caleb, and any other children we're lucky enough to have."

He's quiet for another moment. I don't look away from him, and his face finally relaxes, and he nods slowly.

"I can admit that you're not who I would have chosen for her. It's nothing personal, mind you. But it seems that you're who she's chosen, and I'm not going to try to stop it. I'm proud of my daughter, Drew, and I know that I may not be good at showing it, but I love her. I want what's best for her."

"It sounds like all three of us are on the same page there."

I see Rome nod out of the corner of my eye.

"If it's my blessing you want, I'll give it. Do you have an engagement ring chosen for her?"

I blink, surprised by the question.

"I was going to shop for that this afternoon, actually."

Chandler and Rome share a look, and then Chandler opens his desk drawer and pulls out a small box.

"You can decline this offer," he says as he flicks open the lid. A large diamond, surrounded by more diamonds, winks out at me. "This is a vintage Tiffany & Co. ring that belonged to my mother. I never offered it to Adelaide. It's only been worn by my mother."

"Did your parents have a good marriage?" I ask him.

"Yes. When she died, my father never stopped grieving, and he died less than a year after her. He just couldn't live through life without her."

"London loves that ring," Rome adds. "She used to get into trouble as a kid for sneaking it out of the safe and staring at it."

"Well, that pretty much seals the deal, doesn't it?" I

grin at both men. "If she loves it, and it's a family heirloom, that's the ring she should have."

"When will you propose?" Rome asks. "Christmas morning? That's tomorrow."

"I thought about that," I admit. "Then I considered doing it at the game on Sunday. She's bringing Caleb."

Both of their eyebrows shoot up at that.

"But I don't think she'd want something so public. So, I think I'll do it on New Year's Eve, at home, just the two of us, after Caleb goes to bed."

"She'll love that," Rome says. "I like you, Drew. I know you don't need my blessing, but you have it."

"I think I do need both of you behind me because she loves you both a lot. What you think matters to her."

"Will you talk to our mom?" Rome asks. "She's in town."

I shake my head. "No. I won't go into that because it's London's story to tell, but no. Adelaide isn't any of my business."

"I was wrong about you," Chandler says as he stands and offers me his hand. "Of course, it goes without saying that if you fuck this up, they'll never find your body."

I don't bother to laugh. "As it should be, sir."

"Since you're going to be family, you can call me Chandler."

CHAPTER 20

LONDON

"No one cares that we're here." I'm standing next to Sophie, loading up a plate with food. "I dressed down, like you said to, and Caleb and I wore our hats. No one paid any attention to us."

"I'm *so glad* that Drew suggested this," she says with a smile. "The press will be looking for you in the owner's suite, and that's *if* they were looking for you. You guys are totally safe here."

"It's fun," I admit. The guys are out on the field, warming up and getting ready for the start of the game.

"Oops, I'll be back. I have to go down and kiss Ike before the game."

Sophie licks her finger and hurries out, escorted by security. I carry my plate, and another for Caleb, over to the seats that face the glass so we can look out onto the field and watch all the action. My son chose a spot next to Drew's dad, and they're chatting it up like they're old buddies.

It warms my heart.

"Here's some food for you, buddy. You didn't eat your breakfast."

"Mom, I'm too excited to eat," Caleb informs me. "This is the best Christmas present ever."

"No way," I reply, shaking my head, and finger the necklace that my son got for me. "This one is."

He grins happily and turns to his new hero. "Did you see the present I got my mom for Christmas?"

"It's a nice one," *Old* Caleb replies and winks at me. "We're all glad that you joined us."

"I am, too," I reply and turn my attention to the field when the crowd erupts with applause. Up on the screen are Sophie and Ike, kissing. She says something to him, he nods, and then he turns to the field, ready to go. "I wonder what she says to him."

"Mom, she totally told him that he's got this. Can't you read lips?"

I laugh and ruffle my son's hair. "I guess I can't. Be sure to eat the vegetables *and* the pizza, please."

"She's such a mom," he mutters, making Drew's dad laugh loudly.

"It's her job, man. I like broccoli." He pops a piece into his mouth and chews happily. My Caleb looks down at his own broccoli and takes a bite.

"I guess it's not so bad. Come on, Seattle!"

Content that my son is happy and enjoying himself

with Drew's dad, I walk back up to where some of the others are gathered near the food.

"This is quite a spread," I comment, just as Sophie walks back in.

"I don't know if you've noticed," Lucy says, "but the Montgomerys can pack away the food."

Before I know it, the national anthem is played, the coin is tossed, and the game is underway.

"It's so much better in person," I hear my son say, and I smile over at Brynna.

"He's *so* excited to be here. It makes me feel a little guilty that I didn't let him come before."

"Don't feel guilty for trying to be a good mom," Brynna replies.

"You did the right thing," Olivia says, surprising me. "The press is a bunch of assholes. My dad did everything in his power to keep us away from them, too. And now, you have a place to bring him where he's safer."

"He probably appreciates it more now," Stella adds with a nod. "Also? How cute is he? He's wearing a Montgomery jersey!"

"He insisted," I reply with a soft smile. "Because it's Drew's last name, and he said he had to represent Drew."

"Okay, I'm officially in love with him," Stella says, looking over at my son all dewy-eyed. "That's the sweetest thing I've ever heard."

I'm surprised halfway through the second quarter

when the door opens, and my brother walks through it.

"Rome! What are you doing?"

"I had to at least swing over and say hello," he says. "This seems to the be place to be."

"It's *so* fun, Uncle Rome," Caleb announces. "Come sit with me!"

"Don't mind if I do." He snatches up a piece of pizza and makes his way down to sit with his nephew, just as Ike throws the ball for a thirty-yard pass, and it's run into the end zone for a touchdown.

"That's my man!" Sophie yells, jumping up and down. "Hell yes! Good job, baby!"

There are high-fives all around, and I look down in time to see Ike hurry to the sidelines, and Drew pats him on the helmet as he leans in to talk to him.

Watching Drew on the sidelines, doing his job so effortlessly, is incredibly sexy. His face is hard, his firm body strong as he stands with his arms crossed, chewing gum and watching the next play unfold.

The quarterback throws the ball, but it's intercepted by our guys, and we have the ball back.

Drew starts talking into his headset, pacing along the sideline, and then claps his hands, and the next play begins.

"I think you're good luck," Rome says to Caleb, making him preen. "You can stay."

"I want to come to *all* the games," Caleb says and tosses a puppy dog look my way. "Can we, Mom?"

"We'll see."

"You're always welcome in here," Sophie tells me. "I'm here for every home game. I try to go to the away games, too, but I'm always up here."

"Thank you."

It's the fastest few hours of my life. The game passes so quickly, and at the end of the fourth quarter, with less than two minutes left, we're down by three points.

"We need a touchdown, baby," Sophie says. Her hands are clasped under her chin, and she's rocking back and forth with nervousness. "Come on, Ike. You can do this."

But on the next play, Ike is thrown to the ground *hard*.

"Fuckers," Hudson mutters. "That's a shitty hit. It should be illegal."

I nod in agreement and breathe a sigh of relief when Ike stands up and seems to shake it off. In fact, he looks *mad*.

"That's the face," Sophie whispers. "That's right, babe. You got this!"

With the next play, Ike doesn't have an opening to throw, so he tucks the ball against his stomach and runs, weaving through the other team's defense, and scores the touchdown.

"YES!" I jump, clap, and high-five everyone around me. It's exhilarating and *fun*.

Caleb's right, we need to come as much as possible. This is *our* team. Making sure they feel our support is important.

Plus, the Montgomery family suite is the place to be. Rome may never go back to the owner's suite.

Of course, the press will catch on and find us all in here, and then we're right back where we were before, but I'll mention that to Rome after the game. I don't want to ruin anyone's fun.

Before long, the clock runs out, and we win the game, headed for the playoffs.

"Merry Christmas to all of us," Sophie says, clapping loudly. "That was a nail-biter."

"Why doesn't everyone come over to our place?" Olivia suggests. "We'll order dinner later and hang."

"I'm in," Hudson says, and several others agree, while others say they already have plans.

I have to meet with my mother in a few hours.

I'm not excited.

"I think we'll have to sit this one out, but thank you for the invitation."

"Come on. We can go see our guys," Sophie says. "Just wear your hat, and no one will care."

"Are you sure?"

"I'm totally sure."

"WE HAD THE BEST TIME." Caleb and Drew are in the game room, racing on *Mario Kart*. "Even Mom had a lot of fun. And Uncle Rome came in and sat with me for a while."

"That's awesome."

"It was fun watching you coach," my son continues. "You looked so serious down there."

"It's serious work." Drew glances my way and winks. "Thanks for being there."

"Sounds like we'll be there often," I reply. "Listen, guys. I have to go to a meeting. I'll be back in a few hours."

"You have a meeting on a Sunday?" Caleb demands, pausing the game. "The day after Christmas?"

"Yeah, I do. But I won't be gone long. You two entertain yourselves, okay?"

"We will," Caleb says as Drew stands and walks over to me. He slides his hands over my hips and leans in to kiss me softly.

"Are you sure you want to do this today?"

"I want to get it over with. She keeps texting me, and it's annoying. Enough already, you know?"

"I get it. Drive safe, and if you need me, just call."

"Thanks." I kiss him quickly, then wave at my son, who's making gagging noises. "See you in a bit."

"Do you have to kiss her?" I hear Caleb ask when Drew returns to their game.

"Yeah, I do."

The drive into the city doesn't take long. I agreed to meet with my mother in the hotel restaurant where she's staying. It's a nice place, and it's far away from my house. Once the car is with the valet, I walk into the restaurant and give the host my name.

"Of course, this way."

To my surprise, Mom is already seated and looking at a menu.

"Can I get you something to drink?"

"Water is great, thanks."

"It's about time you got here. I've been waiting for ages."

I frown and check the time on my watch. "I'm five minutes early."

She rolls her eyes and slaps her menu on the table. "Already arguing with me, I see. Is this how it's going to be, London?"

"You tell me, *Mom*."

"I can't believe the way you've treated me this week," she begins, not even waiting for the appetizer before the claws come out. "As if I'm a *stranger*. I came here during the holidays to spend time with you, and I haven't seen you at all."

"If you'd had the decency to give me a heads-up that you intended to come here, I would have saved you the trip."

"Are you saying you don't want me here?"

"Yeah, that's what I'm saying."

The waiter approaches, but I shake my head, and he takes the hint and walks away.

"What's going on with you, Mom? Why are you really here? Don't give me the bullshit story about the holidays, because we both know that you've never cared about being with your children at Christmas."

Her jaw drops open, then she shuts it again and hides her face behind her hand in a fake sob.

"Oh, for fuck's sake." Wishing I'd ordered something stronger than water, I take a sip and sigh.

"He doesn't pay *any* attention to me," she whines. "He's gone all day, and he golfs on the weekends."

"He's gone working, most likely. You married a man in his thirties. What did you expect him to do?"

"To be with *me*. He doesn't have to work."

"Mom, he had a successful career when you met him. You can't expect him to give all of that up just because you're needy."

"I'm *lonely*," she corrects, her voice ice cold. "That's something you should understand."

"I don't need a man to not feel alone." I shrug thoughtfully. "In fact, I have a pretty full life with Caleb and my own businesses."

"Right. I don't buy it."

"No, you wouldn't." I shake my head at the waiter again because I have no intention of staying much longer. "You know, I've been angry at you for most of my life. Angry because you were never there. You were a shitty mother, who had no real interest in loving and caring for Rome and me."

"What in the hell are you talking about? I gave you the *best* nannies."

"I was angry," I continue, "because you were selfish and thoughtless, and you embarrassed me. Hell, you still embarrass me. Look at what you did the other night."

"I didn't know that you were hosting a party—"

"What I'm saying is, I'm letting the anger go. It's too much weight to carry for a person who doesn't care. I'm not angry anymore. In fact, I don't feel much of anything, and that's how I know it's time I tell you this: I'm done. I don't want any relationship with you anymore, no matter how that looks. Don't send gifts for birthdays or holidays, and don't call me when you're feeling ignored. I don't want to hear from you at all anymore."

"You're my *daughter*."

I think of Brynna and all the aunts in Drew's family, and I shake my head. "Not in any way that really matters, and I refuse to be your crutch. It's mentally exhausting, and it isn't fair. So, as of now, I'm finished, Mom. Go back to Europe with your husband and live your life. Or don't. I don't really care."

With her mouth gaping, I stand, grab my purse, and walk away from the table, from the one woman who never loved me the way that she should have, and from all the guilt that I've carried because of her.

I'm shaking it all off and getting on with my life.

The lights are all on when I get home, which doesn't surprise me. Drew and Caleb are still in the game room, with a few more plates of snacks, still racing.

"That was fast," Drew says when he sees me walk in. "How was it?"

"Liberating." I smile down at Caleb, who's watching me warily. "What's wrong?"

"Drew told me that you went to see Grandma Adelaide. Was it bad?"

"No, it wasn't bad. For me, anyway. Who's winning?"

"She wasn't mean to you?"

I blink down at my son and then frown over at Drew.

"Kids hear more than we think."

"She yells at you on the phone," Caleb says softly. "And when she looks at you, her eyes are mean. I don't like her."

"Well, you don't have to worry about any of that anymore, because I just told her that I want her out of our lives for good. Pretty much for those exact reasons. Sticking up for yourself to people who don't love you and who don't have your best interests at heart is okay, my sweet boy. Even if those people are related to you."

"You *told her that*?" Caleb demands, his eyes wide in surprise.

"Yep. I told her she doesn't get to be mean to us anymore."

"I'm really proud of you," Caleb says and wiggles over to sit next to me and lay his head on my arm. And I know, in this moment, that I did the right thing.

"Thanks, buddy. Now, should I kick your butt at *Mario Kart*?"

"You don't even know how to play."

I scoff at that and pick up a controller. "Wanna bet?"

"Yeah," Caleb says. "Let's bet."

"Okay, how much?"

"How about twenty bucks?"

"You're on, little dude."

CHAPTER 21

DREW

"Only you would move in the middle of a winter storm." Liam glares at me as he carries a box from the condo to the truck. "And on New Year's Eve."

"I can't control Mother Nature or the calendar," I remind him. "At least we're not hauling furniture. I'm leaving that here for Lucy."

"You have a lot of shit for someone who hasn't lived here long," Keaton says, carrying two boxes stacked on top of each other. "We need to get finished before the roads ice up."

"We have about three hours before that happens," Hudson says.

"Who are you, the National Weather Service?" I demand and watch as Hud's eyes fill with laughter.

"Maybe," he replies. "Or I'm just old, like you, and I can feel it in my bones."

"Funny."

"It was pretty funny," Liam says with a chuckle. "So, you've boxed everything up except the furniture. Even towels and shit?"

"Yeah, Lucy wants her own stuff, and I don't blame her. And I'm taking all the workout equipment in the second bedroom."

"Fuuuuuck," Hudson groans as he walks by with another box.

"Think of it as a free workout," I suggest, and suspect that if he had a free hand, Hudson would flip me off.

It takes the four of us about an hour to fill the moving truck with boxes, and then we're on our way, driving in the sleet to the new-to-me house.

London's waiting in the doorway, ready to help.

"Don't worry about taking your shoes off," she assures us. "We can vacuum later. Just get that stuff in here so you're out of the cold."

"I can help," Caleb announces, running by in his sneakers. "We're putting everything in the dining room."

"I guess he's the foreman," Hudson says with a wink. "I'm following you, buddy."

After another half hour, all the boxes are unloaded into the house, and I'm closing the door on the back of the truck.

"Thanks for the help."

"I'll take the truck back," Liam offers.

"I'll let you," Keaton says. "Sydney and I are headed back to Nashville tonight. She has a show at the Opry tomorrow."

"Will it be on TV?" London asks. "I love listening to her sing."

"If it's not on TV, it'll be live streamed," Keaton says with a smile. "She even roped me into playing piano for this one."

"You play the piano?" Caleb asks. "That's so cool. Mom, I want to learn to play."

"I'll look into lessons," London assures him. "I'll watch for the show. Have a safe trip out there in this weather."

"Yeah, hopefully, the plane can take off so that we don't have to wait until tomorrow. I fu-freaking hate winter."

"You can say fuck," Caleb says, making his mother gasp in horror. "I hear it all the time."

"You do *not*," London says and pulls Caleb against her and covers his mouth with her hand, making him giggle. "You little twerp. No cake for you."

He just laughs some more, clearly not worried in the least.

"There's cake?" Liam asks, interested. "I mean, I'm not in a hurry."

"Cake for everyone!" Caleb exclaims and runs back toward the kitchen. "I'll cut it."

"No knives," London calls after him, hurrying toward the kitchen.

"They're pretty cute," Keaton says with a smile. "You look good here, Drew."

"I feel good here." I sigh, hanging back. I can hear London and Caleb chatting in the kitchen. "I already told my parents, but I thought I'd let you guys know, since you're my best friends, that I'm asking her to marry me tonight."

"That's...wow," Liam says and pats me on the shoulder. "That's great, man. Congratulations."

"I think marriage is contagious," Hudson says with a shiver. "It seems to be running rampant through the family."

"That's not such a bad thing," I reply and laugh when he cringes.

"Does Caleb know?" Liam asks.

"Yeah, he's in on it. And he's *not* good at secrets, so I didn't tell him until today, and I'm sticking close to him, just in case."

"Come on, you guys," Caleb calls out. "We cut the cake."

After another hour, and an entire chocolate cake, the guys leave, and I stand in front of a mountain of boxes with London at my side.

Caleb abandoned us to play video games.

"This is going to take some time." I glance down at her. "I'm sorry it's such a mess."

"It's not a mess. It's just boxes. We'll get it figured out. I see this one is marked linens. What kind of linens?"

"Sheets, towels, kitchen towels. Stuff like that."

"Uh, Drew?"

"Yeah, babe."

"Have you ever lived with a woman before?"

"Aside from my sisters and mom? No, ma'am."

"Well, how this works is, *I* pick that stuff out. Yes, this is *our* house, but when it comes to décor or linens, that's my department."

"And I'll happily let you have that department, but I couldn't leave it with Lucy. She wants her own stuff, too."

"Oh, good point. Well, do you mind if we donate it?"

"You don't even want to look through it to see if there's something you want to keep?"

She just stares at me, blinking slowly.

"I'm going to take that as a no." With a laugh, I kiss the top of her head and then lift the box. "Where do I put the donation pile?"

"In the garage," she says, pointing to the back of the house, and I carry it out there, setting it in a corner.

"One box down," I say when I return.

"This one is labeled office," she says.

"Yeah, it's office stuff. You don't happen to have a spare room in this house that could be my office, do you?"

"As a matter of fact, I do," she says and crooks her finger for me to follow her through the kitchen and living area, to a small room that faces the backyard. "I didn't know what to use this room for. It's small, but it's definitely big enough for a desk."

"It's actually perfect. I won't have to use it every day, but it's great for the times I'll need it."

"I'm going to start a list of the things we need," she says, taking out her phone. "First on the list is a desk and chair."

"And a lamp."

She makes the note. "We're pretty good at this whole *working as a team* thing."

I grin, relieved that she thinks so, because if all goes as planned, she'll be my fiancée by midnight.

Within an hour, we have a plan for all the boxes—some of them are put away, and others are added to the donation pile.

"Okay, I feel better about this." I wrap my arm around her shoulders. "It's organized chaos now."

"As opposed to regular chaos," she says with a grin. "Yeah, I get it. Let's take a break and eat something more than chocolate cake."

"It was an *excellent* cake."

She grins. "I know. But now I think I want pizza. Or maybe tacos. I'm in the mood for junk food."

"Pizza," we hear Caleb yell from the game room.

"It's good to know he can hear us from in here." I nuzzle the sensitive spot under her ear with my nose. "What do you want on your pizza, sweets?"

"Everything except anchovies."

"A woman after my own heart. I'll order it and go get it. That way, we won't have to wait as long for it."

"We'd better hurry," she says. "We're supposed to get some ice with this storm."

"We've got time," I reply. "It's not even dark out yet."

London brings up the app for the pizza joint on her phone, and after consulting with Caleb about what he wants, we place the order.

"I want to go with you," Caleb says. "I can hold the pizzas."

"Fine by me," I reply.

"Maybe you should stay home," London says with a frown. "Both of you, and we can just have it delivered instead."

"It'll be thirty minutes round trip," I assure her.

"I know, I just...I don't know... I have a bad feeling about it."

"Mom, you worry too much," Caleb says. "Me and Drew will be fine."

"Drew and I," she corrects. "Okay, you're right. I'm going to stay here and bake a pie. I have been a baking machine lately."

"The only complaint about that is the amount of time I have to spend at the gym, working it off," I reply and lean in to kiss her. "We'll be right back."

"Okay, thanks for picking it up."

Caleb and I put on coats and scarves in the mud room and head into the garage.

"Can I sit in the front with you?"

"No, sir," I reply, shaking my head. "You know the drill."

He sighs but gets into the rear seat behind the passenger seat so that he can see my face in the mirror. When he's strapped in, I start the car and pull out of the garage and frown when I skid just a bit in the driveway.

"Looks like the ice is already starting," I mutter, making a mental note to be extra careful on the short ride.

"It got so *dark*," Caleb says from the back seat.

"The clouds are angry," I agree and slowly make my way down the driveway. We're both quiet all the way to the pizza place, and I breathe a sigh of relief when we make it unharmed.

If I'd known it was this treacherous, I wouldn't have bothered with the pizza, and we would have figured something out at home.

But we're here now, so we'll make the best of it.

Caleb and I only have to wait about five minutes for our order to come up.

"You're our last order for the night," the manager says. "I'm letting my people go home. I don't want them out in this weather."

"Good call, man. It's worse than I thought it would be. You be safe."

"You, too."

Caleb and I make it back out to the car, and I make him laugh when I seat belt the pizza in on the seat beside him.

"This way, it's safe," I say with a wink, and then climb in and start the car. We've just made it to the end of the parking lot when Caleb gasps.

"Oh, no! They forgot the breadsticks!"

I push on the brake and look back at him, but the car doesn't stop. I slide out into the road, and an oncoming car, going way too fast for these conditions, can't stop in time.

They hit me hard, broadsiding me and sending me into another car across the road.

Caleb screams before everything goes black.

"DREW!" Someone's jostling my shoulder and yelling in my ear. "Drew, wake up. Wake up."

I can hear Caleb crying, and I open my eyes to find him unstrapped, tapping my cheek.

"Get back in your seat."

"We're stopped," he says. "We crashed. I grabbed your phone and called 9-1-1, and they're coming. You're not dead."

"No." But my shoulder is singing with pain, and I can feel blood running down my face. Fuck, I hope I don't have a goddamn concussion. "I'm not dead."

I can hear sirens in the distance and try to focus on Caleb.

"Are you hurt?"

"No, it didn't hit me," he says, but I can hear the fear in his voice. His eyes look a little shocky. "You passed out."

He starts to cry now, and I reach back to take his hand. "Hey, it's okay. I'm okay. Are you sure you're not hurt anywhere? You're not bleeding?"

"No." He wipes his nose with his hand. "I'm not bleeding. Did I do the right thing?"

"You did *great*." I try to move my left arm, but it is completely out of commission. "You're so damn smart, kiddo. I'm proud of you. You did exactly right. I'm sorry I can't get out and help you, but my arm is kind of hurt right now."

"You have blood on your face."

"Yeah." I swallow hard, trying not to think about what that might mean. So far, I'm not dizzy, and my head only hurts where it's cut, so I'm going to hang on to that. "I'm gonna be okay. I don't think we should get out of the car until help gets here."

"I think they're here," he says, pointing out the window. When I look, I see a firetruck and two ambulances arriving. Now that I'm looking around, I see that two other cars are dented up, but the drivers are out and talking to the first responders.

One of them points to me, and a fireman hurries over as fast as he can on the ice and tries to open the door. It's so crunched up that it takes him four tries.

"My arm," I say immediately. "Head laceration. I don't know about concussion. But I want you to see to my son first. He's in the back seat. Caleb, they're going to help you now, okay?"

"I'm not hurt," Caleb insists as the men hurry around to his side and open the door. "It's Drew. It's my daddy."

He's crying in earnest now, pointing to me, and it tears at my heart. I want to wrap him up and assure him that everything's going to be okay.

"We'll take you both in the same ambulance," the EMT assures me as he helps me out of the car. "Let's get you in there and out of this ice."

The men work fast to get both Caleb and me into the ambulance, and as they do their best to get us to the hospital, they see to the cut on my head.

"Your shoulder is dislocated," I'm informed. "They'll set it at the hospital. Caleb seems to be fine."

"I told you," Caleb insists and lays his head on my chest.

"Buddy, do you still have my phone?"

"Yeah."

"Give it to me."

He does as I ask, and I dial London's number, but she doesn't answer. I try again and curse when it goes to voice mail again.

"She doesn't have the ringer on," I say, and am swamped with a wave of pain. "Shit, I'm going to pass out."

"We're almost to the hospital," I hear someone say. "Take a deep breath."

"I'll do it," Caleb says. "Mom!"

I open my eyes and take the phone. "Baby, there's been an accident."

"Drew? Are you hurt? Is Caleb hurt?"

"We're headed to a hospital. Shit, I don't know which hospital."

"Seattle General," I'm told.

"I heard him," London says in my ear. "I'm on my way. Calling your parents."

"Okay." I let the phone fall and give in to the wooziness. "Shit. Sorry, buddy. Gonna pass out for real this time."

"Drew," I hear Caleb say. "Mom, he's hurt. I'm okay. It was really scary. Yeah, we're in an ambulance. Okay. Okay, Mom. Love you, too."

He lays his head on my chest again.

"She's coming. Mom's coming."

CHAPTER 22

LONDON

"*I knew* they shouldn't have gone." My heart is hammering a million beats a minute. I just need to get to the hospital.

But, in one piece.

"Where are you?" Caleb demands. Drew's dad insisted that he stay on the phone with me while I drove to the hospital, and I'm so glad that he did. I don't feel so alone.

I give him the exit number that I'm passing and white-knuckle the steering wheel.

"Take the next exit," he tells me. "Park at Sound Fitness. I know the owner, and your car will be safe there. I'll be there in five minutes, and I'll pick you up."

"I won't say no," I reply and do as he says. The roads are *terrible*. So, so scary. "I've never driven on anything this scary before."

"It's going to be okay," Brynna says, her voice soothing. "You got to hear both of their voices. I need you to breathe, honey."

I deliberately take a long, deep breath as I pull into a parking space at Sound Fitness and then let it out.

"I'm here. I've parked."

"ETA: three minutes," Caleb replies. He sounds so calm and collected. So in control. It bolsters my own courage, and when I see them turn into the icy parking lot, it's all I can do not to burst into tears.

"I will not cry," I mutter to myself. "My boys do *not* need to see me cry."

I get out of the car and ease my way over to get into the back seat of Caleb and Brynna's SUV.

"Thank you."

"We're not too far from the hospital," Brynna reassures me and reaches back to take my hand. I cling to her like my life depends on it. "Hold on, sweet girl. We're going to get you to them."

I can see the worry on her own face. *Her* baby is in the hospital, too, and I know she has to be sick with fear.

"I told them not to go," I say and wipe my hand over my face. "I had a feeling, a gut feeling, that something bad was going to happen."

"Beating yourself up is a waste of time," Caleb says shortly. He doesn't take his eyes off the road as he maneuvers us through downtown to the hospital.

Before I know it, we're underground in the parking garage, and I can breathe a sigh of relief.

But when we run into the ER, I'm stunned to find that it's packed.

"I'm going to the desk," I announce and rush through the people and to the front desk, where several people are intaking patients. "I'm sorry to interrupt, but my son was just brought in on an ambulance. He's a minor."

"Name?" one of them asks.

"Caleb Ambrose."

She picks up the phone and speaks to someone, then looks up at me. "They're bringing him out to you."

I almost collapse with that news. If they're able to bring him out, he's not hurt.

"And what about Drew Montgomery?" I demand. "He's with my son."

"Are you family?" she asks.

"Well, I—"

"Yes," Caleb says from behind me. "She's his fiancée."

She speaks into the phone again, asking about Drew, then looks at me again. "He can't have visitors quite yet."

"Shit," I mutter, and pace until my son comes walking out of a door, holding the hand of a nurse. "Baby!"

"Mom!"

He runs to me, wraps his arms around me, and buries his face in my stomach, crying. I look up to the nurse. "Is he hurt at all?"

"Not even a bruise," she says. "But he's very brave. I'll be back in a few when Drew can see you."

"Please hurry."

"It shouldn't be long."

"Oh, baby, what happened?" I ask as I lead him over to where Caleb and Brynna are waiting.

"We got the pizza," he says. "And we were going to pull out of the parking lot, but then I distracted Drew because I said that they forgot the breadsticks, and he couldn't stop, and the other cars couldn't stop, and it was like pinball. His side got hit, and he's *really* hurt. His head was bleeding, and they said his shoulder is disassociated."

"Dislocated?" I ask him.

"Yeah, that."

"Please don't let him have a concussion," I say, closing my eyes. When I open them, I look right into the very worried gaze of Brynna.

"And then," Caleb continues, "the firemen came, and Drew told them to get me first. He said, 'Get my son first.' He called me his son, and it made my stomach jittery, but in a good way, and then I called him dad, and is he going to be okay?"

"Yes, baby." I brush his hair off his forehead and hug him close. "He's going to be okay."

Brynna's crying now, and her husband looks miserable, but the nurse returns and flags me down.

"We've got him," *Old* Caleb says, wrapping his arm around my son. "He's safe with us."

"Please keep us updated," Brynna requests, and I nod as I follow the nurse back to where the rooms are. It feels like we've walked a half mile when we reach a room with a curtain pulled, and I walk in, expecting the worst.

But Drew smiles at me from the bed. He has a bandage above his left eye, and his arm is in a sling, but he's sitting up and is fully alert.

"Well, hi there, beautiful."

"Oh, my God." I hurry over to him and kiss his cheek, then his lips and hold his face in my hands. "You scared the *fuck* out of me, Drew Montgomery."

"Yeah, me, too. Is Caleb okay?"

"He's with your parents in the waiting room. They said he didn't have a scratch on him. He's scared and worried about you." I look up as a doctor walks in. "How bad is it?"

"You're a lucky man," the doctor says to Drew with a smile.

"And I know it."

"Mr. Montgomery has a dislocated shoulder and a laceration above his left eye."

"What about the concussion?" I ask.

"What concussion?" the two of them ask in unison.

"He doesn't have a concussion?"

"No," the doctor says. "And I know his medical history. He doesn't show any signs of a concussion at all, and we've been keeping a close eye on that. His shoulder will take some time to heal, but all in all, he's doing well."

"Does that mean I can go home?" Drew asks hopefully.

"Yes. You're on some good medication, so no driving for the rest of the day. You'll need to follow up with a doctor for that shoulder, and you'll likely need physical therapy."

"We have that covered," I reply, thinking of our extensive facilities at the training center. "What about medication?"

"Ibuprofen," the doctor replies. "You're going to be sore; there's no getting around that. Ice it, take the ibuprofen, and alternate with acetaminophen. It'll help."

"Thanks, doc," Drew says. "Come on, beautiful. I want to go home."

"Take it easy out there," the doctor says. "It's treacherous, as you know. We have too many people in tonight because of it."

"We'll be careful," I promise him and help Drew to his feet. "Your mom was beside herself."

"But you weren't?"

"Oh, I'm still a mess. I had to park my car halfway here, and your dad picked me up."

"Good. I don't want you driving in this."

With his hand gripped firmly in mine, I walk beside him as he's wheeled in a wheelchair to the lobby, and when Drew's parents and Caleb see us, their faces light up.

"Thank God," Brynna says on a choked sob and pulls her son in for a gentle hug when he stands. "Scared me."

"Same," Drew says with a smile. "Come on, guys. Let's go home."

"You know what sucks?" my kiddo asks as he takes Drew's free hand. "We still don't have any pizza."

HE'S BEEN SLEEPING for about twenty-four hours straight.

Caleb keeps wanting to check in on him, and keeping that kid out of my bedroom so Drew can rest is like keeping him out of the cookie jar.

Almost impossible.

"I'll be quiet," Caleb insists. "I just want to see that he's still breathing."

"He's breathing," I assure him. I know that because I just looked in on him myself. "We have to let him rest. His body is really banged up, and sleep is what helps it heal."

"Yeah. Even I slept pretty late today."

"You went through a scary ordeal." I tug him to my

side and kiss the top of his head, breathing him in. "I love you so much, my baby."

"I love you, too, Mom. I liked it that Drew's parents stayed here last night."

"Well, I wasn't going to let them drive home in that mess," I reply. "And I think they wanted to stay anyway, to make sure you and Drew were okay."

"Brynna makes really good pancakes."

"What are we going to do about your sweet tooth?" I ask.

"You're the one who keeps making him cookies."

My head whips to the doorway of the kitchen, and I rush over to Drew, cup his face in my hand, and kiss him.

"You're awake," Caleb says happily. "You slept for a *really* long time."

"Too long," Drew says and pads into the kitchen, sitting on a stool. "Can I have some coffee?"

"You can have anything you want," I reply. "But it's almost eight in the evening. Do you still want coffee?"

"Yeah," he says. "It'll clear some of the cobwebs."

"How's your shoulder?" I ask.

"Aches like a mother," he says and winces. "That's what woke me up."

"You need some medicine." I set the coffee at his elbow and then retrieve some pills, along with water, and set those next to the coffee. "Your parents stayed here last night. They left about an hour ago. The roads have finally cleared up. Just wet now."

"Good," he says and drags his good hand down his face. "What a mess."

"You missed New Year's," Caleb informs him. "I guess I did, too, because I was in bed. It's a whole new year today."

"Happy New Year," Drew says and offers his good fist to Caleb for a fist-bump. "We're going to start this one better than we ended the last one."

"Heck yeah," Caleb replies. "I'm going to go play."

He hurries off, and Drew meets my eyes over his coffee cup.

"Thank you for keeping him safe yesterday." Drew frowns, and I keep talking. "He told us about how you insisted that they check on him first. He loved that you called him your son."

He blinks and looks down into his coffee. "Was I hallucinating, or did he also call me daddy?"

"He did," I confirm. "I love that you two are so close. I can't even begin to tell you how much I love that. And the only thing that helped me keep it together yesterday was knowing that Caleb was with *you*. That no matter what, you'd do everything in your power to keep him safe."

"Of course, I would."

I nod and pour myself a glass of wine.

"I'm so glad you both are all right. But, Drew Montgomery, if you ever scare me like that again, I'll simply murder you myself." I have to set the glass down because my eyes are suddenly full of tears.

Before I can turn around, Drew's there, right behind me, his arm around my stomach, and he kisses my temple from behind. "I couldn't get there fast enough because the ice was so bad, and I was afraid of hurting myself while I tried to get to you. Your parents were *so good*."

"They're great in a crisis," he agrees.

"They were the only thing keeping me calm because the two people that I love the most in the world were on their way to the hospital, and I didn't know what happened or if you were going to be okay. My God, what if you weren't okay? And why am I just falling apart *now*?"

"Because you can," he says and turns me with his good arm and pulls me against him. "Because the adrenaline is finally wearing off, and you know that everything is fine. I'm fine, baby."

"I know." I wipe at the tears and look up at his impossibly handsome face. "I just love you *so damn much*."

"I love you, too. I'm not going anywhere. I don't think I could drive tonight."

"That's not funny." But I offer him a watery smile. "Is your head okay?"

"Yeah, I got lucky there."

"I wish I could just put you in a big plastic bubble so that you're safe." He frowns down at me, and I cup his face in my hands. "You're precious cargo, Drew."

"A big plastic bubble isn't really the fashion statement I'm going for," he says. "But I *will* be careful. It was an accident, London. It wasn't anyone's fault."

"Caleb was worried that it was his fault because he made you slam on the brakes."

"Shit, I'll talk to him." He closes his eyes grimly. "It wasn't his fault. It was just icy."

"I know that. And so does he, but he could probably use some reassurance in that department."

"I'll do that."

"But stay here with me for a minute first," I add, holding on to him and loving the way he feels against me, so strong and real. "I'm not ready to let go."

"You know, I had big plans for last night."

I look up at him, surprised. "You did?"

"Yeah, *big* plans. But this works, too." He reaches up and brushes a strand of my hair off my cheek. "I love you, London. I know that there will be times when our relationship isn't easy. Teenager-hood, for example. Or, if we never win a championship title."

"Oh, God, we're doing this."

His face turns sober. "Yeah, we're doing this. We're absolutely doing this because I love you completely. I love your loyalty, your intelligence, your passion. I love that little noise you make when I first slide inside of you."

I can't help but smile at that.

"There isn't anything that I don't love. And I love Caleb, too. He's the best. I want you both in my life until I take my last breath. And I'd like to have more children with you."

I feel my eyes go round, and Drew swallows hard.

"You mentioned once that you don't plan to have more kids."

"I didn't," I admit. "But that was because I hadn't met anyone I wanted to take that on with. I hadn't met *you*. I would love to have more babies with you, Mr. Montgomery."

"You don't have to say that just to placate me."

"Oh, I don't usually placate anyone." I loop my arms around his neck and thread my fingers through his hair. "Now, are you going to ask me a very important question?"

"I'm getting to it. You're so impatient."

I grin, and when he leans in to kiss me, I pull back. "Ah, ah, ah. I'm still waiting here."

"Marry me, London." He reaches into his pocket and pulls out a ring, offering it to me. "Be mine."

"I *am* yours." I narrow my eyes. "Holy shit, that's my grandmother's ring."

"Yeah, your dad gave it to me for you."

I stare up at him, *stunned.* "My *dad* gave it to you? For real?"

"Yeah. He totally likes me now. You didn't say yes."

"Well, it wasn't much of a question, but *yes.*" His lips descend on mine, and I kiss him like my life depends on it, until he moans, and I realize that I'm gripping onto his shoulder. "Sorry, babe. I got excited."

"I can live with it. Caleb's going to be excited that he doesn't have to keep the secret anymore."

"He knew?" I blink, surprised. "He's horrible at secrets."

"I know." He laughs and leans in to kiss me again. "Let's go tell him the good news."

BONUS EPILOGUE

BRYNNA MONTGOMERY

I've often wondered who the woman would be that Drew chose as his wife. Even when he was a tiny baby, and I rocked him endlessly through the night, I'd gaze down into his sweet face and wonder who she would be. My deepest wish was that she would love him even half as much as I do.

Because if she loved him just that much, he would be so incredibly loved, he'd shine with it.

I also wanted her to like me. I didn't know if I could dare hope that she would love me the way I adore my amazing mother-in-law, Gail, but I wanted her to at least like me. I want holidays and soccer games and special events with the woman that I'd bring into my family as a third daughter.

And I'm so damn delighted to know that I have all of that and more in London.

She's exactly what I would have hand-picked for my

boy if I could have. And her son? Well, there's nothing better in the world than a ready-made grandson, as far as I'm concerned.

"So, it took me getting engaged to get you to come home for a visit," Drew says to Erin, who's grinning at him.

"I would never miss an engagement party," she says and clinks her glass to his. "And I figured I'd better come home to check in. Mom and Dad were getting antsy."

"When do you head back?" I ask her.

"Day after tomorrow," she replies with a shrug. "I have to get back to work. But I love it. Seriously, come visit me soon. I hear spring is really pretty in the valley."

"We will," I promise her and turn to my son after Erin walks away to mingle with some of her other cousins. "I'm super proud of you, you know."

"Why?"

"Well, there is a long list, but since I don't want your head to get too big, I'll keep it short. First of all, London's a gem."

His smile lights up the room as he looks around, searching her out. "Yeah, she is."

"I love her. I'm excited to have another daughter. Secondly, I am *so* proud of how you've stepped up as Caleb's dad."

"I *am* his dad," Drew insists. "Just like Dad is Josie and Maddie's father."

"Yeah, I get that. It's the way it should be. I love the way Caleb idolizes your father."

We glance over to where the two of them have their heads together, watching something on my husband's phone. Suddenly, Caleb jumps up and runs over to us.

"Dad, Old Caleb just showed me a video about Navy SEAL training, and it's *awesome.* Maybe I should be a Navy SEAL, like him."

"You can do whatever you want," Drew says. "Does this mean you don't want to be a drummer in a band?"

"Maybe I'll do both," Caleb says with a shrug, then eyes my husband and me. "I just had an idea."

"What's that?" I ask and notice London walk over to join us. "Caleb has an idea," I inform her.

"Oh, good, what is it?"

"Well, maybe I shouldn't call you guys Brynna and Old Caleb anymore."

"No? What would you rather call us instead?"

"Maybe, if it's okay with you guys, I could just call you Grandma and Grandpa. Since we're getting married and everything anyway."

I don't stop the tears that run down my cheeks, and I see that even my tough, strong husband gets a little choked up as we smile and nod at the sweet boy.

"I think that's an excellent idea," I say to him and bend down to kiss the top of his head. "I would love that."

"Okay, cool," he says with a bright smile. "I have *so many* aunts and uncles now. It's crazy."

"You're not wrong," London replies with a laugh. "It's interesting, isn't it, to go from a tiny family to a really big one?"

"It's pretty great," Caleb replies and runs off to talk to other members of the family.

"I think I have something in my eye," Drew says, making us laugh as someone clinks on a glass, getting our attention.

"My dad's going to speak," London says, her voice apprehensive.

"Hello, everyone," Chandler Ambrose says, smiling charmingly. "It is my pleasure to host tonight's party, celebrating the engagement of my daughter to Drew Montgomery."

Everyone erupts in hoots and applause, and Chandler patiently waits for everyone to finish before continuing.

"I thought that I'd start the festivities off with a gift. It was brought to my attention that London and Drew recently enjoyed some time in Montana and that my daughter particularly fell in love with the condo that they stayed in."

"He didn't," Drew mutters in shock.

"You now own it," Chandler adds. "I hope it brings you happiness for many years, and I may even try my hand at skiing once or twice."

"Wow, thanks, Dad," London says, raising her glass.

"You're welcome. To Drew and London and a lifetime of happiness."

We all cheers in agreement, and when I look at London, I see that she looks...confused.

"What's wrong?"

"I don't know what's going on with my dad, but he's a new person. In a good way."

"Enjoy it," I advise her as the music starts up again. This time, it's a song that I used to sing to Drew when he was a baby.

My son holds his hand out for me. "Wanna dance?"

"I would love to."

As he sweeps me into his arms, I can't help but laugh. "You know, this usually doesn't happen until the wedding reception. Dancing with the mom."

"I don't need a tradition to tell me when I can dance with my mom," he says. "Besides, I like dancing with pretty girls."

"You're a charmer. And that smile of yours gets you just about anything you want."

He flashes that smile at me now.

"I hope that you two make each other happy, baby. As happy as your dad and I are."

"I have a feeling about this one," he says with a wink, but then he sobers and looks over my shoulder to his fiancée. "She's everything I never dared to wish for, Mom."

"Then she's everything you need, my boy."

Are you ready for Liam and Bianca's story? You can get more information regarding their book, **THE SOUL-MATE** here:

www.kristenprobyauthor.com/the-soulmate

KEEP READING for a preview of **WILD FOR YOU**, book one in the Wilds of Montana series, featuring **Erin Montgomery and Remington Wild!**

WILD FOR YOU PREVIEW

Erin

"You're changing the sign!"

I grin up at the man who's screwing in the new sign.

Welcome to Bitterroot Valley, Population 8,746.

"The population changed again," he calls down to me, and I nod.

Yeah, I am one of the new residents who changed the population from 8,731. I moved here in December, and since then, three babies have been born, along with a couple of new families that moved to town.

Just in the past four months.

"How often do you change it?" I call back.

"Once a year, when it's warm enough to climb up on a ladder without freezing to death," he informs me, and I nod, look at the sign once more in satisfaction, and then keep walking on my way to work.

It's official. I'm a citizen of Bitterroot Valley, Montana. I mean, sure, I've technically been that since December when I came here with all my cousins for a vacation and decided to stay, but it feels extra official now, and I couldn't be happier. I knew as soon as we landed here that this was my home.

With a little more bounce in my step, I make my way down the sidewalk. It's finally springtime, which means that the bitter cold from winter seems to be over. We still have a little snow on the ground, and I've been told that the mountains will have snow until early summer, but it's finally warm enough to walk to my job at Bitterroot Valley Coffee Co.

I *love* my job. I've met so many people already, thanks to the coffee shop. I have my regulars who never miss a day, and the best part is, I'm still meeting new people all the time. I've never really considered myself to be a social butterfly, but I admit that it was hard to move away from my huge, loud family to a place where I knew absolutely no one. But, I've started to weave myself into the community, and it's only made me love this little town more.

Not to mention, my new best friend, Millie Wild, works with me. Actually, she worked there first and helped me get the job. We became fast friends, and now I can't imagine my life without her. We're roughly the same age, and it's as if we've been friends forever.

I tip my head back and take a deep breath, pulling in the crisp spring air, and smile.

Yeah, this is exactly where I'm supposed to be.

Before long, I've crossed the imaginary line from residential to downtown blocks, and I walk into the warmth of the café. The smell of freshly ground coffee meets me, along with a wave from Millie.

"Good morning." I grin at her and walk behind the counter, hurrying to the back to stow away my things. Once I've grabbed an apron and tied my hair back, I return to the counter and take in the number of people already sipping coffee, having conversations, or typing away on their computers all over the space. "It's busy in here for a Thursday morning."

"I know," she replies with a sigh and wipes her forehead with the back of her hand. "I should have asked you to come in earlier."

"I totally would have. Why didn't you?"

She turns and gives me a grin. "I know how much you like to sleep in. Besides, it's not normally like this, especially in the middle of the week. Anyway, there seems to be a lull now. How are you?"

"I'm *great.*" I tell her about the population sign change, and she laughs, shaking her head at me. "What? It's a big deal."

"You're just so cute. I love how much you *love* living here, Erin. It reminds me to be thankful for it, too. I guess I forget, since my family has been here for more than a hundred years."

"It's my home." I shrug a shoulder, but I mean it

with every fiber of my being. The bell over the door jingles, and Millie grins.

"What do *you* want?" she demands, her voice full of humor.

"An oil change," her brother, Chase, says with a grin as he saunters in. "And maybe a haircut."

"You won't get either of those things here," Millie replies, rolling her eyes. She reaches for a to-go cup to start making her brother's favorite coffee.

"How's it going, Erin?"

"I'm great, thanks. And you?"

Chase smiles and leans on the counter. I've met two of Millie's brothers so far, and they're both *gorgeous*. Chase has a smile that could likely melt all the snow on the ski mountain. Not to mention, he's a cop, and that uniform is *hot*.

"I can't complain."

"Have you arrested anyone today?"

Chase shakes his head mournfully. "So far, everyone has been law-abiding. Well, except for Mrs. Wilburn, who refuses to drive the speed limit on her way into town."

"Is she a speeder?" I ask.

"No, she won't drive above twenty-five," he says with a pained expression. "*Anywhere.* So, she backs up traffic and they call me."

I press my lips together, trying not to laugh, but I can't help it.

"It gives you something to do," Millie says as she passes her brother his coffee. "Do you want a muffin? Jackie Harmon brought some fresh huckleberry lemon ones in this morning."

"I don't pass up Jackie's muffins," Chase says with a nod. "I'll take two."

"I've got this," I assure Millie and, with tongs in hand, gently place the enormous muffins into a bag for Chase. When I pass the bag to him, his fingers brush mine, but there's no spark there.

Too bad. Chase is definitely a sexy guy.

"Well, ladies, it's been real. Call if you need anything. I'm walking down the block to check out the new restaurant going in."

"What kind is it?" Millie wants to know.

"Italian," I reply before Chase can. "I walked by last night and spoke to the owner. It's called *Ciao*. I guess it's a sister restaurant to one of the same name in Cunningham Falls."

"That's kind of cool," Millie decides. "Do you know when it's opening?"

"I didn't ask. Do you know, Chase?"

"Next month," he confirms with a nod. "It's always good to have something new come in. Have a good day."

Chase walks out, and I grab a rag to wipe down the espresso machine.

"Do you have a crush on my brother?" Millie asks

"Are you kidding? Hell no. It's way too far out of town for me. I want to be where the action is, and I'm not really needed out there. I do spend a few days there in the spring, when it's time to brand and castrate the calves."

I turn and blink at her. "That sounds...horrible."

Millie chuckles and tucks her dark hair behind her ear. "I'm just used to it. Been doing it all my life. Anyway, that covers everyone in my family. Tell me about yours."

I open my mouth, but then a group of about eight people hurry inside to order coffee and food, and we're busy for the rest of the morning.

***

Since Millie has the early shift at the coffee shop, she gets off work early, and I stay by myself for the last two hours to close on my own. On our off days, the other two girls, Candy and Marion, who happens to be the owner, work the same shifts.

At first, I was surprised that there are only four employees, but given that the café is closed on Mondays, it works out well for us. We all get along well and keep the place running smoothly.

I enjoy the couple of hours by myself in the afternoon. By then, things are usually pretty quiet in here, so I can clean and mop without too much interruption.

Until *he* comes in. Every single day. Right about...*now.*

The bell over the door dings, and I glance up to see

my least favorite customer walk through the door. He's tall, probably in his mid to late thirties, and always wears a baseball cap. Today, he's just in a denim shirt with the sleeves rolled just below his elbows, with dark blue jeans and boots.

He's a cowboy, that's for sure.

And he's handsome.

If you like the grumpy, surly type.

"Hello," I say with a forced smile as I lean the mop against the wall and walk behind the counter. I've never asked his name because he's never been talkative enough to make conversation. "What can I get for you today?"

"Coffee, black," he says.

"Sure. We have huckleberry lemon muffins today. I have three left, if you'd like one. They're popular."

I smile, but he doesn't smile back. He does, however, eye the last of the muffins in the case.

"I'll take them."

"All of them?"

He levels a look at me. "Yes. All of them."

"Okay. Must be hungry." I happily ring up the muffins and coffee into the computer, and while he does his thing with his credit card, I bag up the treats and pour his coffee. "It's sure a nice spring day out there today. You know, for as cold as it got this winter, I'm surprised by how quickly it's warming up."

"Hmm," is all he says in reply as he taps the screen on the computer, finishing the sale.

"Okay, well, here you go. I hope you have a nice afternoon."

"Yeah." He grabs the brown paper bag and his coffee and turns to go. "You, too."

The door closes behind him, and I let out a long breath. I can usually get a smile out of people, especially if I meet them more than once, but this guy is impossible.

Grouchy cowboy.

I shake my head and get back to work. Before long, it's time to lock the door and set the alarm, which Marion put in just this past winter, and set off for home. I like to walk through town, taking the long way back to my place. I found the cutest apartment above the garage of an elderly guy in town. I like to take him soup and a cookie from Mama's Deli just down the street. He always tells me that I shouldn't bother, but I can tell by the way he lights up that it's his favorite part of the day.

I never see anyone come to the house to visit him, and he reminds me of my grandpa back in Seattle.

"Hello, Erin," Jeannie, the manager of the deli, says when I walk in. "I have his favorite today. Beef with barley."

"Oh, that'll make his day." I smile at the other woman as I pull out my credit card, but she shakes her head.

"It's on me today. It's Mr. Sherman's birthday."

My mouth drops. "It *is*? Well, shit, I didn't know that."

"Of course, you didn't. How could you?"

"How do *you* know?"

Jeannie sighs, then shrugs. "I never forget a date, and my parents must have mentioned it at some point. Before he died, my dad and Mr. Sherman were friends."

"Jeannie, does Roger have any family here? I never see anyone come to see him."

"No." Jeannie shakes her head as she adds an extra cookie to the bag. "Roger and Sue never had any kids, and Sue's been gone, jeez, twenty years now, I guess."

"That's so sad. He's a really nice guy."

Jeannie looks over at me in surprise and then laughs.

"What? He is."

"Well, he may be nice to *you*, but he's always been kind of a grumpy old man. He's your typical *get off my lawn* guy, you know?"

I shake my head. "No, I've never seen that side of him. That's so funny. Hey, throw in a chocolate cupcake, and I'll pay for it."

"That's sweet. I even have a candle you can have."

"That's awesome. Thank you. Well, I'd better hit up one of the shops for a gift for him on my way home. Thanks, Jeannie."

"You're welcome, honey. Go enjoy that weather."

I nod and, with the hot soup and cookies in one

hand, set off across the street to a shop that sells both women's and men's clothes, and find Roger a nice scarf. It's blue and will be handsome on him.

With that finished, and content because they offered to gift wrap it for me, I hurry home and make Roger's house my first stop, before going into my apartment.

"Hello?" I call out as I open the door. Roger told me a while ago that I didn't have to knock, since I come over so often. "It's just me."

"Oh, hello, dear."

He says it that way every day, as if it's a surprise to see me, even though he sees me every day. His eyes light up when he sees the wrapped box in my hand.

"You didn't tell me that it's your birthday." I set the bag of food on the table and hold the wrapped box out to him. "But thankfully, I have my ways of finding things out."

"It's just another day," he begins, but I shake my head.

"No, sir, it's your *birthday*. You've been incredibly kind to me since I moved here, and you're one of my closest friends. I celebrate my friends on their birthday."

His eyebrows pull together as he stares down at the box, and then he looks up at me with soft brown eyes.

"Thank you," is all he says.

"You're welcome."

"Now, since it *is* my birthday, I'd like you to stay for dinner. Jeannie always packs enough soup for two."

"It's your favorite today," I inform him. I don't personally love beef with barley, but for Roger, I'll choke down a small bowl. "What did you do today?"

"I took my morning walk," he says as I bustle about his kitchen, pouring our soup and getting us settled at the table. "They changed the sign again."

"I saw it! I was so excited because *I'm* one of the new people they added."

"Too many people moving into our town," he grumbles as he sits at the table with me. "Now, you, I don't mind, but we have too many move-ins trying to change our town. Make it bigger and what they think is better. If they want Bitterroot Valley to be like California, they should stay in California."

"Maybe you should run for mayor. Or city council."

Roger scoffs as he takes a bite of his soup. "Been there, done that. Many years ago. No one wants to listen to the opinions of an old man."

"I do. Here, open your present."

I notice the slight tremor in Roger's hand as he tears the wrapping paper. I've noticed the tremors getting worse for a while now. When I first moved in, he didn't have any shaking at all, and now his right hand is never still.

If he *was* my grandfather, I'd ask him if he'd been to the doctor, but he's not my grandpa. And it's none of my business.

"Now, what did you do here?"

"It's just a scarf," I say with a smile. "I thought you'd look handsome in it on your morning walks. Until summer, anyway."

He immediately wraps it around his neck and smiles over at me like a kid at the best birthday party ever. "I love it. Thank you."

"You're welcome."

I spend a few hours with Roger, helping him plan some gardens in his backyard, and we even watch an episode of an old TV show that he likes. After surprising him once more with the cupcake and the birthday candle, I head over to my apartment above the garage.

It's just a one-bedroom space with a tiny kitchenette, but it's what I can afford without dipping into my trust fund.

And I'm determined *not* to dip into that at all if I can help it. My dad was so mad at me when I wouldn't let him buy me a fancy house on the ski mountain or in a gated community. But I didn't want that.

I want this, to live within my means, *in* the community.

I want to do this on my own.

And, speaking of my parents, it's time for my weekly video call with them. So, I change into comfier clothes and settle on the couch with my phone.

Mom answers on the first ring.

"There you are," she says with a smile. "I wondered if you were going to call tonight."

"I'm only a half hour late," I reply and shake my head. Then I look closer. "Mom, do you have *pink* in your hair?"

"Yep." She turns her head so I can see it more clearly. "I used to put colors in my hair all the time before I had you girls, and I've decided I want to do it again. How are you, baby girl?"

"I'm great. I *am* sorry that I'm late. It's Roger's birthday, so I spent some time with him after work."

"Is it wrong that I kind of love that you've befriended an old man in this new town of yours, and I don't have to worry about some man your age?"

"It's not wrong. Roger's sweet. Anyway, what's Dad up to?"

"I'm here," I hear him say from somewhere else in the room. "I'm coming."

Suddenly, they're both on the screen. Dad might have a couple more gray hairs mixed in with the dark brown, and I'm sure that's all thanks to me and my move to Montana.

"Hi, Daddy."

"You look good," he says. "Are you exercising?"

"Of course." I can't help but laugh. Leave it to my dad, the former professional quarterback, to worry about that. "It's even warm enough to start walking to and from work again. I'm on my feet all day. What's new with you guys?"

"There's always *something* going on with the family," Mom says. "You know how it is."

"Yeah, everyone's been great about texting me updates. But what's new with *you*?"

They look at each other, and I frown.

"Are you getting divorced?"

Dad laughs, and Mom just stares at me in shock. "What? Why in the world would you ask something like that?"

"I'm as obsessed with your mother as I was the day I married her," Dad assures me.

"You look...serious. Is Zoey okay?"

"She's great," Mom says. "Dad and I are thinking about selling the house and moving into something just a little smaller. We're empty nesters, and we don't need this huge house anymore."

My heart pings at the thought of them selling the house I grew up in. All of my firsts live in that house.

"At least it's not divorce," I reply with a forced smile.

"But it makes you sad," Mom guesses correctly. "I know you."

"It makes sense for you. If that's what you guys want to do, I say do it. Buy something fancy and modern, but a little smaller. I can't wait to see it."

"Zoey had a harder time with the idea," Dad says. "In fact, there were tears and threats."

"She'll get over it." I sigh and then yawn. "You don't have to save my old stuff. Donate it or toss it."

"That's my sentimental girl," Mom says with a laugh. "I miss you, baby."

"I miss you, too. When are you coming to see me?"

Dad's eyes narrow. "Maybe sooner than you think."

Are you ready for Wild for You? You can get all of the information for this small town, single dad novel here: https://www.kristenprobyauthor.com/wild-for-you

NEWSLETTER SIGN UP

I hope you enjoyed reading this story as much as I enjoyed writing it! For upcoming book news, be sure to join my newsletter! I promise I will only send you news-filled mail, and none of the spam. You can sign up here:

https://mailchi.mp/kristenproby.com/newsletter-sign-up

ALSO BY KRISTEN PROBY:

Other Books by Kristen Proby

The With Me In Seattle Series

Come Away With Me - Luke & Natalie
Under The Mistletoe With Me - Isaac & Stacy
Fight With Me - Nate & Jules
Play With Me - Will & Meg
Rock With Me - Leo & Sam
Safe With Me - Caleb & Brynna
Tied With Me - Matt & Nic
Breathe With Me - Mark & Meredith
Forever With Me - Dominic & Alecia
Stay With Me - Wyatt & Amelia
Indulge With Me
Love With Me - Jace & Joy
Dance With Me Levi & Starla

You Belong With Me - Archer & Elena
Dream With Me - Kane & Anastasia
Imagine With Me - Shawn & Lexi
Escape With Me - Keegan & Isabella
Flirt With Me - Hunter & Maeve
Take a Chance With Me - Cameron & Maggie

Check out the full series here: https://www.
kristenprobyauthor.com/with-me-in-seattle

Single in Seattle Series
The Secret - Vaughn & Olivia
The Scandal - Gray & Stella
The Score - Ike & Sophie

Check out the full series here: https://www.
kristenprobyauthor.com/single-in-seattle

Huckleberry Bay Series

Lighthouse Way
Fernhill Lane
Chapel Bend

The Big Sky Universe

Love Under the Big Sky
Loving Cara
Seducing Lauren

Falling for Jillian
Saving Grace

The Big Sky
Charming Hannah
Kissing Jenna
Waiting for Willa
Soaring With Fallon

Big Sky Royal
Enchanting Sebastian
Enticing Liam
Taunting Callum

Heroes of Big Sky
Honor
Courage
Shelter

Check out the full Big Sky universe here: https://www.kristenprobyauthor.com/under-the-big-sky

Bayou Magic

Shadows
Spells
Serendipity

Check out the full series here: https://www.

kristenprobyauthor.com/bayou-magic

The Curse of the Blood Moon Series

Hallows End
Cauldrons Call
Salems Song

The Romancing Manhattan Series

All the Way
All it Takes
After All

Check out the full series here: https://www.
kristenprobyauthor.com/romancing-manhattan

The Boudreaux Series

Easy Love
Easy Charm
Easy Melody
Easy Kisses
Easy Magic
Easy Fortune
Easy Nights

Check out the full series here: https://www.
kristenprobyauthor.com/boudreaux

The Fusion Series

Listen to Me
Close to You
Blush for Me
The Beauty of Us
Savor You

Check out the full series here: <u>https://www.</u>
<u>kristenprobyauthor.com/fusion</u>

From 1001 Dark Nights

Easy With You
Easy For Keeps
No Reservations
Tempting Brooke
Wonder With Me
Shine With Me
Change With Me
The Scramble
Cherry Lane

Kristen Proby's Crossover Collection

Soaring with Fallon, A Big Sky Novel

Wicked Force: A Wicked Horse Vegas/Big Sky Novella
By Sawyer Bennett

All Stars Fall: A Seaside Pictures/Big Sky Novella
By Rachel Van Dyken

Hold On: A Play On/Big Sky Novella
By Samantha Young

Worth Fighting For: A Warrior Fight Club/Big Sky
Novella
By Laura Kaye

Crazy Imperfect Love: A Dirty Dicks/Big Sky Novella
By K.L. Grayson

Nothing Without You: A Forever Yours/Big Sky
Novella
By Monica Murphy

Check out the entire Crossover Collection here:
https://www.kristenprobyauthor.com/kristen-proby-
crossover-collection

ABOUT THE AUTHOR

Kristen Proby has published more than sixty titles, many of which have hit the USA Today, New York Times and Wall Street Journal Bestsellers lists.

Kristen and her husband, John, make their home in her hometown of Whitefish, Montana with their two cats and dog.

facebook.com/booksbykristenproby

instagram.com/kristenproby

bookbub.com/profile/kristen-proby

goodreads.com/kristenproby